D1617353

Audition

Walter Bonora

ISBN: 1536912727
ISBN 13: 9781536912722

Acknowledgements

To CAMILLE AND Mano for all their generous support, to Rick for being the best and most loyal friend a person could ever have, and to my wife Roseann, for believing in me and offering great insight into shaping my work.

Books on any subject are not easy to write. The journey to publication often takes authors on a long and bumpy road. Along the way, we meet hundreds of people who help shape our work. To all of you, a heartfelt thanks.

For my dear friend Mona
Hope you enjoy

Whoever fights monsters should see to it that in the process he does not become a monster

Prologue

A DARK CLOSET is no place for a young boy.

But he had to sing. Mother would not let him out of that closet until he sang "We Can Fly" from "Peter Pan" to her satisfaction.

"*Again.*" The woman's disembodied voice sent a chill up the young boy's spine.

His eyelids twitched. Tears slid down the side of his face. He wanted to be somewhere else, somewhere fun. A place where little boys and girls played. *He did not want to be in this closet.*

His lips quivered. He could understand the tears, but not the quivering lips. This punishment was a first for young Mitchell. The little boy had never been locked in a closet before.

But he had known fear. His mother had stood over him with a wooden spoon, not long ago, and threatened to smack his hands until they bled. *Until you bleed.* He remembered the sick feeling in his stomach.

And another time he was so scared he wet his pants. Mother had whipped his behind with his jump rope until he couldn't sit anymore. *Until you can't sit.*

Young Mitchell forced himself to continue the song. "*Think of Christmas, think of snow. Think of sleigh bells, off we go, like reindeer in the sky...we can fly, we can fly, we can fly...*"

"From the top," his mother ordered.

"*Think of Christmas, think of snow, think of ...think of...*" Young Mitchell started to sob.

"*Again.*" The viciousness in Mother's voice unnerved the young boy. It wasn't anything like Dorothy's sweet voice in "The Wizard of Oz." Why couldn't his mother's voice sound like Dorothy's?

Mother sat in her chair outside the hall closet, disheveled and grim. Tentacles of stringy gray hair fell over her face and down her shoulders. The bathrobe she wore hadn't seen a washing machine in weeks. She lit another unfiltered cigarette and blew smoke through blistered lips. And in that moment she recalled a night in her childhood when her older brother had given her a nasty gift. He was a school bully who also derived great pleasure in tormenting his sister. One evening, he had found a dead rat in a gutter near their apartment. He chopped off its head, wrapped the headless body in a newspaper and stuffed it inside a box. Then, after dinner, while their parents indulged in their usual ritual of heavy drinking in front of the television, he walked into her bedroom and gave her the box, with its morbid content, as a prank gift. He told her it was something that reminded him of her. *A headless rat.*

She often thought of that evening. It fueled her nastiness.

"*Again,*" she hissed.

The young boy wiped his tears. "Mommy I can't."

"Yes you can," she said, coughing up phlegm.

Young Mitchell swallowed hard. The quivering in his lips had stopped. This gave him some measure of relief, though he didn't know why. "*Think of Christmas, think of snow, think of sleigh bells...off we go...we can fly, we can fly, we can fly...*"

Mother was never far from a bottle of cheap whiskey. Drinking that stuff was the thing to do for a boozing, self-loathing woman. She took a deep drag from her cigarette, and while the smoke was going down her throat, she took a long swig of her rotgut whiskey. The combination of whiskey and smoke made her feel painfully good. She moved her head back and forth until she felt a crack in the back of her neck. She drank. Mother relished her whiskey.

Then her cough assaulted the air around her.

Again!

Act One

Chapter I

The Tartan Theatre

Los Angeles - Present

A thunderous ovation erupted inside the ornate Tartan Theatre in West Hollywood. Built in the 1920s, it was only a handful of theaters left standing in L.A. from that bygone era. As the curtain came down on his show, Arthur St. George, a British 60-year old B-movie film and theatrical producer stood at the back of the theatre and wiped tears of joy from his eyes.

His latest stage venture, Edgar Allan Poe's "Murders in the Rue Morgue," was met with an ovation that neither he nor the critics in attendance had expected. The curtain came back up and four curtain calls followed.

In his moment of elation, he recalled the alarm sounded by Los Angeles critics a year earlier when news broke that St. George was about to begin rehearsals for his musical adaptation of the Poe classic thriller. Many critics and theatre insiders thought that the idea of turning a classic into a musical had been beaten to death. They had felt it was overkill and another attempt to cash in on the success of timeless hits like "Les Miserable" and "Phantom of the Opera."

There were also the flops, like "Jekyll and Hyde" and "The Invisible Man." But St. George was never one to pay much attention to critics. Throughout his career, he had mounted productions or produced films born out of an uncanny sense of what sells. He was panned by film critics for producing a low-budget film about creatures arriving on earth from wormholes in the atmosphere, burrowing into the ground and emerging later to feast on human souls. The movie, simply titled "Wurms", became one of the most successful low-budget horror films ever made. St. George took great pleasure in that victory over men and women who in his opinion knew very little about that which they were reviewing. Panned by critics – success at the box office nonetheless.

The Los Angeles opening night performance of "Murders in the Rue Morgue" was, in his boastful opinion, a smash. The audience loved it, and to St. George, that's all that mattered. Like many a showman before him, St. George believed in giving the public what they wanted. If a producer stuck to that idea, the producer would always succeed. He believed in entertainment for the sake of entertainment. And he was often heard repeating the words of legendary film producer Samuel Goldwyn. "If you want to send a message -- call Western Union."

Backstage, the place was all excitement as St. George made his way through the joyful cast and crew. He leaned against the doorway of the green room and felt a surge of pride.

The excitement spilled over to Janet Zeller's plush condo on a tree-lined street at the edge of Beverly Hills. An old friend of St. George, the fifty-year old former ballerina had offered to host their opening night party.

Her three-bedroom unit was located inside a luxury, doorman building. The condo's balcony faced west, so she was rarely without a spectacular sunset. Zeller had long abandoned the world of dance to enter the art world. She owned one of the more fashionable galleries in Beverly Hills that featured French and Italian nouveau impressionism. She had come to know St. George through the Beverly Hills cocktail circuit, and the two had remained close friends.

Zeller gave him a warm, affectionate hug. "Ya done good Arty," she said, toying with him.

"Not bad for a poor boy from Liverpool."

"The way you staged the ape killing those two women rivals anything I have seen on stage in a long time."

Trays of hors d'oeuvres greeted hungry cast members. A tall, blond actor carrying a tray of glasses filled with champagne navigated through the living room.

"Nectar! Nectar of the Gods!" he said in high theatrical fashion. The blond passed by Lionel, a nervous black actor who was speaking with Tina, the production's make-up artist. "How did I look? No dark shadows? No double chin?"

"Lionel. You are a work of art," Tina, said. "My work of art." Relieved, Lionel took a glass of wine from another passing tray.

Across the room Cynthia Dardi tersely whispered to the male lead. "Don't ever step on my lines again."

"The less you speak, Cynthia, the better for the show," the lead actor said. Others within earshot couldn't help chuckling.

St. George, moving through the revelers, heard that remark and it was all he could do to keep from laughing. Cynthia was the one pain-in-the ass in an otherwise wonderful cast. If there was a poster child for prima donnas, Dardi's picture would be plastered on billboards from coast to coast.

As he relished that thought, sensual and buxomly Leslie Brister sauntered up to him. Her tight, red, cleavage-bearing party dress barely hung below her panty line. "My place? Tonight?"

"Perhaps," he said, unimpressed. St. George was accustomed to her advances. He had cast her on her acting skills, and they were considerable. Her burning sensuality gave her the edge over other actresses who had auditioned for the part of a troubled, Parisian cabaret singer, but didn't have the sex appeal necessary for the role.

Holding a glass of champagne, Dardi pushed her bony frame past Leslie, and tossed her a disapproving look. Leslie smiled confidently at St. George, as though Dardi's presence was of no consequence. "I'll be waiting," and she moved past him.

"Her tits really annoy me, Arthur," Dardi snapped.

"Would you like me to have them removed?"

"Detonated would be better. I'd love to see all that silicon explode all over the art work."

"I think she annoys you because she is a scene stealer. She does have a commanding presence."

Dardi's brow furrowed deeply and with a heavy gulp of champagne she pushed down the bile rising in her throat. "Arthur. I want to talk to you about some changes in Act 2. I am not happy with my death scene."

"Not now," St. George replied wearily. "I know this is difficult for you Cynthia, but do try and enjoy yourself."

Chapter 2

As the party wore on, St. George had become worn out. He had decided it was time to leave. He looked for Zeller and found her in the foyer saying good night to other cast and crew-members. "Janet. I am going to sneak out."

"Arthur. You barely said two words to me all night."

"But what little I said was poetry that could render an eloquent man speechless. Wonderful party. Always a joy to see you."

"Do I get the lead in your next epic?" Zeller said putting her arm around him.

"Do I get one of those Robel seascapes hanging in your gallery?"

"Oh. You are a devil."

They gave each other a big hug and a kiss. St. George said good night to the remaining revelers, and walked out of the condo.

>≔◉ ◉≕<

The producer headed down the hallway to the elevator and pressed the down button. The champagne had taken a firm hold of his mind, and things were starting to appear a little fuzzy. While he waited, he felt the presence of someone behind him.

Turning around, he was startled to see Leslie Brister facing him. She was also feeling a little loopy. "Going my way?" she said, pushing her chest against his.

"Don't know." The elevator door opened. A well-dressed man came out of the elevator and stepped around them, moving hurriedly away.

St. George and Leslie slipped into the elevator. She ran her fingers up his chest as the doors closed. "Stop playing hard to get." Her fingers found the nape of his neck. Her index finger slowly walked up the back of his head.

"I wasn't aware I was doing that," he said.

She ran her fingers through the back of his silvery hair. And while the fingers kept busy, her lips gently touched his cheek. "I want you, and I want you to want me."

"Yes. Well, I am a bit tired."

"Oh Arthur…"

The elevator reached the lobby, the doors opened and Leslie stumbled out of the elevator first followed by St. George. She pulled her tight dress down a little. They crossed the lobby and breezed past a doorman who forced an awkward smile.

Outside in the crisp night air, Leslie made one more attempt at luring St. George to her apartment. "C'mon Arthur. It'll be a night you'll never forget. You'll want more and more of me. Like tasting strawberries dipped in zabaglione."

"So sorry, love. I think I really am pooped."

"Arthur. You have a beautiful, sexy woman dying to rewrite the Kamasutra with you, and all you can say is you're pooped?"

"Not tonight dear."

"I'm crazy about you. Always have been." She pouted and puckered and looked absolutely delicious.

With incredible resolve, St. George resisted her advances. "I truly am exhausted love. I don't think I'll be much good. Another night, perhaps."

"Oh Arthur, you are so damned British," she said.

As she turned in a huff and stormed back to the building, St. George smiled and said to himself. "No. I am too damned gay."

Chapter 3

THIS ONE WAS a beut. Sam Valente hadn't expected to find a damned menagerie in the narrow, single-room apartment in downtown Los Angeles. Horned toads in a terrarium; a boa constrictor in another one, and a green iguana in yet another, and all in the front of the apartment. Pushing 45 and after 14 years working some of L.A.'s most heinous crimes, the stuff no one else in the department wanted, this was a first for the detective.

An archway, somewhere in the middle of the room, gave the apartment the illusion of having two rooms.

Birds. Three in one cage off to the right in front of the archway. He didn't know what they were. Maybe some kind of finch or sparrow. They wouldn't shut up.

Three aquariums. One filled with stupid little gold fish; one filled with disgusting green algae like puke stuck to the glass; but another contained several piranha. Now where did they come from he wondered.

Some kind of snake sleeping in a terrarium. A white laboratory mouse spun on a wheel in his little cage in a manic rodent, aerobic workout. And the birds kept screeching.

Valente spotted a familiar face, took a step towards him, when a spotted cat hissed at him from inside its cage directly under the arch to the left. "Jesus!"

"That's an ocelot," said an evidence technician.

The creature hissed at him again. Valente felt that if the cage weren't there he'd be the ocelot's lunch.

The smell of Lysol hung in the air as he moved under the archway. Just ahead, tied to her bedpost was the naked body of Sheila Barrow. Or what was left of her.

Valente had received the call at 7:30 p.m. Forty minutes later he pulled up in front of the three-story apartment building on a trash-filled street in downtown Los Angeles. Not a palm tree in sight. Busted up store fronts, abandoned warehouses, and faded brick structures – could have been any derelict neighborhood in New York or Chicago. Not sunny L.A.

A crime scene unit had already arrived along with a local patrol unit who got the call. A medical examiner and a couple of EMTs were also at the scene.

Other than the police presence and a rusted Chevy with busted tail lights, the narrow street was deserted. Whatever drug dealers inhabited the area had long made a fast exit when they heard the police sirens.

The fiftyish manager, a whiskey-soaked Midwesterner had let in the detective and then went back to his bottle.

Valente tapped the shoulder of Todd Grant, the officer at the scene who met him in the stairwell. "Got anybody coming to get these animals out of here. We need to find out where the exotic ones, like that damned ocelot, came from."

"We're on it," Grant said.

"Any other surprises creature-wise I need to know about?"

Todd Grant simply shrugged. "Nah. This is it detective."

Sheila Barrow's face had been burned beyond recognition. Burned and then extinguished. And there was something else about the body. "Right arm cut off at the elbow," Grant said. He had the tanned, matinee looks common among some of LAPD's younger cops. A flash from the unit photographer's camera sent Valente's eyes back to Barrow's body.

Upper left arm was tied to the bedpost. Next. Abdomen sliced horizontally from one end to the other. An evidence tech nearest the corpse looked at him. "What the hell sets a killer off like this?"

"My friend," Valente said. "If we knew that we'd all soon be out of work."

Valente often had a knack for making light of an otherwise horrible situation. It kept him going and in an odd way, focused. He moved closer to the victim and considered this most unusual crime scene. Exotic animals in cages, and a much disfigured corpse facing him. He jotted down some notes. Only the face was burned, he wrote. *Why just the face?* More flashes from the camera.

"Make sure you get the residue from her face?"

One technician looked at him, insulted. "Of course detective. We won't miss anything."

"You got any prints?" Valente asked.

"Not yet," replied another evidence tech. "But if there's one here, I'll get it."

"Time of death?" Valente asked.

"Couple of days, at least," Grant said.

"Who found her?"

"Heating guy doing a maintenance check of the heating system throughout the units," the sergeant replied.

"A dump like this gets a maintenance check?" Valente said.

"I guess. A lot of complaints led to some action by the city. Anyway, heating guy called us. We took his statement."

Valente checked the narrow kitchen. A small, pale-green Formica table and two folding vinyl chairs stood off to the left. The faint smell of grease was noticeable but not unpleasant. There were far worse smells at a homicide scene.

He peaked into a tiny bathroom that smelled of kitty litter. The medicine cabinet was neatly organized with a bottle of mouthwash, an allergy prescription, and two tubes of toothpaste, a razor and some hand lotion. Nothing out of the ordinary, except... the toilet seat was up, not down.

Was the killer male? Did he take a leak and do what all men do - leave the toilet seat up?

Back to the front room where on a second look, he recognized Danny Lupe, crouched under a desk, wiping it clean. Lupe was an expert evidence tech with whom Valente had worked several crime scenes. He was the meticulous, highly intelligent sort who was not much fun at a party because all he could really talk about was his work. Valente also noticed this part of the apartment appeared to serve as a combination study, dining alcove and zoo.

"How you doing Danny?"

"Just another day in paradise."

"Anything interesting here?"

"You're kidding right?

"Besides the animals," Valente said, impatiently.

"Could be. Check them out." He pointed to a stack of books on the floor next to the desk.

Valente crouched next to them. They were logbooks. He opened one, and flipped through pages of appointments, delivery dates, and the animals to be delivered. "She was a dealer?"

"Don't know. Maybe she bought and sold to zoos."

Valente looked up at him. "I doubt it. What would a zoo want with her?"

"Maybe collectors?" Lupe asked.

Valente considered that for a moment. Maybe she sold hard-to-get exotic animals to eccentrics.

Lupe continued carefully wiping the area under the desk. "Some clowns, for example, want a lion cub for a pet, forgetting that the cute little cub will grow up some day and eat half their house."

Valente liked the collector idea as his eyes roamed down a page of the logbook and over to the next. Then he stopped. "Here's a request for a baby snow leopard."

Lupe bumped his head under the desk. "Snow leopard? How the hell could she get her hands on one of those? You don't get more endangered than those cats?" Lupe said.

Another tech handed Valente the victim's driver's license found in her purse. "She looks better here," the officer said. Barrow was wholesome looking, round-ish face, a small birthmark on her lower left cheek; green eyes, short cropped brownish hair, and from the birth date on her license, 44 years of age.

On a bookshelf, there was a framed photo of her and a female friend standing next to a fountain, posing and smiling.

Lupe took the log book out of Valente's hand. "What about this snow leopard?"

"Danny. Relax. You're gonna pop a blood vessel. It looks like someone was inquiring about the animal. Doesn't say she delivered. You see." Valente moved his index finger down a column on the right side of the page. "There's a delivery date by the animals delivered. No date by the snow leopard."

Valente could see the tension in Lupe's face relax a bit. Lupe was known around the department as a huge animal lover and donated money regularly to various wildlife causes. "Some really sick people out there," Lupe said.

Something about the entries in the book caught Valente's attention. No names or addresses by the phone numbers. Just delivery dates. Did she keep that information somewhere else?

Officer Grant moved past Valente. "It's like Noah's fucking Arc in here. Place's gotta be 600 square feet and she's got 900 square feet of cages."

Valente couldn't argue with that observation. He handed Grant the logbook. "Check those numbers, though I bet they are all unlisted, but check anyway. Let's see if our lady was dealing in the sale of illegal animals."

Chapter 4

THE CHILL IN the air sent a subtle shiver through St. George as he strolled down the quiet sidewalk looking for his car. The street ran parallel to noisy Wilshire Blvd. With its stands of palm and oleander, the street stood in stark contrast to the concrete and bustle on Wilshire. He liked the oleander.

St. George never dreamed he would fall in love with a city that in truth wasn't one. It was urban sprawl connected by tributaries of freeways. He recalled what playwright Tennessee Williams had once said about Los Angeles – that it was a thousand lost villages in search of a city. Still, St. George was oddly fascinated by all those lost villages.

A growing theatrical community had made its presence felt, which pleased him. And though Los Angeles had its many faults, it was also blessed with palm trees and oleander everywhere, like on the street he was walking, filling the air with their sweet fragrances. And something else he had never had in Liverpool – endless sunshine and a cozy, split level, detached home with a front and back yard fringed with swathes of luxuriant tropical vegetation. From the second floor of his Santa Monica home, a partial view of the Pacific punctuated his life. Dank and gray Liverpool had offered no view of blue water.

While enjoying these ruminations, he suddenly had the odd feeling that he was being followed.

This time, if it was Leslie, he would be more forceful with her. He looked up and down the street and saw that, save for an elderly couple walking their dog, the street was deserted.

No Leslie to worry about. St. George felt better about that, because he wasn't in the mood to discuss his sexual preferences at this late hour. St George was old-school. Like many of his generation, he lived his life in the closet.

St. George reached the corner, where he thought he had parked his car. It was nowhere in sight. *Too much damned champagne.* "Where are you, my lovely chariot?"

He looked back, in the direction from where he came, but did not see his car, so he turned left and headed down another street. By now he was disoriented and frustrated and suffering the curse of every late-night reveler begging the question, *where did I park my car!*

As he peered into the darkness ahead, he saw a shadowy figure watching him or so he thought. But as he got closer, he noticed the man was soon joined by a woman. The couple got into a modest SUV.

St. George mumbled a few obscenities about not being able to find his own car. He crossed the street, thinking maybe he had parked his blasted car there. But after slowly scanning that side, he realized all was hopeless. He leaned against a lamppost to catch his breath. And in a moment he suddenly started laughing.

The entire absurdity engulfed him – that of a fabulous evening heralded by a thunderous opening night reception, with promises of more such evenings to come, only to end up looped and lost somewhere in Beverly Hills – a drunken producer in search of his Mercedes.

This time he heard something definitive. *Footsteps.* Behind him. He turned around.

No one. He looked up and down the street. Nothing.

"Leslie," he called out. "Is that you?" Then a thought struck him. He called to her. "Maybe I should go back with you. I can't seem to find my car."

A car drove past him, and soon another. He wondered how long it would be before he found his car, or Leslie would appear. He continued down the sidewalk. Again he heard footsteps, and heavier this time…coming closer.

St. George's breathing got heavier. The air had grown colder. He could see his breath wisping out as he searched the street.

St. George reached the corner and stopped. The traffic ahead at the next intersection gave him a sense of security. For once he welcomed Los Angeles traffic. He could hail a cab, though he never recalled having seen one trolling the streets of those lost villages. But tonight, hope reigned supreme.

He looked once more behind him. The sidewalk was empty. He felt some comfort that he was not followed, and that Leslie had not materialized. All he could think about at this moment was to curl under his linen sheets on his comfortable bed at home. He lit a cigarette, and took a long satisfying puff.

With suddenness he could have never imagined even in his wildest theatrical stagings, two gloved hands gripped his throat. His eyes widened painfully. The cigarette popped out of his mouth as his assailant pulled him back into an alley with the ferocity of a carnivore.

St. George's struggles proved useless to an attacker far stronger than him. He felt himself being lifted to his feet and then turned around, facing a hooded figure with the death grip. Like a noose, the hands tightened around St. George's neck. Tighter, tighter, until there was little air left to breathe. He tried to get a fix on his assailant but his face was hidden under the hood. St. George wanted desperately to see the face of his would-be killer. The attacker's hands nearly penetrated his skin. St. George's feet dangled a few inches from the pavement. Suddenly, his assailant slammed him against the wall behind him, knocking out what little air was left in him.

St. George had often wondered what went through the mind of a person who knew they were about to die. Arthur St. George thought of his mother. When something scared him in the night, and he woke up screaming and crying, she came to him dutifully and lovingly. She would hold him in her arms, and whisper, "There, there, Arty. Everything's going to be O.K. Mummy's here."

Only mummy wasn't here. St. George's feet stopped dangling, until there was no movement. The attacker released his grip, and St. George dropped to the ground, his head slumped forward.

The killer placed his index finger under St. George's chin and slowly lifted his head. He looked at him for a moment. The eyes inside the hood registered momentary regret. He cocked his head to one side as though thinking maybe killing him was a mistake. And then, with a rush, the killer escaped through the alley, staying well in the shadows.

⊷═◉ ◉═⊷

Outside Sheila's Barrow's apartment building, Valente leaned against a wall and took a very deep breath, and then exhaled. He noticed the top of city hall was barely visible over the crumbling buildings and houses in the neighborhood. Across the street, two homeless guys carried pieces of cardboard over their heads. Further ahead of them, he saw a homeless encampment under a freeway. Presumably the two men were headed there to erect their cardboard condos.

Valente didn't normally answer routine homicide cases, only those of an extreme nature, which was why he was called to Sheila Barrow's gruesome murder scene. He was the department's top gun working the cases nobody had the stomach for.

He took another breath of air that gave him momentary relief.

I'm forty –five, look damned good for my age, and in pretty good shape. Why do I feel like a bus just hit me? And that damned ocelot.

His cell phone chirped. He looked at the number. "Shit," was all he could muster.

Chapter 5

BLOOD EVERYWHERE. ON the kitchen counter dripping to the floor. Blood spread under the kitchen table like a stream finding its way to a river. Blood, and more blood. Pieces of brain matter splattered on that same bloodied floor. The kitchen looked like a slaughterhouse.

The severed head of a young man was propped next to a pot of boiling water. The brain had been removed and crushed, hence all the brain matter all over the kitchen floor. A severed hand rested against the severed head.

The large man, with his back to the camera, dumped human entrails into the pot. He lifted his roundish head – potato head his ailing sister used to call him before he finally sawed her in half - and sniffed the air around him. He emitted a guttural snort, like that from a wild boar. And the screen dissolved to the next scene.

This horrific movie pleased Mitchell Shanker who was held in rapt attention by the gruesome film. Blood was important to life, and the lack of it was equally significant. The image on the screen flickered, and then got a little snowy. Shanker reached for his remote and rewound the tape. He was probably one of the few people left in Los Angeles who still had a working VCR.

He rewound to the point where the machete came down on the victim's neck, ripping the head from his body. Then came his favorite part - taking the head and then removing the brain. By removing the brain, you symbolically say – this is no longer human. This is just flesh and tissue.

Shanker loved this movie.

Chapter 6

VALENTE PULLED HIS unmarked car into the staging area near an alley, about an hour after leaving the Sheila Barrow crime scene. Several EMTs were on site along with two squad cars. A fire truck and ambulance were nearby. He looked at the alley. One of his partners was coming towards him as he parked his squad the area. The police tape had already been erected keeping the media and on-lookers away. A group of witnesses were off to the right, giving statements.

As Valente got out of the car, a young, eager journalist approached him. "Can we have a statement, sir."

"I just got here genius."

"We don't get too many murders in Beverly Hills."

Detective Ed McCarty, carefully holding onto a half-eaten hot dog, came between Valente and the reporter. "Move on fellow. Behind the line. We'll get to you later."

The reporter was about to protest but was humbled by McCarty's not to friendly glare, and retreated behind the police line.

"This is what we've got," McCarty said swallowing the last morsel of his hot dog. He was a beer and butter guy with steady blue eyes, ruddy cheeks and a hefty frame. A Boston transplant, he was Irish all the way and wore his ethnicity like a medal of honor.

"Vic was strangled in that alley."

He and Valente crossed a police tape blocking the entrance to the alley and headed towards the victim lying in a body bag next to a dumpster. A chalked outline marked the area around the body. A police photographer was snapping shots. Before entering the alley, Valente noticed a small group of people huddled together around a squad car giving their statements to two beat cops.

"You know who the stiff is?"

"No," Valente said.

"That's Arthur St. George."

The name rang a distant bell. "The producer?"

"Yep. That Arthur St. George," McCarty said. "We got his I.D."

Valente unzipped the body bag revealing the corpse's face. "Who'd want to kill a producer?"

"In this town? You gotta be kidding, right?"

The paramedics re-zipped the bag and wheeled him out of the alley.

"You know what I think?" McCarty added.

"I can't wait for your next consonant."

"Since he is connected to show biz, maybe he was into weird shit. Most of them are. You know drugs, orgies, wild parties, men doing women, men doing men, dogs... bestiality - who the hell knows... Maybe something got out of hand. What do you think?"

"I think millions of years of human evolution have passed right by you. But you're a helluva crime scene detective."

McCarty appreciated the compliment, though he was still trying to figure out the evolution thing.

"O.K. Let me be more delicate and politically fucking correct. Just like a man or a woman could kill the other in a passionate rage, known in many circles as a crime of passion, I think this individual, of a possible weird leaning, might have been snuffed by his significant other, or maybe a weird friend into all that crazy stuff I just mentioned. How's that?"

"Possible," Valente said.

"Jesus. Don't get too enthusiastic. Don't want you getting an aneurism."

"You guys got here pretty fast," Valente said.

"Yeah, a couple walking to their car saw the body, called it in. And before you ask, yes, we got their statements. And of course, the media with all their police trackers, are here waiting to have their usual orgasms over this stuff."

"So he was killed, what? maybe an hour ago, two hours ago?"

"Do I look like the human clock? But we're canvassing the whole area. Don't worry, if he's still in the neighborhood we'll get him."

McCarty had played fullback for a couple of years at Penn State until he blew out his knee. Valente had actually seen one of his games on the tube before he knew who he was. Joined the force twenty years ago, and felt he'd do another five and retire. Over the years, the two had developed the type of friendship centered mainly on sports and an occasional group barbecue. Valente had never been married, and Ed was on his second marriage burn-out.

"By the way. I got the Laker's tickets," McCarty said. "Not the best seats, but who can afford this shit anymore, huh? They keep paying these athletes more money than the gross national product of most third world countries, and who pays. We pay."

"How many times do I have to hear that gripe? Get some new material."

"But he's right *paisan*." Both immediately recognized the velvety voice of Nicole Park, an Asian-American beauty, who was standing just inside the alley. "Ticket prices are out of control." She had a friendly smile and pretty brown eyes like Godiva milk chocolate. But it was her legs that turned heads.

"Well look what the smog blew in," Valente said. His demeanor changed instantly on seeing Park. "Been what? Two years? What are you doing here at this late hour?"

"Looks like we're on a case again." Park had recently been reassigned to homicide after two years working a desk in Intelligence. "Soon as the call came in, chief assigned me to you. We're a team again - you, me, and Mr. Ed. Excited?"

"Be careful, Sam," McCarty said. "She's armed and dangerous."

Valente eyed her suspiciously. "Yeah?"

"Just got back from Quantico," Park said. "Got reacquainted with behavioral analysis."

Valente rolled his eyes. *Behavioral* anything was not high on his list of favorite subjects.

The three had worked several cases together a few years earlier, including two high-profile sex crimes, until Park had asked for a transfer. The human tragedy around working major sex crimes had taken a toll on her to the point where she had requested a leave of absence, and later reassignment.

"All better now?" Valente said, fully aware of her past.

"Of course." Valente wasn't convinced but he would let it go for now.

"So, what's with you and Mr. Ed?" she said.

"Stop calling me Mister Ed."

"Nothing," Valente said. "He just gets to me sometimes. Ed, you got all the subtlety of a toilet seat."

"But few people walk a grid like I do, right?"

"Yeah. You're good," Valente agreed.

"You got that right. Last year everyone missed one little detail in the Roger Hannex case. Not me. We find a butchered body of a woman in Griffith Park. Crime scene gurus went all through the area. Couldn't find a thing. But I did. The killer's government issue ball point pen, you know those old black ones. They're the zippo lighters of pens. Got his pen, prints on the pen, traced him back to his job, and bingo, we nabbed him. Turns out, the dead woman was his wife. How about that?"

"Ed. I wanna be just like you when I grow up."

"Grumpy tonight?" Park said.

Valente felt like he wanted to soak in a hot tub for about three hours. "I just came from the Sheila Barrow crime scene. Not a pleasant sight. Forty minutes later I'm here. Maybe tonight, things are getting to me a little."

"It happens to everyone Sam. You know that."

"Not now Nicole. I don't need your psycho babble tonight."

"Are you ever going to change your image of psychiatry?" she said.

"Yeah. Tomorrow maybe. Not tonight. But you know what? Now that you are assigned to my team, let's go have a drink tomorrow night. Talk about the case, celebrate your reassignment and toast to a new adventure."

Paramedics lifted St. George's body into the ambulance. The vehicle slowly maneuvered out of the area.

"Made some calls before you got here," McCarty said. "His new show opened tonight over at the Tartan. "Murders in the Rue Morgue." He read from his notes. "Says here, it's a musical adaptation of Edgar Allan Poe's infamous crime story."

"A musical version of "Murders in the Rue Morgue?" Valente said.

"*You* read Poe?" McCarty said to Valente in a harsh whisper.

"Of course. Everybody's read Poe." Valente said. "So, any witnesses? Anybody see anything?"

"Not yet, but we are not done canvassing," McCarthy reminded him.

Valente steadily glanced around the crime scene, scanning the street in both directions, before turning back to McCarty and Park. A small group of curious people had gathered behind the police line.

"Anybody over there look like they didn't belong?"

McCarty shrugged. "Not sure. But if he's in the area we'll get him."

Valente looked at Park for a moment. "So, what do you think?"

"Well, tonight was opening night. Start with the cast. See if they know anything?"

"Yeah. That's a good start. Find out if anyone had an ax to grind with him."

And oddly, at that moment, the only thing that popped into the mind of one of L.A.'s finest homicide detectives was the vision of that hissing ocelot in Sheila Barrow's apartment.

Chapter 7

NIGHTTIME FALLS OVER the bay of Naples like a mother gently placing a blanket over her sleeping child. City lights shimmer off the bay's dark waters, and Vesuvius looms large and foreboding. It knows it can reduce Naples to ashes, as it did to Pompeii two millennia before. So for now, the volcano rests, like an ancient goddess daring to be angered.

For Don Pasquale, his reasons for leaving Naples had nothing to do with whether or not the volcano would erupt. He left for one simple reason. Money.

His road to America was a circuitous one. It took him across the Italian Alps into Switzerland. There, he worked for a time in a stuffy restaurant in Lucerne where Italian immigrants were not well liked.

Then from Switzerland to Marseilles where he bribed his way onto a tanker bound for New York. In Brooklyn, he quickly gained employment as a waiter. His good looks, charm, and ability to quickly learn English gained him popularity. On his 30th birthday he was made a manager of a popular West Side eatery, and after a year the owners sent him to Los Angeles to manage their sister restaurant. Within a few years he had opened his own in Santa Monica.

He named it *Don Pasquale's*. The popular *trattoria* offering genuine Neapolitan cuisine, with a dash of Tuscan in honor of his mother, had fast become a fixture on the Santa Monica dining circuit.

The restaurant's ocher walls, blue and ecru floor tiles, and the pleasant aromas of garlic, marinara and oregano made Valente feel serene. The atmosphere cuddled him like a family gathering.

Here is where Valente came to marinate.

When he walked into the restaurant around 10 p.m., the evening after St. George's murder, the place was still packed. A young man, loosely resembling a young Dean Martin, was on the last verse of an old standard. He was backed by a three-piece combo.

The effervescent Don Pasquale, who carried a pronounced pasta belly, and with eyes that shined from too much wine, spotted Valente from the center of the room. "*Amico mio.* Good to see you," he flashed a broad smile that revealed a gap between his upper two front teeth. Valente always felt that Don Pasquale was a dead ringer for the actor Ernest Borgnine.

"Who's the Dean Martin wannabe?" Valente said, taking a small table near the back. Just then the singer began his rendition of *That's Amore.* "He better not screw that up."

"Hey, this is open mic. Almost everyone that goes up there stinks." Don Pasquale had that raspy, smoker's voice common with Italian men who seem to have been born with a cigarette in their mouths.

"Then why do you have it?"

"Gives a few people a chance to live out their fantasies that come alive only in my humble trattoria."

"You should be canonized."

"Maybe later. Tonight I have to endure another bad version of *That's Amore.* What is it with these guys? Almost every Italian American man over forty, who thinks he can sing, has to try that song. Leave it alone. *Please.*"

Don Pasquale's signature dish was linguini with mussels in a white wine sauce. "Start with the linguini?" Don Pasquale said as Valente took a table near the back of the long rectangular room.

"You got it."

A brunette waitress with an hour-glass figure brought bread and a place setting to Valente's table. Her name was Leanna. She smiled and leaned slightly towards him while setting down the bread, giving him a peak into her ample cleavage.

"She is something," he said to Don Pasquale.

"Leanna. Oh yeah."

"They're not real."

"How do you know?"

"My old friend. I'm a Hollywood detective. I can spot a pair of implants like a hawk can spot a field mouse."

Don Pasquale lifted his arms, and waved his hands at him. "Do Italian men think of anything else?"

Valente had discovered Don Pasquale's three years before, and had been a regular ever since. For Valente, it was the next best thing to actually dining in Italy. The food was down-to-earth and the sauces exquisite. All of the dishes had just the right blend of oils, spices, and sauces. His veal cut like butter and his venison with a porcini and blackberry reduction was sinful. The wine list, though modest, included some excellent Brunellos and Barolos. At Don Pasquale, Valente could put the brutal realities of his world behind him for an evening, and think of nothing but Italian gastronomic pleasures.

The off key screeching from the singer attempting to hit a note out of his range interrupted his thoughts. And in annoying counterpoint, his cell phone squealed. As Valente looked at the phone number on the caller ID, his delicious plate of linguini arrived. At that moment his cellphone, and everything it represented, had become the Antichrist.

Chapter 8

Deep inside the cavernous Los Angeles County coroner's office, two levels beneath the ground floor, Valente and Park made their way down a drab, depressing green corridor, past a security guard, and into an autopsy room painted in vomit green. The smell of phamaldohyde hung in the air. The room was predominantly all stainless steel with work stations, two examination tables with drainage holes, water tubs with hoses and two dissection tables.

Chief pathologist Maria Santos was adjusting the volume on a hanging mic when Valente and Park had walked in. She cast them a wry smile.

Valente had no problem with the sight of blood or the stench of bodily fluids. He had been around enough crime scenes and autopsies to not let that bother him. What sometimes made him uneasy was the sight of a body methodically taken apart. In his world view he could care less about the bad guys. But seeing an innocent on a gurney, in this case, Arthur St. George, whose cardinal mistake was being at the wrong place at the wrong time, made him feel bad for the victim's friends and family.

The police department had contacted a brother who had come earlier to officially identify the corpse. It was later revealed that his brother was his only surviving immediate family.

Santos interrupted his thoughts. "Welcome constables."

"You couldn't tell me over the phone," Valente snapped at Santos who was now standing over St. George's sawed body with the standard Y-incision. "I just left a perfectly decent plate of linguini and mussels."

Santos leaned in closer to him, under the bright lights of the autopsy room, revealing a blotchy complexion in dire need of a dermatologist. "I had to see the look on your face," she said.

Valente noticed a mischievous look in her eyes that he did not like. "Well? What've you got? It's late. Some of us do sleep."

"Sleep? What's that?" Santos said. The petite woman packed enough energy to power a city grid. Valente glared at her.

"Be nice Sam or I'll cut open the stomach now rather than after you leave and spare you that horrible stench."

Having witnessed similar exchanges between them before, Park decided to stay in the background for a moment and enjoy their jousting. Santos quickly scanned a medical chart and continued. "There were no hematomas, puncture wounds, or other external bruises. Initial examination, along with X-Ray results, indicate a crushing injury to the victim's larynx. Death by strangulation. Our perp was very strong, constable" she said.

He shot her a look that said *this* *is what you wanted to tell me in person.*

"*Powerful* strangulation, Sam," Santos added. "*Really* powerful. Larynx crushed."

"Really?" Valente said, feigning surprise.

"I'm thorough, Sam. I think that is why you have secretly had a burning crush on me," she winked at Nicole. "If you look here, on my neat, stainless steel organ tray, you will notice a perfect set of lungs. Clean. No signs of cancer." She indicates an adjacent tray. "Here is his liver, possibly showing signs of a few too many bourbons, or scotch, but nothing to alarm anyone. Nothing to suggest self- abuse, though we'll confirm all that when we get the tox report back."

Valente was not in the mood for another night of jousting. He appreciated her talent – she was perhaps the best in the business, but Santos was known around the force as an instigator who often enjoyed intimidating others.

"As I was about to cut further," Santos smiled coyly, and moved over to a microscope on a counter. "I found this." She gestured with her head, couple of times, towards the microscope.

Valente reluctantly peered through the lens. "A damned hair. You could have told me this over the phone. Are you enjoying this because I have a murder to solve."

"It is simian." Both Park and Valente narrowed their eyes. Santos words fell on them like something spoken from a macabre movie. "I found this hair lodged behind his left ear, and a couple more in his head."

She gave them a moment to digest her report. "As you can imagine, I've pretty much seen it all in my little world, but this threw me for a curve. I asked the crime scene techs to call the zoo. They sent someone over to verify. The hairs found on St. George's body belong to a large ape."

Valente wondered whether long nights at the morgue had finally loosened Santos' marbles.

"Sam. You're speechless," Santos said, relishing these moments when she could annoy him. "This has got to be a first." Then she turned to Park, with a wry smile. "I just love getting on his last nerve. Did you know that only two chromosomes separate us from the apes? But in his case, maybe only one."

Valente looked through the scope again, fighting back his temper. "What kind of ape?"

Santos cleared her throat. She wanted the delivery to be perfect. "Gorilla," she said chewing on every letter. "Silverback."

⤙▱ ▱⤚

Valente took the squad car into a sharp turn out of the morgue's parking lot, burning rubber at 40 mph. "Easy, easy, easy," Park screeched.

"Gorillas?!" Valente said as he skidded around a corner. Then images of Sheila Barrow danced through his mind – the woman with all the animals. "What the hell is this? Animal association month? This is nuts."

Then he slowed down as he moved in behind traffic. A silly thought crossed Park's mind. "I can see the headlines. Producer strangled by actor who moved like an ape."

"What do we know about St. George?" Valente said, still smarting from the scene at the morgue.

Park opened her notebook and read. "Producer and director of low budget horror films. Been at it for about 30 years. Originally from London. Still has a small flat there. *Chopped Into Pieces and Still Moving* was one of his 'epics'. *Fraternity of Blood* was another. *Murders in the Rue Morgue* is his second theatrical venture. Before this one –"

Valente shook his head, obviously annoyed. "Not his resume." He turned onto an exit ramp to the Ventura Freeway. "Billy Geller was canvassing right?"

"Yeah," Park said.

"He's one of the best," Valente said. "Takes statements better than anybody on our beat. So what else do we have? Was he screwing anybody he shouldn't have been?"

"Doesn't look like it. He was a little reclusive. Eccentric. Gay. At times sarcastic. Some people in the cast thought he pushed them too hard, but all in all, he was class all the way. He has a brother up north. Half Moon Bay. Roger St. George."

"Anybody talk to Roger?"

"Yes. He gave a statement." Park continued, checking her notes. "He was at his home at the time of the murder. Runs a non-profit marine mammal rescue center. From his statement the two did not seem to have been very close. He didn't elaborate on that too much, but he admired the success he had gained in the entertainment world."

"What else do we know?"

She thought for a moment. "Do you mean did he have any enemies?"

"Everybody's got enemies."

Chapter 9

MITCHELL SHANKER SAT at his desk in a room illuminated only by candlelight. He was a handsome young man in his late twenties. His dark eyes were soft, but penetrating. His skin was pale but not unhealthy.

A bland bookshelf stood at one side of his desk, the shelves crammed with copies of film scripts, plays, books about costume design, and several books on theatre history. One book was always a source of inspiration to him– *Legacy of the Grand Guignol.*

In it, the reader would learn that the French had unknowingly, through the Grand Guignol, kicked off a chain reaction in horror entertainment. The theatre had been housed in the Pigalle area of Paris, and from its opening in 1897 until its closing in 1962, the Grand Guignol specialized in horror shows. Its name was often used to describe graphic, gratuitous horror entertainment that some suggest gave birth to the 20th century's slice and dice movies.

Shanker often read passages from this book. His favorite was the part about one of its most notorious directors – Max Maurey, who succeeded the theater's founder, Oscar Metenier in 1898. Together, with playwright Andre de Lorde, dubbed "the Prince of Terror," insanity became the Grand-Guignol's theme. At a time when insanity was just beginning to be scientifically studied, the theatre's repertoire explored countless manias and featured staged killings, mutilations and scenes of torture so realistic that audience members often fled the theater in terror.

There was a play about a necrophiliac who violated tombs and mutilated bodies. "The Horrible Passion" by de Lorde depicted a young nanny who strangled the children in her care. And there were many more that captivated Shanker. He was a devotee of the Grand Guignol.

The flame on one of the candles at the edge of Shaker's desk flickered. He held a flattened hand in front of it until the flame steadied. Then he began to write a letter.

Dear Mother, I've been auditioning as promised. Did not get the part in that musical but I think I made quite an impression on the director. Please write. I've sent you several letters and have not heard from you.

Love, Mitchell.

He placed the letter in an envelope and sealed it. Then he looked at himself in the mirror.

"Write to me mother."

Chapter 10

WEARING LATEX GLOVES, Valente moved methodically through St. George's small, second floor study. The Santa Monica home was not far from the beach, stirring recurring feelings in Valente about wanting to move from his Los Feliz apartment closer to the ocean. To him, the whole reason for living in L.A. was to live near the water, otherwise why bother. But he hadn't found the right place yet. And buying was out of the question the way prices kept soaring in the area.

He walked downstairs to the living room where a cognac leather couch and matching armchairs caught his eye. The coffee table in front of the couch was of black marble on wrought iron legs. Nice he thought. Very nice.

He noticed some titles on a bookshelf but a cursory review revealed nothing of particular interest. Theater books mainly and several books on film history. He looked behind a large seascape painting hanging on the wall over a fireplace. Nothing. No hidden safe.

"Bedrooms are clean," Park said walking down the stairs.

They went into a den, handsomely decorated in leather. A small mahogany desk stood in the center of the room which also doubled as an office. The walls were adorned with paintings of men in various erotic positions. The room seemed oddly like homage to photographer Richard Mapplethorpe.

"I'm thinking a jealous lover?" Park said.

Valente had his eye on an explicit painting of three young men entwined in sexual positions that would bring down the wrath of every evangelist in America. "How many ways can you bend the human body?" he said quietly. Then he quickly changed his tone. "I'm not sure about the lover thing. But you know what's been nagging at me?"

Park raised an eyebrow. "No *paisan*. What's been nagging at you?"

"What's been tugging at my chain is those gorilla hairs?"

"I have to admit, our unsub is original"

"How did those hairs get there?" Valente continued. "If we were dealing with a psycho sitting at home staring at his butcher knife and waiting for a dog to tell him when to kill again, that would be one thing. And often those types make a major blunder. But I don' think that's our perp."

"Oh?"

"This guy has access to places most people don't?"

"Like the primate house at a zoo," she interrupted.

"He's clever. Organized, and smart."

Park opened a drawer to a file cabinet, thumbed through several file folders. "You listening?"

"Yes. I can do two things at once," she said.

"So I ask again. How did he get those hairs, and what is he telling us?

Park stopped rummaging through the files for a moment. "He's leaving us clues. That's obvious. But for what? Maybe he wants to get caught – assuming this won't be his first and last victim."

"Whoa, pretty lady. Don't go serial on me yet. You need more than one murder to qualify as a serial killer."

"Yes. I think it's three."

Valente found a stack of photos on a shelf. They were 8 X 10 headshots of actors. "Did you call the zoo?"

"Yes. Shaka, Naka, and Oomgawa, or whatever their names are, were sleeping soundly when St. George was murdered. I also inquired if anyone could have gotten near a gorilla to pluck some hairs. No one gets near the apes except the handlers and the vets, and they all have alibis."

"Nevertheless, our perp got those hairs." While he thumbed through the stack of 8 X 10s, something in the file cabinet grabbed Park's attention. A small photo album under a row of hanging files. She opened the album and was startled by its contents. "Will you look at this."

Valente moved next to her, carrying the stack of photos from the wall shelf. The photo album she held was filled with pictures of St. George in various erotic poses with a young man who was a stunner. Park looked at Valente with a little air of confidence. "So? Jealous lover?"

"Maybe, but again, why the gorilla hairs?" Valente set the stack of photos on the desk.

"Call these actors. Start with the reject file."

"What about super stud in the album?"

"Him too."

Valente turned from her and walked over to a window. He seemed distracted. "Sam?"

He kept staring out the window. "Most of the time, I love my work. I honestly don't wake up with an ax to grind. Maybe just a small hammer. Never had a drinking problem, burned out cop syndrome; didn't wreck several marriages, and all that stuff. Seems like every movie about a cop is about a guy on some kind of burn-out. That ain't me. But when a case gets really weird, when I feel that we are entering a territory without a constitution, I get really antsy, like I want to get out of this business. And this? This is getting weird."

Park thought for a moment. Planting the gorilla hairs was certainly not the M.O of a garden variety killer. "You could be right, but then again this murder could be just another crime of passion. Nothing weird there."

"Something isn't right Nicole. First, I'm at the apartment of a strange woman who dealt in exotic animals. Someone burns her face, slices off her right arm and cuts through her abdomen. Talk about that perp making a statement. Then gorilla hairs are found on St. George."

"You think there is a connection?"

⋄⇒▶ ◀⇐⋄

Outside St. George's house, Valente and Park walked to their unmarked squad car parked across the street. For the first time tonight he noticed her sleek figure, beautiful legs and soft hair blowing in the breeze. "Stop looking so sexy."

"I guess that's a compliment."

"Hey, I like beauty. My girlfriend, she's good looking. You're beautiful. Too beautiful to be a cop. You ever try modeling?"

"In my early twenties, I tried it for about six months."

"Only six?"

"I couldn't stand being around all those neurotics." Park felt uncomfortable talking about her modeling days. Like many attractive women, she was insecure about her looks. She wanted to be recognized for her brain, and not her body. But she still loved those moments when heads turned whenever she walked into a room, though she would never admit it to him. The curse of good looks she thought. Women want to be taken seriously but they also want the attention. "Could we get off the subject of my legs and continue on the work at hand."

So Valente turned a little more serious. He had something about her he needed to get of his chest, and figured might as well do it now. "Nicole, off and on we've been together working crimes for about five years, until you took that leave of absence. I need to know that you are back in the saddle. Understand? Nothing in our business changes. Blood and guts are spilled every day. Been going on since apes learned how to walk upright. This isn't about you trying to prove something. This is about us finding a killer."

Nicole did not immediately respond. She had expected that. He needed to know that he can depend on her. She had her fall. She had requested time away from homicide. She had gone through all the requirements for someone who had work issues and needed to sort things out. Hours of departmental required counseling and working a desk job had proven beneficial. In fact, the boredom made her work doubly hard to get back to homicide. Her emotional break was a reaction to all the horrors she had witnessed, but she knew it was a temporary thing. Despite the suspicions of others in the force and the man in front of her, she was tough and could handle the rigors of the job.

"I'm O.K. Sam," she said plainly. "Better than OK."

Valente looked at her for a moment. He believed her. "Good. So like I said, call in those actors. Let's see what will turn up."

Chapter II

IT WAS THE black bird on the cover of a book that had grabbed his attention. A menacing raven glared at him from *The Complete Works of Edgar Allan Poe*. The book sat under a lamp and the raven, the bird on the cover, dared him to open its pages. Ron Styles would soon take the dare. But for now he gazed at the bird and considered the possibilities. He lit a cigarette, took a deep drag, and glanced outside his window. All was still and dark.

Styles had been obsessed with Edgar Allan Poe since he was a junior in high school. He had read all of Poe's short stories, and most of his poems. His favorite piece had always been *The Black Cat*. He had poured over biography after biography of the Baltimore writer.

Poe died too young, Styles felt. Like many great artists, Poe was a tormented man out of step with his time – a tortured soul who, like many of his kind, saw the world through different glasses. Poe often looked at his world through the glass of a bottle of absinthe.

Nonetheless, drunk or sober, he wrote some of the most compelling thrillers in the English language. Poe is considered by many the father of the detective novel, and his character Dupin, an original exponent of scientific deduction, appeared a generation before Conan Doyle's Sherlock Holmes. In "Murders in the Rue Morgue," Poe created one of the greatest masterpieces of the genre.

Styles stared at the raven on the cover of his book as though waiting for it to screech. He lit another cigarette and let the smoke slowly stream out over his lips. He traced the trajectory of one stream of smoke as it wafted towards the ceiling and disappeared.

Ron Styles was the owner and artistic director of the McLean Theatre Company in Carpinteria, a beachside community north of Los Angeles. Often he needed hours of quiet time before enduring the horrendous traffic from his condo in Woodland Hills to the theatre. Moving closer to work was in the works.

Having had the good fortune of a small inheritance, Styles had purchased the theatre several years earlier after a fire had consumed the structure. A man with a burning passion for theatre, Styles spent most of the rest of his inheritance on the restoration of the only professional theatre company in Carpenteria and its neighboring areas. Many in the culturally-starved town saw him as a savior. There were no prominent art galleries, no museums, and no fashion boutiques. Just the usual strip malls, and fast food and retail outlets. So Carpinteria had relied on its theatre to quench its thirst for the arts. For many residents, it tied the town together.

The theatre reopened a year after the fire and until recently had played to sold-out crowds. Styles proudly, and sometimes arrogantly, promoted himself as one of the few champions of regional theatre in America. He had gained some national recognition for his work at the McLean Theatre and had received an award from the Los Angeles League of Theatres for best regional company. But to the displeasure of most who knew him, he moved through his world soaked in self-importance.

Like many artists, Styles often needed a challenge. He had reached a point in his career where he tired of producing crowd pleasers. The "Damn Yankees," and "Man of La Manchas" and "The Odd Couples" were all becoming a blur to him. He needed to push the envelope, and of late, had taken some costly risks. He wanted to brave artistic waters that went beyond the conventional tastes of his subscribers.

Three years earlier, Styles had set sail on those waters with a new drama about the Beat generation of the 1950's. The show sank in a week. Then came a production of Samuel Beckett's absurdist drama, "Waiting for Godot," which barely ran a month.

Facing the dilemma of fulfilling his thirst for something bold with that of satisfying his patrons' desire for standard fare, he spent months searching for a vehicle that would accomplish both.

And then came the news of Arthur St. George's murder. Having been consumed with running his own theatre, he had paid little attention to the trade reports of St. George's staging of "Murders in the Rue Morgue." He had received an invitation to the opening night performance of the musical but it got lost in a stack of mail. When news of St. George's murder broke, Styles was at first saddened by the loss, but suddenly awakened to the possibilities of staging another of Edgar Allan Poe's works.

Over the years, some of Poe's stories had been adapted to film with varying degrees of success. In the 1960's "Fall of the House of Usher," "The Pit and The Pendulum," and "The Mask of the Red Death" all starring horror film icon Vincent Price were a sampling of the Poe stories adapted to film. And in every decade since, film makers in Europe and the United States revisited Poe. But, until St. George's production of "Murders in the Rue Morgue," there had never been a major stage production of a Poe story, at least not to Style's knowledge.

So, in the wake of St. George's murder, Styles had decided to cash in on the popularity of the musical and adapt another of Poe's works. He just hadn't figured out which one until the black bird on the cover of his book shone a light.

And the bird, never flitting, got the attention it snarled for. Styles picked up the book again, and let his fingers skim over the pages until they found their mark.

And the words he had not read in years filled and thrilled him unlike anything he had felt before. *The Raven's* opening line that he had read many times in his youth – *once upon a midnight dreary* – still gave him a thrill.

Except for the lamplight over his desk, there was darkness all around him. He let the author's words penetrate deep within. *Once upon a midnight dreary, while I pondered week and weary…*

Should he turn the poem into a drama? Or would he consider a musical? He stared at the raven on the cover of his book, and smiled. "Thank you."

Chapter 12

THE ANGRY MOTHER dragged her screaming son by the hair down a dark hallway in their home. She was more frightening to him than ever before. Never had her eyes had such a look, like that of an animal on the hunt. He had only seen this look in movies. In *scary* movies. She looked like she wanted to eat him.

"I'm sorry mommy," he said with tears streaming down his face. "I'm sorry."

"You failed *again*." Her entire face jutted forward like a reptile preparing to suck in its prey.

They reached the end of the hallway, and to something terribly familiar to the frightened child. The dark closet. Mother opened the door, threw him inside and slammed the door shut.

The young boy cried out. "Mommy I'm sorry. I'm sorry."

She plunked down on the ever present chair near the closet. "No you're not. And tonight you're going to know what sorry is."

"Please mommy. I'm scared. I'm scared. I'm scared."

"*Shut-up!*"

Mitchell woke up in a cold sweat, trembling. The nightmares just wouldn't go away.

Chapter 13

"Do you recognize any of them?" Park asked.

The handsome blonde looked again at the four photos in front of him. "Nope. Can I go now?" Park waved him off. "Sure."

The West Los Angeles Community Police Station rarely saw the type of action a precinct does in South Central L.A. or New York's South Bronx. So, when St. George's murder happened on their turf, the precinct had become a circus. With nearly 270 sworn police officers and about 25 civilians, the station provided service to approximately 225,000 residents in a 65 square-mile area that includes Santa Monica, Marina Del Rey, Culver City, Westwood and Beverly Hills.

Valente watched the ongoing interrogations from his desk. He noticed one of the younger detectives questioning a handsome, chiseled actor. "Did you know St. George, personally?" the young detective asked.

"No. I just read for a part in one of his films three years ago. Am I a suspect?"

And then a black actor mouthed off to another officer. "We're all neurotic man. I ain't met an actor yet working with a full deck. Know what I mean? Man, all those white boys, and a couple of us blacks, making 20-30 million dollars a movie---ain't that some shit? ---they're all messed up. But murderers? I don't think so. We're actors; we ain't killers, though I'd like to shoot my damned agent sometimes."

Valente then caught Ed McCarty in the middle of interrogating an obviously gay actor. McCarty was visibly uncomfortable. This, Valente did not want to miss. The actor made no apologies for his homosexuality.

McCarty was a throwback. A died-in-the wool, all American uncomfortable with anything that didn't smack of manliness. He was a man's man - a card-carrying member of the NRA and a devoted fan of John Wayne westerns. He loved sports, drank beer, and didn't have a feminist bone in his body. In movies, he wanted his heroes to be men, not pencil-thin, silicon- packed models who expected audiences to believe they could take on armies of muscle-bound thugs. He wanted his action heroes tempered in steel, not painted in mascara.

McCarty peered at the blond actor over his glasses. "So…" he glanced at his notes. "Jessie Paget, what do you do when you're not bouncing around on a stage?"

"I don't bounce." Jessie wiped his forehead with his handkerchief and continued. "I deliver medical supplies."

"Who for?"

"Various hospitals. I work for a company that supplies hospitals with a number of goods."

McCarty wrote this down. "Got any names."

"Names?"

"Of the hospitals."

"Don't you believe me, you big hunk of Irish flesh?"

Valente's entire body shook from spasms of repressed laughter. McCarty turned several shades of red.

Jesse leaned forward on both elbows, and rested his chin in his cupped hands. "You're looking at me like I'm a freak. Don't worry big fella. I'm not going to hit you with my purse."

"Excuse me." McCarty got up and walked out of the squad room. He needed some air.

"Hey Ed," yelled one of the cops. "Got any rouge. I'm out."

The place erupted, and even Jessie joined in the merriment. "He's a dinosaur."

Valente decided his legs needed a stretch, and caught up with Park who was heading for the water cooler at the other end of the squad room. "How many more?"

"You said go through St. George's pile of photos. Well in came the pile *paisano*. We got seven or eight left, I think."

Billy Geller, their ace canvasser, met up with them. "Got something for you hot shot." He said to Valente. "St. George hated bad critics."

"Are there any good ones?" Valente said.

"Let me rephrase. He disliked critics he felt were incompetent. He was known for sending rebuttals to critics who gave him bad reviews. He felt that only those who had spent their life working in the particular art they were critiquing qualified them to be critics. One critic once said about a play he had opened that *Arthur St. George made a valiant attempt at nothing.* He became a sort of hero to the struggling artist who did not have the courage to openly attack critics."

Valente had kept his eyes steadily on Geller following his every word. "Good work. And articulate."

"I love movies, theatre…"

"Find out if he targeted any one critic in particular. Someone who might have a score to settle with St. George."

"Already on it." Geller had always been a credit to the force. Squeaky clean, efficient, dedicated. Never a scandal or even the hint of one.

Park wasn't convinced about the critic thing. "You really think a crazed critic is out there getting revenge on St. George?"

"Who knows. Cover all bases all the time."

As Geller disappeared under an archway, Park noticed Lieutenant Lamont Campbell through the plate glass window of his office barking into his phone. A huge ego was in that office housed inside a big frame with busy brown eyes. Campbell, their immediate supervisor, continued his tirade then slammed down the receiver. He opened his door. "Valente, Park. Get in here."

Park walked into his office first.

Campbell's office was a sight in sports decor. Framed pictures of the lieutenant when he was a linebacker at Ohio State University hung on the wall behind his desk. Then, he looked great. Broad shoulders over a solid frame. Confident eyes and a granite chin. Taking a closer look at one of the photos, someone might see an uncanny resemblance to football legend Jim Brown. Now, he looked like a man who could shed the fat from too many years of hot dog abuse.

Campbell made it a point to rarely sit when agitated. He felt he could better assert his rank when standing. "What's this about King Kong?"

"My guess is our killer is toying with us," said Valente.

"Toying?"

"Apes don't strangle people. Something about the lack of a precision grip," Valente said. "And the last I checked, there are no reports of runaway gorillas in L.A. or anywhere else in the United States."

Campbell's eyes narrowed. "I'm not laughing."

"For now we are looking into the possibility of a jealous lover," Valente said.

"I've got Hollywood calling me. That guy's agent just hung up and was not very nice. 'Who would kill him?' he said. 'St.George was one of the nicest people you could ever meet. In a town filled with barracudas, he was a goldfish.'"

Valente and Park looked at him oddly.

"Hey that's what the guy said." Then he added "Someone leaked the news about the gorilla hairs."

"We're doing all we can." Valente said as he and Park started for the door.

"By the way. Check out this call," Campbell handed Valente a note. Valente read the note, then handed it to Park.

Chapter 14

Sometimes the distinction between a good and bad neighborhood in Los Angeles is blurred by too many palm trees and too much sunshine.

But Hermillio, a slice of East L.A. was an exception. Even the rats avoided it. Hermillio was a nightmare of old warehouses, trash-filled streets, boarded storefronts, and people living near the gates of hell. The stench of human waste hung in the air and on any given day; hundreds of used syringes speckled the sidewalks. A dead body could rot in an alley for weeks before anyone noticed or cared.

The fifty-year old, rotund landlady led Park and Valente up the narrow, winding stairs of a four-story apartment complex. The halls smelled of urine and Lysol.

"He would be up late saying the strangest things in English I never hear before. Like poetry or something." Her accent was Eastern European and Park wondered what a woman like her was doing in a neighborhood like this. Park also wondered if the fleshy woman would make it up the last flight of stairs. She must have weighed 250 pounds and began wheezing about half way up the first flight.

"Anyway, I start to listen, and everything he say is about death, monsters, vampires, and sometimes he talk to someone else. His mother I think."

"His mother?"

She fumbled with a set of keys as they moved down a dim hallway. "I think his mother. I never see her, but I think. Then what make me call you is, he moves out, just like that. Leaves me envelope for rent under my door."

She found the right key, unlocked the door and they entered the apartment.

"So he moves out," Park said.

"He move out right before the murder of that famous director. That morning he move," she said.

Valente and Park examined the living room. Bare, except for an old end table pushed against a wall.

They moved into the bedroom. It had been stripped of all furniture and belongings and then a poster on the wall facing them stopped them in their tracks. It was a chilling portrait of a vampire glaring at them through bloodlust eyes. They looked at the poster with an uneasy feeling.

"Get a CSI unit here," Valente told Park.

Chapter 15

THE BATHROOM QUICKLY filled with steam as Park stepped into her warm shower. She let the water stream over her hair then took an aloe soap bar and gently scrubbed her thighs. As she turned to wash a side of her leg she was reminded of the cellulite that wasn't there last year. Then she noticed again, and with a twinge of horror, the slight handle forming around her waist. This was unacceptable.

But Park was not unrealistic. She had a decent figure that certainly could use a few more hours in the gym. But nothing to be ashamed of. In looks and physique, the 38 year-old detective blew away most women half her age. She also liked a good meal and wasn't about to embark on one of the many idiotic diets obsessing Americans. She had always been athletic and figured – what the heck, I'll get to the gym…eventually.

After a few minutes of scrubbing down, she turned off the water, grabbed a towel and dried off. Feeling reenergized, she wrapped the towel around her head, put on a bathrobe and went down the stairs of her split-level home in the San Fernando Valley.

She poured herself a Chardonnay. Her eyes quickly searched the living room for her handbag. She found it on the couch and removed a copy of *The Collected Works of Edgar Allan Poe* she had checked out earlier from a local library.

Park nestled comfortably on her couch and opened the book to *Murders in the Rue Morgue*.

She had never been a fan of Poe. In high school and early college, the author seemed to have always been a favorite with the guys. But she did enjoy several of his poems.

As Park read on, she was reminded of how many of today's thriller writers were directly or indirectly influenced by Poe. His grisly descriptions of the murders foreshadowed, a hundred years earlier, the manner in which similar accounts are revealed in modern crime thrillers.

After a thorough investigation of the house...the party made its way into a small paved yard where lay the corpse of the old lady, with her throat so entirely cut that, upon an attempt to raise her, the head fell off. The body as well as the head was fearfully mutilated - the former so much so as scarcely to retain any semblance of humanity.

The descriptions of the horrifying murders of two women on the fourth floor of a house on the Rue Morgue set in motion the mystery that was to unfold. Park was captivated. Investigators found the old lady's daughter shoved up the chimney of the fireplace in the apartment.

The corpse of the young lady was much bruised and excoriated...the throat was greatly chafed. The face was fearfully discolored, and the eye-balls protruded. The tongue had been partially bitten through.

Barely an hour elapsed before she had completed the tale. And she had to catch her breath. Something about the story gave her a sudden idea. A final sip of her wine, and she picked up the phone and called her partner.

→≡∘ ∘≡←

Valente was doing push-ups in his bedroom when the phone rang. His girlfriend had gone out of town to visit her mother and wouldn't be back for a couple of weeks. He decided to take this opportunity to do the kind of stuff guys do that drive girlfriends crazy - workout, leave the toilet seat up, and sit around in his underwear drinking a beer and watching a ballgame.

Out of breath he struggled to his knees and answered the phone. "Yeah."

"Got company?" Park said on the other end.

"Yeah. Playmates everywhere. It's out of control." He leaned against his bad, taking a deep breath.

"Hi *paisano*," she said.

"You know, I love how you say *paisano*."

"How do you mean?"

"Your voice. It changes registers. It kind of goes up a notch into this sweet little girl voice."

"Yeah?"

"Yeah." For a fleeting moment Valente felt a surge of desire for her. He had known Nicole for a few years but only recently started seeing her in a different light. "So what's up?"

"Do you have a copy of *Murders in the Rue Morgue*?"

"Sure – dozens, all over my apartment. Got a first edition encased over my mantle. What are you smoking?"

Cute, she thought. "In the book, an escaped orangutan did the killings."

"Right. It slipped my mind."

"Not up on your Edgar Allen Poe, huh?"

"Nicole, I read Poe in high school." Then something she had just said struck him as odd. "Did you say orangutan?"

"Yeah."

"Gorilla hairs were found on our vic."

"Right. As you know, Hollywood loves to take a classic and ruin it. In one movie version of the book, the one that I saw on late-night television a thousand years ago, the story was drastically altered. A madman trained a gorilla to do his killings. Maybe our guy liked the movie version better than the book."

Valente digested this, while at the other end Park was having fun impressing him with her knowledge of B-movie horror films. "What's the ape *dujour* in St. George's version?"

"Gorilla."

"Our perp is clever. But so are we. Can I get back to my push-ups?"

"Not yet. I started thinking again about what you said at the morgue. About access. How he got the hairs? Have you considered the possibility that maybe our guy is working with an accomplice?"

"Don't tell me you're starting to believe the gorilla nonsense."

"Of course I'm not. I mean a human accomplice," she said. For a moment she wanted to clock him...

"What I meant by access," he continued, "was another party who supplied him the hairs. I wasn't suggesting that two people were involved in the killing.

He waited for a moment, letting her think about what he had said. "What about your jealous lover theory?"

"I don't know. Right now anything is possible. Like you said. Why the hairs? Would a jealous lover go to those extremes?

Valente was getting fatigued. "Get some rest Nicole. This is just the beginning. We've got a long road ahead of us. Goodnight."

"Goodnight."

She replaced her receiver and thought about what he had said. *Just the beginning...* The last thing she wanted was spending weeks, months, even years hunting a madman.

Chapter 16

THE SILVERBACK TRAINED his suspicious eyes on the curious visitors. In an outdoor pen under an early morning sun, he watched guardedly over his family of two females and four youngsters. He stood between them and the two investigators speaking with Susan Bressler, senior primatologist at the Los Angeles Zoo. Bressler was in her mid thirties. She was a pensive type who did not warm easily to strangers. The silverback kept a steady eye on them.

"I need you to check your files," Valente said. "Go back a couple of years. Check your part-time staff. Find out if anyone's behavior has changed; has anyone been acting strange, distant, depressed. Often these characteristics are indicators. Anything that could shed…"

"Officer. I've already told your partner on the phone…"

"Doctor Bressler. I know. But new things develop during the course of an investigation. Sometimes the smartest, most accomplished can harbor a darkness you and I can't possibly imagine. Will you cooperate?"

At this point the wiry primatologist felt silly about being resistant. There had been media inquiries the day before, calls from journalists, and pranksters teasing her about a gorilla gone mad and on the loose, all of which had made her edgy. "Of course, I'll cooperate. Stupid of me."

'See if anyone on the staff suddenly quit. If anyone's behavior changed."

For the first time Valente noticed the silverback watching him. "Oh, and don't worry. That big guy over there has nothing to worry about," he turned towards her. "But we need to check every lead, no matter how far-fetched. If one of your people decided to pull a prank, or be the unwitting accomplice in a crime… well, like I said, we need to check everything."

"I understand."

Chapter 17

As VALENTE WALKED into the police station, he wondered what kind of a sick mind would implicate an ape. Why throw suspicion away from humans only to create a potential frenzy against one of nature's most endangered creatures. He had tossed that question around in his mind several times after leaving the zoo.

He was about to enter the squad room when a voice trailed behind him. "Hey Detective. Detective." Valente turned and saw a young guy jutting his head out of a room a little further down the hallways. "They're starting a computer scan on fingerprints taken from the possible unsub's apartment."

"Good. It's about time."

A familiar voice called out to him. It belonged to Ed McCarty. "Sam. Got a couple more Laker tickets. You interested?"

Valente waved him off, and turned into another office where Joyce Tyrel, also a member of the Intel unit, was running fingerprint matches. Park was in there with her. Names scrolled across the screen as Valente hung over the young woman's shoulder and watched the names appear. "Let me know when you got something."

Valente checked the wall clock and saw that it was nearing noon. He needed to file a report, and check again with the primatologist at the zoo for any updates. He was about to leave the room when Tyrel called out to him. "Here we go."

A photo of a man appeared on the screen with the following information:

NAME: MITCHELL SHANKER;
ADDRESS: 1644 N. Byron Way,
            Hermillio, Ca.

"Not bad looking," Park said, somewhat surprised.

He had short, dark hair cropped over the ears. Brown eyes were set in an unblemished face with a strong jaw line and chin. With some make-up, he could have graced the pages of any men's fashion magazine. "This guy got a record?" Valente said.

"Nothing. Not even a parking ticket," Tyrel replied.

"Why do we have his prints?"

Tyrel scrolled further and saw an entry that stated he had prior military service. "U.S. Army. Got out on a medical. Looks like he was a boot camp bust. I guess he couldn't take the heat."

Word had reached Campbell's office that a match had been found and he was downstairs in a hurry. "Got an address?" he said as he came into the room.

Valente shrugged his shoulders. "Same as the one you gave us." Then a thought suddenly struck him. What if the guy got stupid? What if *now* was the time for the perp to get lazy and make the mistake that would lead to his arrest?

He called over to Park. "Post surveillance outside his apartment."

"Don't get a hard on," Campbell said.

"Sometimes these creeps get homesick. You know that Lieutenant. I don't have to tell you. He's smart, but like all these types, he has his limitations. I'm betting he's figuring we would never waste time going back to his apartment. That we have other leads to follow and that we would never guess he would be so stupid as to go back to his former place of residence."

"Like I said. Don't get yourself a hard-on." Campbell walked out of the room, taking his scowl with him.

Valente shook his head in disbelief. "Did this guy get half his brain sucked out of his head?" But he wasn't going to let Campbell ruin his day. "Would you get that unit out there? Two-man teams, round the clock. Let's say for a week, for starters."

"OK."

When she walked out of the room, Valente looked at Shanker's photo that seemed to stare at him from Tyrel's monitor. Valente lowered his eyes and forced a crooked smile. *Do you know who I am? Have you ever taken a moment to consider the consequences of your actions? No? Time to start considering shithead.*

Chapter 18

YOUNG MITCHELL SHANKER was terrified when he stood before the casting director. He knew he would perform badly and he knew that his mother, who was in the waiting room, would punish him severely.

But he went on, reading the silly lines of a cereal commercial. The casting director listened patiently to the child's horrendous reading, and then pleasantly dismissed him.

That night, in his mother's kitchen, pleasant thoughts were but a memory.

She stood by the sink, looking at an iron plugged into the wall. She held Mitchell close to her side. Her eyes were glued to the iron. Eyes as black as a shark's - blacker than the closet she would no doubt lock him in.

But mother had something else in store for young Mitchell. Tonight would not be a night for the closet. Apparently the closet was not having the desired effect on young Mitchell's discipline.

"You are going to get better, Mitchell. Acting is in our blood. And it will be in your blood."

"Mommy."

Mother kept her eyes focused on the iron. Then, as though brought out of a trance, she unplugged the hot iron.

She rolled up Mitchell's sleeve, and slowly moved the hot iron toward her screaming child's arm as --

Mitchell woke up trembling. Soaked in sweat. He sat in bed and stared at the wall in front of him. Sweat poured down his face. His breathing was fast with short, quick breaths.

He looked at his forearm. Though less prominent, the scar from the hot iron was still there.

⇢⊫◉ ◉⊨⇠

He needed his basement. There, Mitchell sought comfort from the barbarities that defiled the world around him. In this living coffin, he gathered his strength and his courage.

The basement was cramped and untidy. The walls were filled with posters of horror films, particularly the older ones like the original *Dracula*, *Frankenstein*, *The Mummy*, and posters of Vincent Price films such as *The Abominable Dr. Phibes*, *The Tingler*, and *Theatre of Blood*. Notably absent were posters of slasher films. He viewed those films as a cheapening of the genre, and did not want any of those posters hanging alongside the masters.

Mitchell slowly passed in front of each poster, as though paying homage to them. After the procession he stopped in front of a mirror and admired himself. Dressed in a black suit with a black cape, he felt absolutely majestic. Power was in his hands, and greatness in his soul.

Then he glanced at a wooden sculpture of a raven perched on his window-sill. He stared at the bird for a moment.

With a flourish, he threw his cape over his shoulder, and sat down at his desk to write. He took a quill pen out of its inkwell and began.

When he finished he folded the letter into an envelope and sealed it. Again he looked at himself in the mirror.

"Write to me mother."

Chapter 19

In 18TH CENTURY Paris, the Marquis De Sade had a rather unique take on love, and he was jailed for it. He felt virtue could not triumph in a world filled with vice. So to him, love was nothing more than a word used by perverted seducers to lure young women into a world of sexual deviance. Women existed for man's perverse pleasures. They were nothing more than a sublime creature to be bent in every way imaginable. Such was love for the Marquis de Sade. Romance writers and poets through the ages have told the world how they define love.

For Nicholas Teague, and his lovely Marilyn, their love was defined on weekends. Nicholas and Marilyn were two, very sexually charged young adults. Weekends gave them a sense of independence, and isolation. On weekends they loved each other passionately. During the week they barely saw each other. They were friends with privileges.

Their love-making was intense. At times magical, and often edgy. Such was love for Nicholas and Marilyn.

They had been at his Sherman Oaks, ground floor bungalow apartment for three hours. They were about to explode into their third orgasm.

Nicholas was a stud. He stood firm at six feet, granite chin, broad shoulders, and washboard stomach. An athletic body in actor's clothing. Marilyn knew she had a catch, and she wasn't about to let him go. He made love to her unlike any man before.

Unfortunately, in the throes of passion people lose their perspective. In the case of Nicholas and Marilyn, neither was aware of the penetrating black eyes watching them from the blackness outside his bedroom window.

Suddenly he exploded into her, and instantly she was a raging she-wolf clawing into his shoulders, biting his neck as she reached her climax.

And then the phone rang.

Panting heavily, Marilyn spoke. "Don't answer."

Nicholas looked scornfully at the phone as though it were a mischievous kid brother pulling a prank.

"Don't answer. Let it ring," she said, nearly out of breath. But the persistent pest kept ringing.

Always hoping for the phone call that could change an actor's life, Nicholas reached over and picked up the receiver. "It could be my agent," he said.

"There is no God," she moaned.

"Hello," Nicholas said. The nasal voice from the other end was unmistakable. *"Nickie!"*

He winced. "Mom?"

"Of course it's your mom."

"Hi mom."

"You sound out of breath."

"I was running to catch the phone. Didn't want to miss your call."

Those eyes kept watching them. Determined eyes that held two perfect bodies in their sights. Then, for a moment, the eyes registered sadness. The mind behind the black eyes drifted. *What is it like to be with a woman? How does her naked body feel? What does it feel like to be inside her?*

"You saw Vampire's Blood?" Nicholas said. "Where?"

"Benton, Nebraska," his mother said.

"Where the hell is Benton?"

"I never knew we had a Benton in our state either" she said. *"It's about three hours from Lincoln."*

"You and Dad drove all the way out there?"

"Sure. We brought Aunt Margo along."

"Thanks Mom. That was really sweet."

"You were wonderful, but the film was a little too violent for my tastes."

"I shot that movie over a year ago, and it finally opened…in Benton?"

Marilyn got out of bed. "You want a beer?" she said walking out of the room.

"Yeah."

"Tell her hi for me," his mother said.

Feeling a little embarrassed, Nicholas called out to her. "Hi from mom, Marilyn."

"So. Did you guys see the movie?" Nicholas did not hear his mom. He was thinking about some rough kitchen sex.

"Nickie. Hello."

"Yeah. Mom. What?"

"Did you see the movie?"

"Not yet."

"Why not?" said his nosy mother.

"It didn't open here. Low-budget horror films rarely get wide distribution. I guess I'll see it when it comes out on cable or DVD."

"Well that's odd," his mother said.

"Happens all the time Mom."

Marilyn opened the refrigerator and took out two beers. Nicholas' conversation with his mother was barely audible. She opened a drawer, looking for a church key. No opener.

"Hey Mom. I got another call. Gotta go Mom." Nicholas wanted desperately to get back to Marilyn.

"Dad and I are proud of you son. You did good."

"Love ya mom."

"Wait Nicholas. Before you hang up..."

"Yes, mom."

Her search for the bottle opener continued. Marilyn had opened every drawer when she noticed the living room curtains swaying to a gentle breeze.

That was odd. The windows were closed when they had arrived. Nicholas was always careful about keeping doors locked and windows shut, particularly when they were about to have one of their raucous nights.

Marilyn stepped around the kitchen counter. She was about to move toward the window when it dawned on her that the lights were out. They had left the lamp on one of the end tables turned on. The only illumination came through the window from the spill of a nearby street lamp. She tried the wall switch. No light. She looked up and saw that the ceiling fixture was minus a light bulb.

Something else caught her attention. Shattered glass covered the floor beneath the window. And then it hit her. She was standing in the living room alone, and naked.

Fear suddenly consumed her, and she was about to call out to Nicholas when a hooded image emerged from the darkness. Its gloved hands grabbed her throat and spun her around, so that her back was against his chest.

⋅⊷⊜ ⊜⊶⋅

"Mom. I love that you are so concerned about my career, but don't worry. These movies often lead to bigger roles. Kevin Bacon? His first film was *Friday the 13th*. Remember…? Right, you never saw it. But look at him now. And Jack Nicholson? He started in horror films. He was in the original *Little Shop of Horrors*, the one directed by Roger Corman…"

With one hand around her throat, he squeezed tighter and tighter. He noticed her stunning figure cast against the bluish street light spilling into the room. But the attacker was unmoved. The body that would weaken the knees of most normal men had no effect on him.

She tried to break free. Then she felt something cold, and sharp entering her lower back. A pain unlike anything she had felt before.

With his free hand, Shanker pushed the knife deeper, cutting the life out of Marilyn. Then with one ferocious turn, he twisted the blade.

"O.K. Love ya mom. Bye…" He hung up and sat upright in bed for a moment. At times he missed the simplicity, and naiveté of small town folk. Then he realized that Marilyn had not yet returned. "Marilyn. How long does it take to get a beer?"

Chapter 20

NICHOLAS STARTED TO feel edgy from sitting on his bed those few minutes, naked, and not hearing a sound from the living room. What was keeping her he thought? He stared at the doorway to his bedroom, hoping she would appear. "Marilyn?"

Silence.

"Marilyn?"

He got out of bed. "Marilyn. What are you doing?" He put on his pajama pants and moved towards the doorway.

The movement was swift, and fierce. Nicholas was thrown against a nightstand. When he looked up he saw the cloaked stranger standing in the doorway to his bedroom.

Was this a scene from a movie thought Nicholas? Was it one of his actor friends pulling some kind of a sick prank? It was almost comical. The man dressed in black, framed his doorway. From under his cape, he lifted a long, bloodied knife.

Whatever thoughts Nicholas might have had about this being a friendly prank quickly disappeared. "Where's Marilyn?" Nicholas said his voice cracking.

Holding the knife at an angle, Mitchell lunged at him. Nicholas caught his arm with the knife and the two flipped over the bed, and onto the floor.

Miraculously, Nicholas landed on top of his assailant, and quickly delivered two blows to the man's jaw.

The knife fell out of Mitchell's hands, and he watched, in horror, as it slid across the floor.

Then he grabbed Nicholas by the shoulders, shoved him against the bulkhead, and scrambled for the knife. When he saw the intruder reach for the knife, Nicholas dove on his back, and grabbed his extended arm.

The two struggled for the knife.

Mitchell was not prepared for the strength of his worthy opponent. He thought he would have an easy time dispensing of him. To the contrary. The actor was in good shape, and strong.

But Mitchell did prevail, with the knife firmly in his grip. He got to his knees with Nicholas behind him who had one hand around his neck, his fingers digging into him, while his other hand gripped the hand holding the knife.

Mitchell flung Nicholas over his back crashing him into a chair.

The fight continued in a macabre duel of strength and smarts. Every time Mitchell lunged with the knife, Nicholas found a way to sidestep him.

Mitchell was coming unnerved and getting confused. But then he noticed something. A look in Nicholas' eyes. *Fatigue.*

Mitchell found an opening, and dove head first into his stomach, knocking the wind out of him.

Nicholas stumbled against the wall. Mitchell lunged with the knife. Nicholas ducked, but could not avoid the knife as it penetrated his left shoulder. The pain enraged him. He delivered a volley of punches to Mitchell's face, and then kicked him squarely in the chest, sending him crashing through his closet doors.

⇥⊙ ⊙⇤

Disoriented, Nicholas staggered down the hallway. "Son of a bitch." Everything spun around him. The pain in his shoulder was excruciating. Mitchell had cut deep, penetrating muscle tissue.

As he struggled down the hallway, he could only think of Marilyn.

He reached the kitchen and tried the light switch. Nothing. Then he froze. There, on the floor, slumped against the window was Marilyn's limp form.

"Oh God. Marilyn."

He rushed to her side. As he was about to embrace her, he abruptly pulled away. For a few seconds he stared at her. She sat there with an almost serene expression, in a pool of blood. Blood everywhere. Dripping from the wound in her back and unto the floor. Her throat had also been slit from end to end.

His knees buckled and he dropped to the floor. Then he felt a wave of nausea and vomited.

His head hung low. He gasped for air. "Marilyn," he said in a harsh whisper. Nicholas was losing strength with every passing second. The pain in his shoulder was nearly paralyzing, but he knew that somehow he had to go back into that room and destroy the monster that had done this.

However, like an exhausted boxer, staggering into the final round, Nicholas had no legs left. The wound to his shoulder was taking its toll. He sucked in air as best he could and forced himself to his knees.

And then it happened.

Mitchell had been watching, waiting for a final confrontation. *Timing is everything.*

Nicholas got to his feet and staggered towards him. "I'm going to kill you."

For a fleeting moment Mitchell admired the wounded warrior. So week, yet so determined. His two seconds of sympathy quickly passed and he gave Nicholas a hard shove to the floor.

Nicholas rolled over on his side, exhausted. He felt his skin prickle. Gasping for air, he forced himself up on all fours. He would try to make one final lunge.

But Mitchell would not wait. He had him where he wanted him. He ripped the kitchen phone out of the wall, and slammed it against Nicholas' head.

Chapter 21

NICOLE AND VALENTE were working late at the squad room. He took a sip from his third cup of coffee. Nicole stood next to the window, staring at an empty street below. All quiet there, but somewhere else, probably chaos. *Life in the big city.* Further down the squad room, a deputy was packing his shoulder bag and calling it a night.

She turned to Valente and noticed him calmly sipping his coffee and reviewing the case file. "That is your last cup or you won't fall asleep until next week."

Valente stretched and smiled appreciating the levity. "So what did you learn at Quantico?"

She dropped in a chair facing him across his desk. "A whole lot of crime scene stuff. Profiling...that sort of thing. Did you know that a very tiny percentage of serial killers are raised in a normal, healthy environment, and they just do their killing because they like it?"

"I heard that on one of those the psycho-of-the week crime shows?"

She fiddled with her hair – index and thumb rubbing a few strands together - something she often did when she was processing stuff in her head.

"Nicole. We are not at serial level yet. Why are you cutting to that chase?"

"Just got a feeling."

"O.K. Hold on to that, but in the meantime, what do we know so far?"

"He's local. He knew the producer. Maybe even some of the cast. He knew where to find him. And he had to have been familiar with Poe, or at least *Murders in the Rue Morgue,* to come up with the hairs. That is one coincidence I am not buying. That is a direct correlation to that story."

"What about that vampire poster?

"I'm not there yet," she said calmly with a smile.

Valente thought for a moment. "Maybe he is not only a jealous lover, but an actor who tried out for a part in his play and didn't get the role?"

Nicole's eyes widened a bit. "Well, that would be convenient."

"Yeah. The has-been who never was," Valente said.

"Obviously, at some point, he had a psychotic break," Nicole added. "And unfortunately for St. George, our producer may have presented the final stressor in Shanker's life."

Valente thought about those possibilities for a moment and couldn't argue. Whatever demons lived inside this guy are now calling to him.

He slid the file he was reading across his desk towards Nicole. "Evidence report back from Sheila Barrow's apartment. No other evidence or DNA of anyone. Whoever did her, wiped the place clean. And I don't think our guy is that good. For now, I am going with the ocelot lady was a professional hit, and Shanker took out our producer -- a jealous lover with a sick imagination. You good with that for tonight?"

'Sure. For tonight."

Chapter 22

HIS EYELIDS FLICKERED twice. A brief flash of light. Then darkness. A fire burned somewhere in his mind. Images of burnt corpses passed before him. They were all naked, young men and women in various stages of burn. Then one saluted him, smiling – bleeding lips on a melting face.

His head roared. Pain was unlike any he had known. But he knew he was not dead. Death is painless.

Nicholas had no idea where he was, how long he had been there, nor how he had arrived, but he sensed he was prone on something cold and flat.

What had happened, and did it really happen? Was it a bad dream? No. Dreams don't make you bleed.

Something else. He could not lift his arms.

Slowly he opened his eyes. All was a blur at first. But then his surroundings became clear. The overhead light illuminated what appeared to be a stark room. The stiffness in his head and neck, and his lethargy restricted his movements, so he decided not to exert a lot of effort while checking details of what he could see in the room.

Something buzzed in front of his eyes, like a mosquito, only it didn't land and bite him. Then it quickly disappeared.

With difficulty, he lifted his head. He noticed his wounded shoulder was now bandaged. He saw a narrow, rectangular window above him, so he figured he was in a basement. In front of him was a long counter on top of which lay several surgical instruments, a wash basin, and what looked like a glass container. Over to his left was a door, and where it led he could only guess.

He felt something tight on his left arm, and saw that it was a tourniquet. An I.V. was drawing blood out of that arm. He now realized that he was prone on a gurney.

Then it became apparent why he couldn't lift his arms. They were securely fastened. He tried to rest his arms free, but he winced from the unbearable pain that shot through his wounded shoulder and down his arm. The pain made him remember the fight, the knife wound to his shoulder and the whack to his head. *My God, Marilyn*, and his eyes welled with tears.

A shadow passed before him and then became life. The evil that had wrecked his body and taken his lover stood before him in all its blackness. "I should have played the vampire."

Nicholas wanted to fire a thousand questions at him before ripping out his heart. But he was able to manage only one. "Why Marilyn?"

Mitchell flinched. For a moment the menace in his eyes vanished. "She got in the way. My apologies."

Nicholas looked at his arm, then at the I.V., and felt the crunch of horror from seeing his blood being drained from his body. And the terrifying truth became all too clear. He was going to die.

"I was right for the part. Not you, Nicholas Teague." Mitchell pounded his fist on the counter. "Nicholas Teague! What kind of a name is that for a horror-film actor?"

"Why ...are...you doing this? What did I ever do to you?"

"*Teeeeegue*," Mitchell hissed. "Vincent Price. Now *that* was a name. Christopher Lee, Peter Cushing, Boris Karloff." He swallowed hard, proudly stood tall, and lifted his head. "Mitchell Shanker."

Nicholas felt himself slip in and out of consciousness. And in his deteriorating state he could only utter one word. *Please.*

Mitchell leaned into him, close enough to where Nicholas could smell him. "That's what I said, alone, every night after every audition. *Please.*"

Shock comes with the recognition that there is no hope. But for Nicholas, there was no shock. Strangely, there was acceptance. In his last moments of lucidity, he accepted the inevitability of death. And he was able to force a smile.

He smiled at the absurdity of his predicament. And he felt exhilarated by having lived a great 26 years on this planet.

Unlike many people cursed with the nightmare of a broken home, Nicholas had been blessed with a loving family. He loved his parents and wanted nothing more than to make them proud. He loved his mother's high-pitched voice and his father's saintly patience.

His struggles as an actor had been minor compared to those of others. Relative success came at the young age of 20, when he was cast in a small, recurring role on a soap opera.

That led to bit parts in low-budget films. And lastly, his first substantial role as a young vampire in yet another low-budget modern vampire film titled *Vampire's Blood*. A role he felt would lead to more successes. So for most of his young career he had been spared the ordeal of having to bartend, or wait tables to pay the rent. Nicholas had no regrets.

Mitchell removed the I.V. sack, and attached another one. Nicholas' lips moved slowly, but no words formed. The room went dark as he lost consciousness. He had slipped into a world of dreams. The last burned body floated before him. A young girl, barely 16, smiling as her face caught flame.

"*Vampire's Blood*. I should have played the vampire. Not you." Mitchell then made two, round incisions at the base of his victim's neck. He went to the sink, rinsed his hands, and then dried them. Before he left the room, he turned once more to Nicholas. "I should have had that role. I should have played the vampire!"

Chapter 23

HALDEN CEMETERY WAS nestled on the outskirts of Pasadena. It was not a large municipal cemetery, nor did it have a number of celebrities buried there, as in Forest Lawn. Halden had maybe two hundred gravestones and a few, remaining empty plots.

Valente maneuvered his car through the cemetery's lone parking lot at a little after 3 a.m. He turned down a narrow road that led to the bottom of a hilly area where the police line began. The grounds were nicely manicured, he thought, but like all cemeteries, the place gave him the creeps.

Several squad cars and an ambulance had already arrived. Dawn was about an hour away.

He walked past the police line, past several EMS officers, evidence technicians and a couple of crime scene detectives. He spotted Ed McCarty taking down the statements of the two patrolmen who were first on the scene. Valente walked up the grade, turned around some gravestones where Park met him. She handed him a thermos filled with coffee. "Thanks," he said.

As he was about to drink, he froze at the sight ahead of him. An evidence tech had just snapped a Polaroid and moved to one side.

It was in that moment that Valente saw Nicholas Teague's naked body propped up against a gravestone in a seated position. His head slumped to one side. At first glance, there didn't appear to be any marks on the body. The body just sat there, peacefully. But as he got closer he noticed where a bird or two had pecked at Teague's torso and thighs. There was also the puncture wound in his shoulder and some facial bruising.

"What now?" Valente said. His tone suggested to Park that he really did not want to know the answer. He wanted this to be over quickly, but he somehow sensed this was not going to be an easy case. Somehow he knew that this killing and that of St. George were connected. And this worried him.

Coroner Maria Santos tapped him on a shoulder giving him a start. "Most of the blood's been drained out of him constable," she said. She pointed to the bend in his elbow where the I.V. had been hooked. "See the needle marks?"

"Why aren't you home in bed dreaming about having a boyfriend?" Valente said.

"Oh. That was low. But, come. You'll find this really interesting." Santos led him closer to the body, turned her flashlight to the base of Teague's neck. "Puncture marks, bite marks, fang marks, whatever you want to call them. So some pervert wants us to think he is a vampire?"

Valente paid little, if any attention to her. His mind was on something curious about the ground.

"Where's the blood?"

"Sam. His body was dumped here," Park said. "His blood was removed somewhere else."

"Any prints off the body?"

"None. Prints on skin only last about an hour. He's been here a least three, four hours." Valente appreciated the reminder of fingerprint technology. At this late hour he was firing whatever questions came to his mind.

"Wipe this area clean. Our perp left something – a fiber, shoe print, hair follicle – something. He didn't just beam himself in."

"It's him, isn't it?" For the moment, Valente ignored Park's question. "Any witnesses?"

"We're in a cemetery at 4 in the morning." Park said.

"Cute," said Valente. "Who found him?"

"Night watchman doing his rounds. Called the police."

The color of Nicholas Teague's body had turned a bluish gray. His sunken face and eye sockets resembled a thousand corpses Valente had seen from years visiting autopsy rooms. "Who is he?" Valente said quietly.

"That we do have," Park replied. "His name is Nicholas Teague. We found this. It was lying by his foot."

She handed him a plastic evidence bag that contained an I.D. card. "Before you ask. There were no prints on the card."

Valente looked at the plastic bag. "Our killer is smart, organized, meticulous…"

Santos interrupted, "I'll be going now, constable. As soon as I get the body, I'll give it my fullest attention, but unless there are any other surprises, we can simply say that the cause of death is massive loss of blood brought on by a very thirsty vampire."

Park finally had had enough. "Santos, please. We don't need this now."

Santos' expression went grim. "It helps me get through all this shit."

Valente couldn't take his eyes off Teague's body. It actually pained him to see a life end so young and full of promise. For a moment Valente felt saddened, which went against everything he had been taught. *Give up the dead* he had been repeatedly told by his instructors when he was a rookie at the academy. *Do not form a connection.* Every day good people die for no reason.

Valente looked at Park. "Now you might be right. Now, we can start thinking serial." And as he was about to elaborate, Nicole noticed something on Teague's body. "What is that?"

Valente turned to the corpse and saw what had grabbed Nicole's attention. Something forced its way out of one of the holes in Teague's neck.

An evidence tech who was near the body, took a closer look. "Some kind of larvae."

"Are you a forensics entomologist?" Valente said.

"No sir I am not."

"Do we have an FE here?"

Josh Arkoff, the FE on site, was collecting entomological specimens at a gravestone four meters from the body when he heard Valente ask for an FE. His eyes lit up when his presence was requested. "I'm right here."

"You an FE?" Valente asked.

"That's me. The bug man," he said, forcing a nervous giggle.

"Good." Valente said. "A larvae, or something just crawled out of a hole in the vic's neck. Bag it and determine whether the bug is local, or from somewhere else. If we can determine the thing's origin, maybe we can establish a primary crime scene."

With hair that stuck out like hay, and a face badly needing a shave, Arkoff presented the image of a studious man whose personal appearance meant little to him. But the enthusiastic, 34-year old forensic entomologist, who spends most of his working hours in a research lab and rarely goes to a crime scene, loved when he was the center of attention, however brief the moment.

Arkoff removed a pair of tweezers from his medical kit. Carefully, he picked up the slimy larvae and dropped it into a small plastic vile. The creature would then be taken to the lab where it would be placed in an incubator and kept alive for as long as it took to establish its habitat.

"This could be just a garden variety slug found everywhere in this region," Arkoff said. "But on the other hand, the little slime ball could be a peculiar parasite of some kind."

"Can you identify the thing now," Valente said.

Arkoff looked inside the plastic vile. The larva was no more than a centimeter in length, pale white and barely moving. "It's hard to tell. I'd say, offhand, a grub of some kind, but I won't know until I put him under a light."

"What's your name?"

"Josh Arkoff."

"Josh. We are in the middle of what's probably going to become a nightmare of a murder investigation. I don't want assumptions. I want results, OK?"

"Let me finish my evidence collection, and I'll get back to you post haste." He returned to the other gravestone to finish collecting his bug samples.

"Thanks Josh," Valente called out to him, and then when he was sure Arkoff was out of earshot he turned to his partners. "Is he any good?"

"Bugs are his life," McCarty said. "I think Arkoff did his dissertation on the mating habits of Presbyterian horny beetles. This guy eats caterpillars for breakfast."

Park and Valente couldn't help themselves. McCarty could be charming in his Paleolithic way.

A yawning patrolman called up to them from a squad car at the bottom of the hill. "Valente. You got a call on the car radio."

"Who is it?"

"Campbell. Said he tried to reach you on your cell." Valente checked for his cell phone but realized he had left it in his car.

"He wants an update," the officer said.

"Now?"

"You know Campbell," McCarty said. "The guy is the police department's largest source of natural gas. You want to solve an energy crisis, just stick a tube up his ass. You better take it before he gets an aneurysm?"

While Valente walked down the hill to take Campbell's call, he suddenly remembered the evidence bag in his hand. He shook the bag so he could get a clearer look at the card inside. It was Teague's Screen Actor's Guild card. "Christ. An actor."

Chapter 24

THREE TIMES OVER the toilet. Nothing much left inside to heave up. In a cold sweat and with a few shivers, Park returned to her bedroom and sat on the edge of her bed. The memories of her past had come back to haunt her. She had to suppress those feelings because she did not want another transfer. She would not let herself fall again. Park had worked hard to overcome the bad memories. The shattered lives. The slaughter of the innocents as she called it.

There was the pre-school teacher from Irvine, Ca. who buried seven kids. The badly decomposed bodies were found a year later in a semi-circular grave near her home. Forensics had determined that the children were buried alive. But through a crack in the legal system, the pre-school teacher was acquitted. Park had wondered for nights who was the real monster – the teacher, or the system that let her go. Six months after her acquittal the teacher was found in a ditch, her head crushed under a block of cement. Her attacker was never found but there had been rumors that her killer was a parent or relative of one of the murdered children.

There was the strange case of Elgin Bunt, the Mother's Day killer. For six years he killed two elderly women on Mother's Day. First he raped them, then he tied them to their beds with telephone cords. Then he slit their throats and wrote Happy Mother's Day in their blood across the wall over their beds. When he took the stand he kept repeating the words Happy Mother's Day. Though his defense attorneys tried to cop an insanity plea, the jury found him guilty and he received multiple life sentences.

And every year after that trial Park burst into tears when she visited her mother on Mother's Day.

Most crime scenes tell a story. And like most stories, crime scenes have a plot, characters, a beginning, middle and hopefully a conclusion. Imagery is vivid in most crime scenes and the images of killers destroying the lives of the innocent were hard for Park to banish from her mind.

Teague's crime scene was another chapter in the story unfolding before her. Park knew that in order to bring the story to its rightful conclusion she had to get into the mind of the killer. What profile did he fit? Was he the type that started fires, an often common trait in serial killers when they are young. Son of Sam started over 2000 fires throughout New York before he evolved into a serial killer. Others begin as stalkers, or peeping Toms, before escalating to burglary, rape, and eventually murder. For now, this perp's MO is no doubt about power and control, and could even be classified a sadistic killer. Park was not sure. Was he simply bent on revenge? Was he out to take down Hollywood and all it represents?

Perhaps she needed this purge so that she could face her demons and then ultimately *this* very real demon. Nicole Park failed once before. She had let the horrors of her job knock her to her knees. She was allowed a leave of absence, and allowed to return in her role as a profiler, and detective. This time, she would not fail.

Chapter 25

DOZENS OF CANDLES illuminated the graveyard of dreams. Candles rested in ornate candelabras, and some in simple holders or plates. A stained glass design of a gargoyle perched on a church spire hung in one window.

Shadows fanned across the many horror film posters. And there was a new one - the poster from the Hitchcock classic, *Psycho*. "I thought you would like that mother," he whispered to himself while admiring the poster.

Crown molding ran along the baseboards. A rusted, antique stovepipe sat in one corner of the basement room, and a dusty, 16th century Venetian armoire stood against another wall, left here by the shady owner who had skipped town on a foreclosure. Other than the dust on the armoire, the room was remarkably clean.

The house had been abandoned for more than a year in a small parcel of Los Angeles not yet discovered by developers. That would change soon, he knew, but the old colonial would serve his purposes until the wrecking ball came, and he would be long gone.

Mitchell put in a CD, and turned up the volume to Mussorgksy's *Pictures at an Exhibition*. . Music inspired him. He particularly loved Bach and Mozart and of course, the Mussorgsky epic. He felt as an actor he could prepare better for a role while music played in the background.

Tonight he would rehearse verses from *The Raven*. He filled his glass with cognac, took a sip, and began to recite:

"Deep into that darkness peering,
Long I stood there wondering, fearing
Doubting, dreaming dreams no mortal

Ever dared to dream before.
But the silence was unbroken,
and the stillness gave no token..."

Mitchell tried to be as dramatic as possible. His voice resonated over the music. And he felt a sudden surge of triumph. No longer would he walk in the shadows of the giants like Vincent Price, Christopher Lee or Peter Cushing. They were the great ones, but they had had their day. It was time for him to reign supreme, both in film and on stage. He would be the new, crown prince of the horror genre.

He closed his eyes and remembered the casting notice in *Variety*. All parts open for The Maclean Theatre's staging of Edgar Allan Poe's *The Raven*. That was a few weeks ago. Much had happened since then. He extended his arms out from his side and pretended he was walking on a tightrope high above ground. *All parts open.* Mitchell hated casting notices that read all parts open because in truth most roles were already pre-cast. Why can't these bastards be honest? Ron Styles was no different.

When he opened his eyes he faced the darkest corner of the room. The light from the candles illuminated only his immediate area. That corner of the room was in blackness. Nothing moved, but he felt her presence nonetheless.

"How was that mother? Different music. Something more dramatic?" He fumbled through a stack of CDs. "Mozart, Beethoven, Chopin, and another Mussorgsky work - *Night on Bald Mountain*? That one? Wonderful how Walt Disney incorporated that piece of music into *Fantasia*."

He changed the CD and soon the thunder of Mussorgsky's dramatic score shook the room. And his eyes fell on the *Psycho* poster again. A wry smile crossed his lips. "You like it, don't you mother? I thought it was a nice touch."

He looked back at the dark corner of the room, as though waiting for a signal from the unseen guest to begin. Then he turned wildly around, raising his head high. "Spawned from a worm...better to reign in hell, than serve in heaven..."

Mitchell drank from his glass, and stood tall and triumphant. He was lord over his universe. "...At that time a mighty fiend lived in darkness and suffered greatly...the grim demon was called Grendel. This unhappy being had long lived in the land of monsters..."

He fell into his leather chair, cocked his head back, and stared at his candles. The light danced across his face.

He poured himself another drink, and sipped slowly, and thoughtfully. "So, you Ronald Styles, my ancient nemesis are going to stage The Raven. *The Raven. Hah*!

Chapter 26

CAMPBELL KICKED A trashcan across the squad room nearly hitting Valente in his shin and bouncing off a leg of Park's desk. "He left us a clue right on the wall of his goddamned apartment!"

"I'm real sorry lieutenant," Valente said, trying to control his temper. "We find an old movie vampire poster on the wall of an empty apartment, so naturally I'm supposed to assume that somewhere in L.A. somebody is going to have all his damned blood drained out of him."

If a black man's face could turn red, Campbell was nearly at that point. His impatience and explosiveness was legendary around the department. "Don't screw with me Valente. Not now. Not today."

Campbell headed for his office but before entering, turned to them. "And you Park. You screw up again, have one of your I-gotta-find-myself moments, and I'll have your ass walking a beat in South Central." He slammed the door behind him.

"Can he do that?" Park said

"What?"

"Have me walking a beat?"

"Yeah. He's an example of everything that's wrong with affirmative action."

Park did not appreciate the remark. "Sam. You know better than that."

"Give me a break. The damned quota system is wrecking this country."

"Do I detect a hint of racism?" Park said.

"A hint of frustration. I just want what's fair, and I think there were more qualified whites who could have gotten his job."

Then McCarty wheeled over in his chair, salivating, eager to offer his take. Park threw her hands up, exasperated. "Great Sam. You woke up the caveman."

McCarty's grin got wider. "Hey Park. You know what they say about EEO, Diversity and Downsizing don't you?"

"No Ed. I don't," she retorted.

"EEO is hire blacks. Diversity means hire women and Hispanics. And Downsizing is get rid of the white boys."

"Jesus. I thought Neanderthals were extinct," she said.

"It's payback time baby for all the people we white folks screwed," McCarty added.

She turned to Valente because going any further with Ed on this subject would be pointless.

Valente realized that he might have crossed the line. The last thing he needed were rumors flying around the Los Angeles police department that another right-wing bigot had found his way into the force, particularly when, in his case, it wasn't true.

"I don't like it when a perp has the upper hand," he said.

"None of us do,"

McCarty wheeled back to his desk. "It's all getting to us amigos. Why we do this work will keep shrinks in business for years."

Park ignored him. "I did more checking on St. George and Teague. They both were once associated with the McLean Theatre Group, about 60 miles north of here."

"Where?"

She opened a file and ran her eyes down the first page. "Carpinteria."

"Where the hell is that?"

"Between Ventura, and Santa Barbara."

"So our unsub is not only familiar with our general area, but also up the coast a bit." Valente turned to McCarty. "Did anyone stick out when you were canvassing the St George crime scene? Someone who looked like they didn't belong?"

McCarty shook his head. "By the time we got there, it was the cast members and a couple of residents. No stragglers."

"Any word on the bug sample?" Valente said.

"Collecting entomological specimens from a crime scene can result in a lot of bugs," Park replied.

"I know. But I only care about one bug. The one crawling out of the vic's neck. Get on the phone, call that FE. What's his name?"

"I don't remember."

Valente searched his brain for a moment. "Arkoff. That's his name. Tell him to get me the report ASAP."

Park placed a comforting hand on his shoulder. Her touch took a little of the edge off. Valente was fast becoming a man torn between his commitment to duty, and his growing interest in Park that went beyond the professional. And he knew this was not the time, during this investigation, to get romantically confused. So he quickly put those thoughts to rest, for now.

"Where was that theater?"

"Carpenteria" Park replied, "Ventura County."

The county was out of their jurisdiction in the event the case shifted there, but Valente didn't care. He'd take any help he could get. He'd call in the FBI if he had to.

"Let's take a drive. I think a day out of this town will do us both some good.

Nicole smiled at him. "I'm fine *paisan*. I'm not the one hating the whole world right now."

"I don't hate anyone," he grumbled. "McCarty you got the watch. And I want that bug report."

Chapter 27

VALENTE ONCE HAD a dream where a giant held a box full of houses and threw them all over Los Angeles county as punishment for Hollywood's hedonistic life-style. Out of that mess came the traffic snarl and blanket of smog for which Los Angeles is famous.

On the way home he had spent a few minutes on his cellphone with Park going over some details of the case. He wanted to make sure that while they were gone to Carpinteria, nothing stopped in LA. Full court press is what he had said to her.

He slipped in behind a line of traffic up the San Diego Freeway. He went over details of the recent events. Cops always think they've seen it all until something new happens that defies reason. This one was a first in a career that had him working some strange cases.

A few years back there was the Harmon Davie case, the Riverside child murderer who had abducted several children and starved them in his basement. He felt that grown-ups were the cause of all of society's ills and the Lord had told him to kill these kids before they grew up to be murderous adults. Before Davie, there was Jamarcus Collins, a crazed black man who went on a rampage through South Central, killing elderly women who reminded him of his abusive grandmother.

But a guy who drained the blood out of his victim like a vampire, and someone who appeared to be imitating the murders in horror or thriller stories? – that was certainly new to him. *Life imitates art in horrific fashion*. And there was something Valente had to eventually accept. He and his team would probably have to seek the advice of a profiler, and he had no stomach for them. Why? In Valente's opinion – what good has it done. You poke psychological holes in a jailed serial killer and meanwhile right around the corner another atrocity happens. He re-called an old theatre adage that has application in all phases of life – the make-up may change, but the face is the same.

The traffic was driving him nuts. He needed to marinate.

Don Pasquale's was still lively when he walked in near closing. No singers to-night, which was a relief. Three or four tables towards the back – couples enjoy-ing a romantic evening - and one table with three guys talking business.

Leanna, the hour-glass beauty was serving a couple at a table. Valente wasted no time. He moved towards her. Fate smiled favorably on him. The lovely bru-nette saw him, and excused herself from her table. "Where have you been? I've been looking out for you. Hoping to see you here."

Valente was startled but recovered quickly. "I'm here now. You got any plans after you get off?"

"No. Are we making plans?"

"How about I buy you a drink?"

"Sure."

At that moment, Don Pasquale decided to come between Leanna and Valente. "Leanna. Please, the customers. Sam will be here when you're finished."

He turned her around and gave her a gentle shove towards the tables, then he looked at Valente, almost paternally. "Put Federico back in your pants."

"You're a cruel man. You know we are genetically predisposed to chase women."

"You got a point. Why are you here so late? The kitchen is about to close."

"I'm not hungry."

"You came for Leanna?"

"Not at first, but now that you mention it…"

"Have some vino. Take the table in the front."

"Yeah. I need to think."

Like most homicide detectives, Valente was married to his cases. The strange turn of events of the last couple of days certainly had his mind racing in several directions. A woman, presumably dealing in the sale of illegal animals, is brutally murdered, and may have even been tortured. A theatrical and film producer is murdered and gorilla hairs are found on his body, and now an actor has all the blood drained out of him in vampire fashion. He strongly sensed a connection between the producer and actor's death. But he wasn't sure how the woman, Sheila Barrow, figured into all this. What really had him going, and where he felt this investigation would lead, is that he couldn't recall a case where someone exacted a vengeance against Hollywood in murderous fashion other than the rare crime of passion.

A carafe of white wine later and Valente took a rain check with Leanna. She offered little objection. Probably for the best she had said to him.

Pasquale put a hand on his shoulder. "Go home Sam. Can't have you driving drunk. Anything happens to you, I'll have *agida* for the rest of my life.

Chapter 28

VALENTE AWOKE WITH a start. His first instinct was to look at his alarm clock. *The damned phone ringing at 4:20 a.m.* His hand reached for the receiver. He brought it close to his ear. "Speak," he said, clearing his throat.

"Detective Valente?" said a hesitant voice.

"Yeah."

"Josh Arkoff. Sorry to bother you so early, but I figured you wanted to know as soon as I completed my analysis."

"Who is this?"

"Josh Arkoff. The FE."

"Huh?" Valente said clearing his throat again. He looked at his alarm clock again. There was no mistaking the hour. The large red numbers glowed like a marquee.

"The bug guy. You know, at the crime scene of the guy who had all his blood drained out of him?"

"Oh. Yeah..."

Josh continued. "Anyway. I wanted to review my report one more time just to make sure. I didn't want to miss anything, which is why I took so long?"

"What do you have?"

"You're not going to believe this. In fact I had to do some pretty serious cross-referencing. Just when you think you've seen it all, bang, zoom, to the moon and back..."

"Arkoff. I am real tired. Get to the point."

"Yeah. Sorry. The bug is called *Nycteribiidae*..."

"English please."

"Umm. Oh. Well, there isn't an English translation for *Nycteribiidae* other than bat fly."

"Bat fly?" Valente repeated, not sure where Arkoff was leading him.

"What we have here detective, is the larvae of a bat fly. There are two families, one is *Streblidae*, and the other, the one we found, is *Nycteribiidae*. You with me?"

"Barely," Valente said as he propped himself up and tucked another pillow behind his back.

"*Nycteribiidae* are wingless, spiderlike insects with long legs and a small head that folds back into a groove in the thorax when at rest. They are external parasites."

"Is that important?"

"Not particularly. Just being thorough. But get this. *Nycteri---*"

"Arkoff. Do me a favor. You're giving me a headache with the Latin. Call him bat fly. I'll know what you mean."

"O.K. This bat fly, which has been known to attach itself to a variety of bats, has a particular affection for the Mexican free-tailed bat."

"Is that important?"

"Maybe. Those bats live in Central Mexico and in the Chihuahuan Desert. They don't venture this far north."

"Do you have any idea where someone could get a hold of the larvae of a Mexican bat?"

"Sure. But you would need access. A zoo would have them, private collectors, a research lab."

"Research lab?"

"Sometimes. But, if your killer was really obsessed with the Mexican free-tailed bat, then it's possible he may have gone into the Chihuahuan Desert to retrieve their larvae."

"I doubt that. But I like your research lab suggestion. Anyway, thanks Josh. I'm going back to sleep."

"Wait. There's one more thing."

Valente frowned. "Always is. What is it?"

"I also found six, dead wasps in a cluster behind a gravestone,"

"Is that unusual behavior for wasps?" Valente said with a tinge of sarcasm.

"Well, like -- hello. It's not like they all flew in formation and died at the same time falling into a cluster next to a gravestone."

Valente heard the indignation in his voice and tried to put him at ease. "Arkoff. Relax. I was kidding. So, it can be assumed that they were planted there. But why?"

"Maybe to confuse you guys. Wasps don't die together in a cluster, and there hasn't been any spraying."

"What do you mean?"

"Well I checked the whole area to see if there were any other dead wasps. I did some cursory analysis. I phoned L.A.s park commission and Department of Public Works to check if they had done any spraying that could have killed the wasps. Nothing. No spraying, and those were the only wasps I found."

"Good job Arkoff."

"Thanks. Oh wait one more thing."

"Sure."

"Don't forget, sometimes killers plant intentional clues to throw you guys off the trail, along with clues that could lead to their apprehension. I would forget about the wasps, but I wanted you to know because I figured you could be dealing with a very clever man."

Valente smiled. The guy was trying a little too hard, maybe. "Thanks Josh."

"Goodnight."

Valente replaced his receiver and rolled over on his back. He noticed a crack in his ceiling.

The larva is connected to the bats, he thought while following the line of the crack. The wasps are there for the killer's own amusement. Is he telling us that someone is supplying him with animals? Valente thought again about the bats, and then checked the caller I.D. on his phone.

Arkoff picked up his receiver.

"Arkoff," Valente said quietly. "Tell me about parasites."

"Huh?"

"Parasites. Tell me about them,"

The enthusiastic forensic entomologist finished off the remaining Chamomile tea and eagerly continued. "They are an organism that obtains nourishment from another living organism. The host, which may or may not be harmed, never benefits from the parasite. And the parasite cannot survive apart from their host."

Those last words struck a chord. *Cannot survive apart from their host.* A parasitical serial killer?

"Detective. Hello? You still there?" Arkoff's voice rung in his ear.

"Yeah."

"And parasites are highly specialized."

"Thank. Oh and Josh. Run a chemical analysis on that larva."

Chapter 29

MITCHELL SHANKER LOVED to watch the sun creep down and bleed into the horizon.

Sunset brought about the end of a sunny day. Blue skies and California sunshine were symbolic of a lifestyle Shanker would never have: a Bel Air address; a house with a pool; tanned bimbos in string bikinis; a convertible. It was his distain for things beautiful that led him to become a research assistant working with some of nature's most appalling creatures. RETLAN laboratories in Riverside provided him that opportunity. Like all unsuccessful actors, he had to find a way to make a living. Years before, the Army did not work for him.

Planning his medical discharge from Uncle Sam's Army was a thing of beauty. He had laughed quietly at the faces of the military tribunal, as he called them, who had found him unfit to continue military service. During boot camp in Florida, Shanker had done a great job of convincing his drill sergeants that he just didn't have what it took. He had forced himself to hyperventilate during inspections, induced vomit during marches under a hot sun, banged his head against his locker screaming for freedom, screamed in sheer panic while on the firing range, and he continually failed to complete the obstacle course. It was a performance worthy of an Oscar, and the Army had had enough of him. He knew the Army had plenty to choose from. Why waste time with a person who could eventually be more trouble than he was worth.

After his medical discharge, he enrolled at Iowa State University. There he studied chemistry, biology, and other science courses. But he hated the Midwest, and the small town where he grew up. As a 10-year old he had developed an interest in biology that ranged from insects to invertebrates, and some bird species.

Strange for a young kid who used to place live tadpoles on the barrel of his .22 rifle and pull the trigger. He did this when his mother wasn't looking though he seriously doubted if she cared. She spent her days in a bottle dreaming of him becoming a movie star.

Shanker never finished college. He dropped out and headed for Los Angeles. Hollywood was calling. He was armed with enough academic knowledge to con his way through an interview at RETLAN Laboratories.

In the research lab he did not have to deal with the outside world. He did mindless work, during which he became lost in his thoughts. Here he was able to dream the dream of stardom. Here he forged his plan to become Hollywood's reigning horror actor. And in here he didn't have to deal with all that Los Angeles sunshine.

The work at RETLAN was routine and could be easily accomplished without devoting his full attention. As a lab assistant, his duties varied greatly. He was responsible for maintaining research animals which included feeding them and cleaning their cages. Some of the animals in the lab included rare and exotic species of snakes, bats and rodents. He particularly hated the bats because of the annoying flies found on them.

He also stocked the lab with supplies and chemicals, and routinely cleaned much of the equipment. Originally, the opportunity to work in a genetic lab sounded interesting, but as with most jobs, it soon became mundane. Now, the only real enjoyment he got from his work was injecting lab mice with DNA extracts synthesized in the lab which caused the mice to go into manic convulsions.

He would soon transfer to the invertebrate section where he would catalogue invertebrate specimens taken off the platform legs of offshore oil rigs operating in the Santa Barbara Channel. To the scientific community, it is no secret that like the rainforests, the oceans harbor life forms with untold potential for pharmaceutical and commercial uses. The scientists would determine if any of the invertebrates harbored curative powers for ailments like arthritis and some cancer causing tumors. Of course, Shanker wouldn't be anywhere near the research. His job would simply be to separate the live ones from the dead ones.

But for now he had to contend with the annoying flies.

He was suddenly distracted by a commotion behind him. Garrison Clayborne, a scientist with more acronyms after his name than Shanker thought possible, entered the lab. Clayborne was Shanker's supervisor. The easily excitable fellow was followed by two men. "Careful. Careful" he barked to the movers carrying a large covered terrarium. "Do not drop that, or it will be hell for all of us." He joined the two men carrying the crate to lend a hand. "Mitchell? Where are you? Ahh. There you are. Wait 'till you see what I've got."

Shanker was one of Clayborne's favorites. The fascinating, sixtiesh herpetologist with degrees in zoology, micro-biology and a Ph.D. in chemistry, wasn't one who warmed easily to people, but he had taken a liking to Shanker.

"Come in here." They entered an adjoining lab through swinging doors. "Put it over there. Please." Clayborne had to remember not to be so gruff. Though he meant well, his behavior could be off-putting to some.

The two men lifted the terrarium and set it on a lab table. Shanker looked on curiously. Clayborne handed the men a wad of cash and quickly dismissed them.

As they left the room, Shanker asked him, "What's in the box?"

Clayborne stuck his head out of the room. When he was certain the two men had left, he turned triumphantly to Shanker. "A rare find. The mother of all venomous snakes." With grand theatrical fashion he removed the cloth covering the terrarium. "The black mamba."

Shanker's eyes widened. The agitated snake moved back and forth in its glass prison. Shanker registered obvious concern. "That's the precise look you should have, Mitchell," the scientist said. "For centuries this serpent has sent terror through the hearts of Africa. Next to Australia's land taipan, it is the world's most venomous land snake. Two drops of its venom can kill a man in a matter of minutes."

Shanker watched and listened in rapt attention. This was certainly the highlight of his week at the lab.

"Do you know why else they are so dangerous? Besides their deadly neurotoxin, the black mamba is very nervous and extremely unpredictable. Most herpetologists don't want anything to do with them because of their jitteriness."

Clayborne's eyes were the most alive Shanker had seen since he had come to the lab two years ago. Clayborne had often expressed his wish to get his hands on a black mamba so he could extract samples of its venom for various neurological experiments. But few people would get near the thing. Today, Clayborne was in mamba heaven.

"And another thing. It is also the world's fastest snake."

Clayborne tapped the glass and watched the snake recoil in a defensive posture. "Mitchell. I can trust you, can't I?"

"Sure Doctor."

"Well. Let's keep this our little secret for now. I haven't decided exactly what I am going to do with him, or how I am going to explain the sudden appearance of an illegal creature in our lab."

"Where did you get it?"

"Mitchell. If I tell you that, then you would be involved. I don't want you to get into any trouble. I'll have it all figured out soon enough. This won't be the first time I've crossed the line in the name of science. Can I count on you to keep this hush hush?"

"You can count on me. But what about those two?"

"They're fine. They wouldn't know a mamba from a salamander."

"Do you plan to keep him here?"

Clayborne couldn't take his eyes off the snake. A year-long search had finally netted rewards even though getting the thing set him back a pretty penny. "You and I are the only ones with the key to this room. So for now, things will be O.K. Remember, hush, hush. I'll be right back. All this excitement fired up my bladder." He turned and left the room

Shanker couldn't quite understand why his brain suddenly felt so animated. Was it the snake? Was he getting new ideas about how to prepare for his next "performance?" Serpents have always figured big in literature, and mostly to no good.

Chapter 30

Los Angeles rush hour had snapped Valente out of his reverie. Why do they call it rush hour? Nobody's rushing anywhere.

While stuck in traffic, his mind went back to a recurring desire - where to buy a beachside condo. Would it be Venice Beach, Marina Del Rey, Santa Monica, Newport Beach, Long Beach? He didn't care as long as it wasn't inland where the smog made him angry. Newport was his favorite

Valente had learned over the years to take his mind to other places when a murder case had started to consume him. He had learned from friends and family in Philadelphia and relatives in Italy, that no matter how tough things got, it wasn't worth losing your mind over. He also had learned not to waste his money on therapists unloading their psycho-babble on him. All he had to do was think about something pleasant to ease the stress. That was his therapy. He didn't need any mental adjustments. He was adjusted just fine.

"Never ends huh?" Park, who was driving the car, said.

"I guess if you have to be stuck in traffic, what better place than here. You get the ocean, sunshine most of the year, low humidity. Roll down your window and feel that breeze; put in a Jimmy Buffet CD, and life isn't so bad."

"Did you just go surfer-dude on me?" Park said.

Carpinteria was about 90 miles north of Los Angeles. He sipped a double cappuccino bought at a coffee shop in Santa Monica. Judging by the traffic they were at least an hour away.

He finished his cappuccino and browsed over a travel brochure of the small, beachside community. Nestled between the Los Padres Mountains and the

Pacific Ocean, the city boasts "the World's Safest Beach." At least that's what the brochure said.

Valente thumbed through the pages until his eyes fell on another newsy morsel. Carpinteria is also noted for its secret swamp, a 230-acre salt marsh hidden behind a chain link fence and an urban necklace of mobile homes, apartments, business parks, and mansions. Few coastal wetlands remain in Southern California and the Carpinteria salt marsh is one that is actually thriving.

The town's other distinction is that it is home to the MacLean Theatre Group. Snuggled in a peaceful woodsy setting, four miles inland from the coast, the small repertory company had developed a favorable reputation over the years. A recent recipient of a small grant from the National Endowment of the Arts, the theatre had also been nominated some years ago for a Tony award as best regional theatre. It did not win the award, but being recognized by the Tony organization helped its growing reputation. And then the fire, which led to two years of inactivity.

Park cast impatient glances at him while he read over the brochure. "Did you know about this salt marsh up here?" he asked.

She shook her head. Park had something on her mind and wanted to share it with him. Park had wanted to discuss an item with him since the St. George murder and chose this time to broach a subject that was not on the top of his list. "Sam. I've wanted to talk to you about something."

"What's up?"

"I think we should talk to a profiler."

"You're a profiler."

"Someone else Sam. Someone not connected to the case. You know? An outside opinion? We're too close."

"Don't get me started. I'm enjoying the ride."

"Sam. The whole department knows you are not big on psychoanalysis. But it's something we need to do."

"Whatever floats your boat, baby."

"Sam."

"O.K. For your benefit, I'll give you my 30-second speech. I don't have much use for all of that psycho talk hovering around murder investigations.

We've been probing the minds of murderous psychopaths for how many years now? And regardless of all the theories, all the analysis, all the studies trying to understand what makes these sickos tick, every day a child is killed and a killer is born."

Park sat quiet for a moment. She couldn't argue with that. She was about to offer another opinion but decided against it. She would save it for later.

Sensing her displeasure, Valente tried to put her at ease. "Now don't go getting your nose out of joint. It's just one man's opinion, and like they say, opinions are like assholes. Everybody's got one. Besides, I gave it some thought the other night."

"And?"

Valente forced a grin. "I guess I can be open-minded for an hour or two. Who did you have in mind?"

Park smiled internally. She had always felt a sense of triumph when she could persuade stubborn people to at least keep an open mind and give something unpleasant to them another chance. "I don't know yet. I'll make some calls, and I will let you know."

Chapter 31

THE LIGHTS HAD been turned down low, casting a bluish, garish glow. A cloaked, hooded figure appeared from shadows and stood behind the man slumped over his desk. The figure spoke one word. "*Nevermore.*"

Slowly the young man at the desk raised his head. He had tired, blood shot eyes with dark circles under them. He hadn't shaved in days. When he heard the strange voice, he looked up and said in a painful whisper, "Stop tormenting me." He wanted to turn but a slow roar was starting in his head. He slowly turned his head to one side and saw that the bottle of brandy was nearly empty.

And then the figure stepped closer to him, standing to his side. It raised a crab like finger. "*Nevermore,*"

Fear consumed the man's body when he saw the thing before him. The gates of hell had opened.

"What have I done? What do you want from me?"

The voice was low, and menacing. "You have defiled the world you inhabit. You must suffer for your transgressions."

"I only want Lenore."

"You want?" The hooded figure moved closer to him, still pointing that crab like hand. "You haven't earned the right to want anything. Lenore is gone."

Then he slowly stepped back from him and in a nasty whisper said 'Come with me."

The young man shook his head and moaned. "Stop."

"Come with me."

"I beseech you. Be gone."

Suddenly there was a loud metallic crack, like a gunshot, then the crackle of splintering wood. The cloaked actor looked up at the fly bars, and then instinctively dove into Kevin Rodgers, the play's lead actor. A large floodlight crashed on the stage four feet from the two actors. They tumbled onto the floor behind the desk. A gray-haired lighting technician suddenly appeared on the catwalk, panic in his eyes.

"Oh for God's sake," came the screech from the back of the theatre. "Stop. Stop. Cut." Carly Hanson, the play's director, leapt out of her seat at the production desk in the middle of the auditorium while technicians and crew members rushed to the stage. "That light could have killed one of them," Carly screamed.

From the fly space came the voice of the mortified lighting guy. "Sorry Carly."

For Ron Styles, who watched the commotion from the lighting booth, the biggest headaches were the technical rehearsals. He hated working with electricians, costume designers, sound technicians and stage managers. He hated the details, the expenses, the inevitable breakdowns that often cost him money he did not want to spend.

In one instance, three years ago, an entire sound board blew its circuits four nights before opening night. Another time, he had to fire his wardrobe supervisor who was stealing props and costumes and selling them to a local costume shop.

His dislike for things technical stemmed from experiences early in his career. A long time ago, when he was barely twenty, he got his first job in the theatre. He was an usher at an Off Broadway house that had since closed. The play opened and closed in a week, and for the next three years, he drove a cab, worked as a messenger in a law firm and tried his hand at acting which proved disastrous. Too many rejections forced him to abandon any dreams of becoming a star. But he was in love with the theatre so he took whatever work came his way.

Initially, Styles took jobs as a stagehand, a carpenter's assistant and as a lighting technician, often called a *lampy*. He hated being called *lampy*, and night after night over cheap wine and salty peanuts in Hell's Kitchen dives, he told himself that working crew was not where he wanted to be. He had his sights set on bigger things.

Then he fell in with a group of aspiring directors who regularly met at a cafe in the Village. There he met a man who would later become his mentor, Albert Bartok. The director hired Styles to serve as an assistant stage manager on a new show he was staging Off Broadway. The play was a success and moved to Broadway five months later. Styles then worked for Bartok on three more productions, before taking the helm as artistic director of the Manhattan Actors Group, an Off-Broadway theatre in mid-town Manhattan dedicated to experimental drama. The group folded less than a year after its inaugural production. The plays were just too bizarre for mainstream audiences. With poor attendance, the company had run out of money and backers.

Once again Styles found himself out of work, and the thought of going back to driving a cab, or waiting tables sent him into a two-month depression.

Then a friend from California called and invited him to work on a play at the famed Mark Taper Forum in Los Angeles. Styles said goodbye to New York and moved West, and his fortunes slowly began to change.

From his perch in the lighting booth, Styles watched a crew member remove the shattered flood light. He was about to erupt into one of his famous tirades when he decided to let his director handle the situation, for the moment. There was a manipulative side to him. Sometimes Styles enjoyed teasing his cast and crew into thinking everything was fine, and then he would descend on them like an angry god.

Carly had arrived on stage, moments after the crash, screaming at the people responsible.

The feisty, 50 year-old redhead found other things wrong once on stage. "This is the door to the study, Bob. It needs to be over there, stage right. I can't have people entering through the walls."

Then she snapped at some cast members who were milling about in the orchestra pit. "Where the hell is Kevin?

"He's a little shaken up Carly," Bart, one of the cast members, said.

"Get him out here. Get everyone back out here. Please."

She leaned closer to Bart and said in a whisper. "I don't want Styles on my back. I don't need his neurotic shit now. *Capisce*?" Big Bart, as his cast members called him, who played the hooded figure, headed for the backstage area when Kevin came storming back on stage. "Jesus. Carly."

Kevin held his hand over a small scrape on his forehead. "Aw," said Bart. "A booboo on your head. Try getting rammed in the chest by a 250-pound line-backer coming at you at full speed."

"I don't' care about your football days at USC."

Carly called out to her lighting director who was walking down the aisle to-wards the stage. "Larry, the backlighting is not quite right. Maybe it's the scrim. Would you please check that."

"Yessir, ma'am"

"Wardrobe. W-A-R-D-R-O-B-E," Carly shrieked.

"God Carly. I'm here." Jennifer Foley stood downstage of Carly with her ever-present tape measure draped around her neck. She was a thin blonde with wholesome, Midwestern looks.

"Jennifer. So far, so good. But I need you to check Bart's cape. It's a little too full. Take it in a bit."

"Yes Carly. Right away."

The lighting technician responsible for hanging the lights on the fly bars came over to Carly. The short, old man with eyes that had seen a lifetime of struggle appealed to her. "I'm so sorry Carly. It wasn't the boom. The wood is very old up there."

"I should fire you," Carly snapped at him.

The man looked meekly at the floor. He was clearly, and honestly horrified about what had happened, and Carly knew that. "Don't let it happen again," she said, with a softer tone.

The old lighting technician's eyes sparkled and he returned to his duties.

"We open next week, Carly." She gritted her teeth at the sound of Style's annoying tone.

"I know, I know," she said turning to him.

Though Styles had a voice that was at times smoky, sultry and sexy, the rest of his appearance and demeanor was completely repulsive to her. His pasty skin, curly brown, oily hair fringed with white at the temples, and tobacco-stained teeth were not easy on her eyes. He also had a slouch that annoyed her. She wanted to shout at him *don't slouch!*

"I am running out of patience, Carly. And let me tell you something else. I am not happy with Kevin's rehearsals. I never wanted him in the first place. But I trusted your judgement. Please prove me wrong. Please. Tell me I made the right decision in letting you cast him."

"You made the right decision, Heir Ronald." Carly turned her back on him in grand theatrical fashion.

Carly Hanson had gone to the mat for Kevin Rodgers. Styles had wanted someone older and more seasoned, but Hanson liked Kevin's youthful innocence, and the fact that he took direction well. She was convinced he would be able to tap into the darker side of his character with her careful coaching. Despite numerous arguments, Styles had finally yielded.

Carly searched the stage for her trusted, reliable, and unbearably efficient stage manager. "Leo, where are you?"

"Back here Carly."

The crisis of the fallen floodlight had long passed for Leo Fellman who had moved onto another crisis. He was searching the prompt corner for his master copy of the script on which he had jotted down numerous notes and instructions for the cast and crew. To a stage manager, losing or misplacing a master copy of a play could be a major headache, much like someone losing their tax returns on April 14.

"Leo. I want the cast on stage in thirty minutes, O.K?"

"Yes. Carly." The sixtyish, silver-haired stage manager was on all fours when he finally found his treasured script under the prompt desk. "Now how the hell did you get down there?"

Chapter 32

THE MACLEAN THEATRE'S small dressing room was crammed with cast members who added finishing touches to their make-up. After the crisis on stage they had relaxed and actually became a lively group again. Two actors engaged in a mock, sword-fighting duel, thrusting and paring towards each other with imaginary swords. They were all enjoying a few moments of merriment, save for one. Preston Hanks. Though weeks before he had felt overwhelmed and exasperated by the rigors of show business, he had landed, and much to his surprise, a small role in "The Raven." He sat at the make-up table, nervously applying his make-up. "I don't like it. Psycho killing actors. Why us?"

"That's why they're called psychos," Bart said, who sat next to him applying his make-up. "Years of insanity have made them nuts."

Preston began to pout. "Very funny."

"Why did you have to bring that up Preston," said Jennifer. "Leave it to you to ruin the moment."

"Well it's all over the news sweet thing."

"I know that. We can't escape the news; it's everywhere, but at least for a while, down here we can."

Preston ignored her. "We don't hurt anyone. We bring entertainment, and joy, and hope to the otherwise desperate lives of so many unfortunate souls."

"We do that?" Bart said.

Brianna, a brunette in her late twenties, adjusted her bra. "That's right Bart. Actors end all suffering in the world. Didn't you know? I read an article about that in Psychology Monthly"

The cast broke up. Brianna was cast as the poet's sensuous and radiant lost Lenore --the reason for his torment and ultimate demise.

"I'm not laughing," Preston retorted.

"Preston. Relax," Bart said. "If any psychos come this way, me and Kevin will dispose of them quickly." Then he lifted his brawny six foot-three frame, and flexed like a body builder in competition.

"Oh sure. And how do you suppose you'll do that? Are you going to chase him away with your bad jokes?"

⊷══ ══⊶

The long, pleasant drive along the coast and then inland a few miles through a winding, hillside road finally came to an end when Park turned unto a gravel driveway that led to the theatre.

Nestled behind a row of palms, she and Valente noticed that the converted, mid-20th century barn needed a nip and a tuck here and there, and perhaps additional landscaping, but otherwise the theatre looked to have undergone a worthy renovation. Two iron lampposts stood on opposite ends of the front steps.

As Park guided the car towards the entrance, the theatre's marquee bore a chilling reminder of recent events. It read: Edgar Allan Poe's *The Raven*.

"Poe's hot these days," Valente said.

"A few years ago, everybody was doing Jane Austen. You know Hollywood. When something's hot, everyone jumps on the bandwagon."

Chapter 33

THE CAST AND crew had assembled on stage. Kevin was the last to arrive. Styles was outwardly annoyed. "You won't be late for opening night, will you Kevin?"

Kevin shook his head, and ignored the sarcasm. He was used to it by now. In fact, no one in the cast paid much attention to Styles' sarcastic outbursts. "Is everybody here?"

"Yes Ron," Carly said, impatiently.

"Good. Now listen up. This show will get more press than anything I've done before. Perhaps this is due in part to the death of Arthur St. George. In a way, we all owe him a debt of gratitude. St George was a true innovator, a credit to our profession. An impresario in the mold of a George M. Cohan, Flo Ziegfeld or P.T. Barnum. A great showman and a great man. I probably would not have gotten the inspiration to do this show were it not for his production of "Murders in the Rue Morgue." Tragic that he is no longer with us.

Carly, and many in the cast, thought Styles was a morbid opportunist who was using St. George's murder to cash in.

"So, I think you can appreciate the importance of being diligent, and professional," Styles continued. "We've got a lot of work to do in a short amount of time. And some big shoes to fill. Let's not make Carly's and my life any more trying. O.K?"

During Styles' address to the cast, Valente and Park had let themselves into the back of the theatre where they waited for him to finish.

Styles continued: "Murders in the Rue Morgue" is having a smash run. Though not a critical success, it is packing the house, and I have every confidence that our play will be a smash, and who knows, maybe even a move to Broadway."

All eyes lit up on stage. The dream of every writer, actor, and director working in regional theatres all across the country is to take their show to Broadway. That does not happen often but when it does, good or bad, it is an experience they will cherish forever.

"You really think we have a shot at Broadway," Kevin asked.

"There's always that hope," Styles said. "We are not an obscure theatre, and I have arranged for some very influential New York backers to come see us. But let's not worry about that now. Let's worry about getting through opening night."

Then he turned to his director. "Carly?"

"Thank you. Places for Act One in ten minutes," she barked.

As the cast dispersed, Brianna took Jennifer and Preston aside. "Styles seems kind of worried."

"Yeah. I guess. He's got a lot invested in this," Jennifer said.

Preston twirled two fingers through a strand of his hair. "Nobody said he had to adapt "The Raven." It's not like there's a shortage of material in the English language."

"But wow. Broadway?" Brianna said.

Kevin was the last to leave. He remained on stage, casting a nervous look at the fly bars up above. "Relax Kevin," Carly said. "I checked them myself."

Walking up the center aisle while lighting a cigarette, Styles noticed Valente and Park.

"Let me guess. L.A.P.D."

They nodded and he was not thrilled to see them. With dripping sarcasm Styles said, "A subtle entrance. How refreshing."

Valente introduced themselves. "Sam Valente, Nicole Park." They offered up their badges but Styles ignored the gesture and breezed past them.

Kevin had noticed the police enter and spoke to Carly in a harsh whisper. "They're here about the killings huh?"

Carly kept a suspicious eye on the police who followed Styles out of the theatre. "I guess,"

Chapter 34

IN THE LOBBY, Styles softened his attitude toward them. He gave himself a moment to change his demeanor, take a deep breath, and try to put on an air of gentility.

"I poured everything into this old place. I'm sure you noticed the upholstered seats, the new carpeting. New marble here in the foyer. And some of the latest state-of-the art equipment my budget would allow. We're still renovating here and there, but for the most part we are on par with some of the most modern theatres. We're digital everywhere – dimmers, effects and recording capabilities. I even bought us a damned fog machine the other day." He almost laughed at that. "And with the NEA grant, I can start renovating the rest. Build another wing. I'd like to turn the whole place into a small performing arts center with classrooms, dance studios, rehearsal rooms and jogging track."

"A jogging track?" Park said, not fully believing him.

"Just kidding about that."

They stepped outside where Styles continued his tour. "You know, in ancient times the Greeks built a stage, carved stone seats into the side of a mountain, and captivated their audiences with brilliant words and perfect acoustics. Today, we need digital technology, special effects, mic'd actors, and enough lights to illuminate a football stadium, and all to mask the lack of a good script. The competition is not for the story. It's for the latest gizmo to wow legions of teenagers raised on junk technology. And still, with so much money spent on all that technology, so many productions reek."

He paused for a moment. "I want to create an environment where the emphasis is on the play, not the technology."

Then he noticed a stand of cypress off to the right. "However, one thing I'm definitely going to need is more parking. Those poor trees might have to come down."

Back in the dressing room, the actors made a final check on their costumes and make-up before rehearsal.

"Would someone tell me why the police are here? I mean it's not like any of us are suspects," Preston said, still in his pouting mood.

"Do you have something to hide sweety pie?" Bart said.

"Yes I do, and it's not for you. But someday. Someday I am going to turn you."

"I don't know how to limp my wrist."

Preston threw a wad of tissue at him.

Brianna breezed over to them. "I read in the paper where Arthur St. George and Nicholas Teague were once members here."

"Nicholas Teague?" Bart said, not recognizing the name.

"The guy that got his blood drained out of him," Brianna said.

"Coincidence! Coincidence," Preston said, waving his hand in the air as though it were a little flag. "You can find a connection to something, some-where, anytime, always."

Both Brianna and Bart simply rolled their eyes.

Chapter 35

JOSH ARKOFF HAD always wanted to make a difference.

Ever since the Tennessee native had seen a dung beetle while on a grade school, class trip to the National Zoo's insect house in Washington D.C., Josh had become fascinated with those critters. While the idea of a creature feeding on the fresh dung of large, plant eating mammals to produce offspring grossed out his school mates, Arkoff, instead, was captivated by that behavioral peculiarity.

By the time he had entered high school, his interest in beetles had grown. He collected stacks of nature and science magazines that featured articles on beetles. Of the nearly 1.5 million classified species of animals and plants, nearly 750,000 of these species are insects and about 40 percent of those are beetles, making them the most diverse forms of life on earth. He remembered a funny quip by one of Charles Darwin's friends on the subject of beetles. When Darwin asked Thomas Huxley what the study of creation revealed about the mind of the creator, Huxley replied, "The Almighty has an inordinate fondness for beetles."

Later, Arkoff's interests spread to other insect species along with crustaceans and small creatures in general. His first couple of years in high school were not without ribbing from some classmates who thought him weird that he had developed such an intense fascination for creatures most people abhor.

Then, one night, in his senior year of high school, Arkoff saw Frank Capra's classic film *It's A Wonderful Life*. It had transformed him. From that moment he kept the film's central theme close to his heart – *everyone makes a difference*.

So, armed with his desire to do exactly that, Arkoff got a degree in biology from the University of Tennessee. While there, a fellow student, knowing his interest in insects, loaned him a book on forensics entomology. Late one night, while studying for a final, he decided to take a break from reading the chemistry that was dissolving his eyeballs, and get into the book loaned to him by his friend. The book captivated him. At last he had found his calling and a way to make a difference: Forensics Entomology.

He applied at several graduate schools, and it was finally the University of Southern California that accepted him. While there, he had become inspired by a leading expert in the field who had always stressed the importance of insect analysis in crime solving.

Josh had been folding his laundry at his neighborhood laundromat in Culver City when he received a call on his cellphone from the lab doing the chemical analysis on the bat fly. During the call his eyes lit up like a pair of white Christmas bulbs.

Josh felt something big was going down in the investigation and he was going to be a part of the equation. The fuzzy-haired geek might actually make his mark in the field of forensics entomology. His mind was racing in a thousand directions when he left the laundromat. In a few minutes he would make the call that could break the case wide open and endear him to the police and his colleagues: the call that would allow him to continue to make a difference. Or so he had hoped.

Chapter 36

STYLES AND THE police moved around the side of the theatre. The sun was shinning bright in their eyes. "With all this sunshine it's sometimes hard to get in the mood evoked in *The Raven*. We should be doing the play in a dark and dreary city like London, or New York."

Valente paid close attention to his every nuance. There was something about Styles he did not trust, but he could not put his finger on it.

"That's where much of the grant money will go." Styles pointed to a rear addition of the building that was incomplete. The walls were up, but the roof was not. Only steel crossbeams were in place.

"I had planned to make that the dance and rehearsal studio I was telling you about. Then I ran out of money, which held up construction until the National Endowment for the Arts grant came through. I don't know what I would have done without them."

They stepped over some rubble as they entered the incomplete structure and walked over a cool, cement floor. A small cement mixer rested in the center of the large room. Several sheets of drywall and rolls of wire mesh stood at the far end opposite them.

"This will eventually be a state-of-the-art, multi-purpose facility, complete with showers and a steam room."

"Mr. Styles," Valente said. "Both of the victims were at one time associated with your group."

Styles frowned. "I guess the tour is over." He took a deep breath and started to talk about what he had hoped to avoid. "Don't you think that disturbs me? Christ we open next week."

They headed back to the theatre.

"We've got to check out all leads," Valente continued. "I'm not at all suggesting that someone is bent on killing off members or former members of your company," Valente said, trying to offer some reassurance. "But you have to admit, there is a coincidence."

"Well the papers suggested ..."

"Yeah. The papers," Valente said with disgust.

"Well? Who do I believe? My phone rang off the hook after St. George's death. Reporters were crawling around here when somehow it leaked that several years ago he had directed a play at this theatre."

Valente had no desire to argue with him about the state of journalism in America so he quickly got to the point of their visit.

"Tell me about St. George," Valente said.

"Not much to tell. He directed an original work, a mystery called *The Presence*, a few years ago while I was in New York on a fund-raising campaign. The play did not do well and closed after a month. I think his mind was consumed with *Murders in the Rue Morgue* and he took my offer to get a paycheck. I never met him in person. He came highly recommended and since I had little time for interviews before my trip East, I hired him based on his resume and the references."

"And Nicholas Teague?"

"Don't know him."

Valente wasn't convinced. "I'd like to look at your files."

"I don't know what good it will do. Hundreds and hundreds of actors have auditioned here through the years."

Now Park was becoming impatient. "Like my partner said, we have to be thorough. The easiest of murder investigations can be a long, painstaking process. We're dealing with an unusual set of circumstances. I'm sure you can appreciate our position."

Styles had no desire to engage either of them in further conversation. He respected the police but had little interest in their day-to-day travails. "You have your job to do." He checked his watch. "And I have mine. They're about to resume rehearsals. We had a slight accident earlier and we're a little behind schedule. You're welcome to join me." He started up the steps to the theater

"Thanks but I think we'll check your files," Valente said.

"Whatever," Styles said. "The office is to the right of the lobby, adjacent to the ticket window."

Park took his arm gently. "I think we should watch a little. Might give us another perspective."

Styles stopped at the top of the stairs. "She's right. A little culture is good for the soul, and it's free."

"What do you think?" she said to her partner.

Valente wasn't sure where she was leading with this, but he agreed. "Alright. But just for a little while."

As they went up the steps, Valente's cellphone chirped. He flipped it open. And before he could say anything a voice screeched into his ears. "*Detective Valente. I found it. You won't believe it. It took some doing but I found it.*"

"Who is this?"

"I'm sorry. Arkoff....Josh..., the bug guy."

"Josh. What do you have?"

"You wanted a chemical analysis. Boy did I get one."

"Good work Josh."

Arkoff could barely contain his enthusiasm. The lonely man loved the attention. "Thanks. Thanks."

"So give it to me," Valente said.

"Well. It's kind of complicated. It's better if I meet you at the lab."

"When?"

"Umm. The man you need to speak to won't be there until day after tomorrow. His name is Thibodeaux. He's an expert in forensics anthropology. We can meet you in the morning."

"In the morning, then."

"Day after tomorrow."

"Right."

"Umm. Detective. Do you think you guys could pick me up? I'm having car trouble."

Valente truly liked the bug geek. There was something disarmingly innocent about the guy. "Sure Josh."

"Cool. Thanks."

"Good news from Josh?" Park said.

"Maybe. We'll know soon enough."

Styles shot them a stern look. "C'mon."

Chapter 37

KEVIN RODGERS WAS the only one on stage when Styles and the two officers quietly entered the back of the theatre. His make-up had not changed. As the doomed, tormented poet, he was made up to look tired, worn, unshaven, with disheveled hair. Dark circles under his bloodshot eyes.

His costume consisted of a white, wrinkled poet's shirt, and a pair of black pants and boots. He sat slumped over his desk. A nearly empty decanter of brandy rested at the edge of the desk.

Carly stood up from her seat in the center row and announced loudly. "Places for Act I. From the top."

The lights went out. Then came the sound of thunder and rain. Slowly one light came up casting a yellowish glow over Kevin. The rest of the stage was dark.

Painfully, he lifted his head from the desk and leaned back on his chair. His eyes peered into a bleak future. He glanced at the bottle of brandy. Maybe a half a glass left. He poured the remaining liquor into a snifter and drank, savoring the fiery liquid, letting it slide down his throat.

"Brandy. You are all that gives me pleasure." And then he spoke the words that began the haunting tale.

Once upon a midnight dreary,
While I pondered, weak and weary,
Over many a quaint and curious
Volume of forgotten, lore.

Carly watched and listened. Her eyes seemed to hear the words as she mouthed the evocative poetry. Styles, who had only seen him in early rehearsals, was suddenly paying close attention. The painful rasp in his voice was strangely impressive. Even Park and Valente were drawn to the young actor's instant command and presence, playing well the part of a broken young man on his last bottle.

"...While I nodded nearly napping,
Suddenly there came a tapping,
As of someone gently rapping,
rapping at my chamber door..."
...Tis some visitor I muttered.
Only this and nothing more..."

He took another sip of his brandy, and leaned back on his chair recalling another time.

"Ahh distinctly I remember
Twas the bleak December..."

...And far away, on the outskirts of Los Angeles, in the basement of an abandoned house, a wooden statue of a Raven sat perched on a windowsill. Mitchell Shanker's voice echoed from the darkness within. The inanimate bird seemed to come to life at the sound of Mitchell's voice.

"...And each dying ember wrought its ghost upon the floor.
Eagerly I wished the morrow--vainly I had sought to borrow
From my books surcease of sorrow--sorrow for the lost Lenore..."

Mitchell Shanker struck a match and lit the tip of a red candle on a long, gilded candle stick. He moved into the center of the room, naked. The candle eerily illuminated his face.

"...For the rare and radiant maiden whom the angels name Lenore,
Nameless here for evermore."

And then Shanker spun violently around to face the raven taunting him from his windowsill.

> "Prophet! said I. Thing of evil -
> Prophet still, if bird or devil.
> By that heaven that bends above us
> By that God we both adore---
> Tell this soul with sorrow laden if,
> within the distant Aiden
> It shall clasp a sainted maiden
> whom the angels name Lenore.
> Clasp a rare and radiant maiden
> whom the angels name Lenore.

> Quoth the Raven, *"Nevermore."*

END ACT ONE

Act Two

The oldest and strongest emotion of mankind is fear,
And the oldest and strongest kind of fear is fear of the unknown

H.P Lovecraft

Chapter 38

FAT, GREASY SHELLY Brooks hated fags. Whenever there was news of a gay bashing, Shelly Brooks celebrated. To him, gays were like vermin.

Shelly Brooks particularly hated homosexuals who appeared normal. He always knew in the darkest reaches of his racist mind that they are not normal. So to him, the ones who acted straight were the worst offenders, like the two guys standing next to him at the Santa Anita race track. This was the ultimate insult.

The race track was a place where real men -- cigar smoking men with a lot of attitude, stained teeth and bad breath -- came to wager their hard-earned bucks on the horses. This was no place for men in petticoats talking about the latest fashions. The track was a place for men who smelled of whiskey and sweat. Greasy men, like Shelly.

When he wasn't blowing his money on hookers and horses, he ran his Hollywood costume shop on Hollywood Blvd. near Vine. He never made it right to the infamous corner where he had first hoped to open his store. He had always wanted the Hollywood and Vine address. Coming from the soot stained streets of Elizabeth, New Jersey to find decadence under blue skies had suited him just fine.

Brooks tried to concentrate on his racing form, scanning the stats of the latest entries. But the two gay men standing next to him at a counter were a distraction. They should have been talking about horses and betting, but instead they were going on about what time to meet at the All Nations Club. The place was a popular gay disco in West Hollywood, and Brooks cringed at the mention of the name. They segued to talking about the opening of a new musical at the Performing Arts Center, and on and on about the director who was so innovative and brilliant. What were they doing here? Brooks wanted to deck both of them, but like most cowards, he internalized his hatred, building stores of bile inside his gut somewhere.

Brooks was about to move away from them when the call to post sounded over the loudspeaker. Within moments of the call, Barf, his excitable track buddy appeared. "Shelly. I got the tickets. Like you said."

"You bet the five horse?"

"Yep. Across the board, and I boxed him with the seven."

"The seven. Jesus, Barf. The seven horse is a dog."

Barf felt sheepish and wimpy. "I thought I'd take a shot. You never know." Then Brooks noticed that familiar look - the one where he appeared to lose all color in his face.

"It's that time, huh?" Brooks said.

"Gotta go." He made a bee-line to the men's room. Joe Halley got his nickname "Barf" because he always threw up before a race.

Brooks went outside to seek comfort amongst the railbirds.

The railbirds were a class of people unto themselves; a subculture found only at racetracks around the country. They were the track regulars who, as a habit, hung over the rail, studying the horses as they made their way in the post parade to the starting gates. There was rat-faced Louie Mott, an auto mechanic; dapper Giorgio Finucci, a card player decked out in thrift-shop Armani's; lone shark Eddie the Thump, and Stumpy Crockett, a worn out groom who worked the backstretch whenever he was sober and who often borrowed money from Brooks.

Like so many others, they hung at the rail, watching the horses' stride, going over the same questions in their minds -- was the horse steady, was he sweating too much, did he walk with confidence. They watched the jockey and studied his demeanor.

They hung there during the race, cheering and urging their horses to victory, and after a race, they remained there, licking their wounds and broken wings.

Year in and year out their faces showed the same expressions: fear, anticipation, anxiety, hope, confidence, disappointment, and despair. A true racetracker wears them all, because a single horse race is like a chapter out of one's life condensed into two minutes.

Daily, the race trackers bemoaned the bets that were never made, the money that should have been bet, the horse that was a favorite but overlooked, and the hunches ignored.

The romance of the thundering horse, the fearless jockey, and the pot of gold that awaits at the finish render inconsequential the remote possibility of success.

But Shelley Brooks could care less about any of them. In fact, he often tired of hearing the same lamentations of *I shoulda bet this horse*, or *I shoulda bet that one*. The graveyards are full of the *I shoulda, coulda's*.

"It's a little chilly out here Shelley," Barf said returning from the men's room.

"I had to get some air. Those two fags in there were making me sick."

"Hey Shel. Ease up. They're people, like you and me."

For a split second, Barf thought Shelley was going to have a seizure. "Like you and me? Are you kiddin' me?"

"Never mind," Barf said.

"You know. They're everywhere. Like Italians. They breed like cockroaches."

"Italians?"

"Yeah. Whatever. Arabs. Muslims, dirt people. You know? I think I got one working for me."

"An Italian?"

"Huh?"

"You got an Italian working for you, you said."

"No I don't. I gotta fudge packer working for me."

"Yeah? In Hollywood? Who woulda thunk it." Barf lifted his jacket collar, feeling the nip in the air. "I'm going back inside. Watch the race on the monitor like we always do."

Brooks followed him, close on his heels. "I'm telling you, I think I got a fag working for me. Says he's an actor."

"Hollywood's full of them. Why are you surprised?"

"Barf you're giving me a headache."

The only person who liked Shelley Brooks was Barf, because Barf was a loser, just like Shelley.

Chapter 39

SPECTROM TECHNOLOGIES IN Alameda assisted southern California state police and the FBI in complex chemical analysis of unusual specimens. The facility had a reputation for using leading edge technology not available to most forensic labs.

At SPECTROM, Valente would meet Martin Thibodeux, a leading authority on forensics chemistry. He would give the police the startling results of the chemical breakdown found in the bat fly --- *Nycteribiidae*.

Josh Arkoff sat in the front seat of Valente's unmarked cruiser as they turned off the Santa Monica Freeway. He had been a bubble of nervous enthusiasm since Valente had picked him up at his place 45 minutes earlier. Though generally not part of procedure, Valente didn't have a problem bringing him along. Valente liked the bug guy. He remembered Campbell's line about St. George. "In a town filled with barracudas, he was a goldfish." Arkoff had big, brown, goldfish eyes and reminded Valente of a young guy who seemed to find wonderment in everything.

"You're gonna love Thibodeaux. He's a real character," Arkoff said reading the unfolded map in his lap. "Oh, sorry over there. Turn right up there."

The front of the building was framed by tall stands of narrow cypress trees, commonly found on the hills of Tuscany. Whenever Valente saw those trees in California, he thought of Italy.

The structure was typical of the mind-numbing sameness of office park buildings throughout the country. Most were of a non-descript architecture, no more than two or three stories high, built in a seemingly serene environment of ponds, trees and lawns that contrasted with the often frenetic pace inside.

When they walked into Thibodeux's lab there was the unmistakable sound of New Orleans coming from a CD player somewhere in the room. Only the music wasn't Dixieland. It was Cajun.

The room appeared sterile, unlike crime labs Valente was accustomed to seeing which are filled with bloodied evidence on work tables. This lab was packed with computer monitors connected to laboratory instruments which appeared to function on their own. Two research analysts were checking specimens under their respective microscopes. Another technician was spraying something for residue testing.

Valente watched as an automated syringe extracted a clear fluid from a small glass bottle on a rotating tray and injected the fluid into a piece of equipment unfamiliar to him.

"Pretty cool, huh?" said one of the analysts. "That's a GC mass spec. You know what that is?"

Don't insult my intelligence, Valente thought as he shot him a disarming look. "A machine that identifies drugs in blood samples."

"Right. But this baby is more advanced than standard mass specs, allowing us to use this on non-traditional specimens, like insects."

From behind a partition halfway down the left aisle, Thibodeaux appeared in a long, white lab coat. "Josh. Nice to see you. How've you been?" he said with a pronounced Cajun accent.

Josh turned his head slightly and said in a hushed tone to Valente. "Don't let the Bayou exterior fool you. The man's brilliant."

Thibodeaux was taller than Valente had imagined. He was also older. Valente guessed 65-70. His disheveled mass of white hair begged for a comb and a pair of scissors. He was somewhat of a legend back home. A Louisiana boy, whose roots dated back to the 1800's, Thibodeaux had an ancestral uncle who had caroused with Jean Laffite. And legend had it that whenever Laffite drank too much, the great uncle would carry him back to his room in a local bordello.

"C'mon down. Got what you need right over here," Thibodeaux said with casual southern gentility. He wore his Cajun roots with pride, but his cramped office just off to the right of the lab barely held a trace of those roots, except for an alligator head angled prominently on the edge of his desk. "I used to wrestle those things when I was a kid. I take it your Detective Valente?"

"Yes,"

"It's a pleasure to meet you detective. Your reputation precedes you."

Thibodeaux removed a computer printout from a file. It was filled with colored lines, graphs and numbers. "I now understand why you are considered one of the best in your field." Thibodeaux said. "You have intuition. The good ones have brains. The great ones have intuition. You had the good sense to have this little bugger tested for chemicals."

Valente shrugged off the compliment. Others like him would have done the same. He amusingly wondered if anything was incubating inside his tangled mass of hair.

"And boy did we find a chemical," Thibodeaux said good-naturedly. He handed Valente the printout.

"What am I looking at?"

"You see here. You see this graph, how these peaks go up and down. These peaks form a chemical fingerprint so to speak. By that, I mean the pattern is unique to *this* chemical. I had to do some digging to identify this one because this was a reading unlike anything I'd ever seen."

Thibodeaux then led them out of his office to a counter where the two assistant researchers were working. He showed them several charts and test results.

"It took me a couple of days of research but this is what we found. Actually my two very competent assistants found it. Mike Hedge, the mass spectrometer fella, and Rollie Alonso."

They made their brief introductions and Thibodeaux continued. "I am old and usually fall asleep around nine. They stay up late. And Rollie over there is never far from a gym or a protein shake. Right Rollie?"

Rollie shrugged his broad shoulders and remained silent.

Thibodeux handed Valente a one-page file. Most of what was on the page read like gibberish to him. "Dr. Thibodeaux. English please?"

"My apologies." He leaned against the counter, folded his arms, and smiled at them proudly. "That, my friend, is the compound *triexeminin oxlinofiero diment*. We generally call it TriOxlin. It is a strictly regulated chemical used in limited recombinant genetic research for cancer treatment."

"Recombinant?" Valente said.

"Yes. Research involving the splicing of genetic material from one individual to another or even from one species to another for cancer research and other medical treatments.

"You said it was strictly regulated. Why?"

"Very high absorption rate. Analysts work with asbestos gloves to reduce the risk of absorption."

"How did this get into that larva."

"That's not quite how it happened," Arkoff offered eagerly. "The chemical got into the fly that laid the eggs that produced the larva."

Thibodeaux appreciated the young man's enthusiasm and added, "We assume that wherever this compound is located, it is in a lab that is doing research on exotic species, one of them being the Mexican free-tailed bat. Probably *Necteribiidae* landed on an open tube or slide of the TriOxlin and absorbed it into its system."

Valente digested all this for a moment. Then he noticed a set of vials containing a yellowish liquid next to Thibodeaux's two assistants. "What exotic compounds do you have in here?" he said.

Thibodeaux leaned around his researchers. "Oh. Urine samples," he said, with a wry smile. He couldn't help himself. "We do get those occasionally – testing for drugs in athletes, and some state and federal workers, that kind of thing. We have to do something to pay the rent."

Valente looked at the charts in front of him. Somehow a bat fly got this stuff into his system and then laid eggs on Teague's corpse. This is getting very weird he thought, even by Hollywood's standards.

"Doctor. Who is using this drug?"

"Do you remember what I said about intuition? I knew you would ask me that, so I took the liberty of calling a colleague in Washington. My friend has access to a national data base of all the research labs that could possibly use this substance."

"And?" Valente said.

"Well he hasn't called me back yet," Thibodeaux said. "He's busy doing chemical analysis for the Charleston police on a murder-suicide case in West Va.

Guy wiped out his family, then took the gun to himself. He'll get back to me as soon as he can."

"Can anybody else get into this data base?"

"You know anybody at the FBI. They have it?" Thibodeaux said.

Chapter 40

ON THE DRIVE back to the police station, a name popped into Valente's head. Ernie Cochran, the one friend he had at the FBI's Los Angeles district office. They had not seen each other in about a year, but they kept in touch with the occasional phone call or e-mail. He would phone Cochran very soon. First he had to deal with something he was still wrestling with. *The visit from the profiler.*

Nicole Park had found one - nationally renowned Ellen Weist.

Several months had passed since Weist last visited Los Angeles. She had been busy helping Chicago's FBI bureau solve a couple of serial killings in the Midwest. Then she had gone on a book-signing tour.

When Valente entered the interrogation room set up for this interview, he noticed Park leaning against one wall, sipping coffee; McCarty sat at a long conference table. A tray of coffee, and a carafe of water were centered on the table. A large chart detailing Shanker's profile hung on a wall.

The diminutive Weist stood in front of the chart, studying it. She acknowledged Valente with a slight nod and returned her attention to the wall chart

- Physical evidence: bat fly larvae, and Teague's SAG card retrieved at the gravesite.
- Shoe prints-size 8 ½.
- A chemical known as TriOxlin.
- There was also the one mug shot.
- A column listing the approximate time of death and location of both victims ran down the right side of the chart.

Valente had only heard about her, but never met her. She looked fit. A runner, he guessed. Or maybe an avid tennis player. She was 43, wore no make-up, and her brown hair was just starting to show some streaks of gray. Valente liked that she didn't seem to care about hiding her aging process. She wore a Navy blue suit with a white blouse. He was impressed by her understated elegance. Her credentials weren't bad either.

She had studied with the FBI behaviorists at Quantico, and held degrees in psychology and behavioral science. Over the years, Weist had developed a reputation building accurate profiles of the cases sent to her. But a few years ago she had created a firestorm of controversy with her book *Troubled Youth/Troubled Minds*. In it, she posed a radical concept of holding a child's parents accountable, whenever provable, for the criminal actions of their offspring, particularly if that child developed into a killing machine.

The reaction by her peers ran the gamut of opinion. Some even suggested sarcastically to simply prosecute everyone who had come into contact with a criminal during the individual's early development, since factors like physical and social environment play a crucial role in shaping a person's character. Although her concept was backed by a series of brilliant articles and papers, most in the psychiatric world remained dubious.

Before arriving at the police station, she had taken the time to read over the police report of the two killings. They were intriguing to her and fraught with wild psychological possibilities.

"You guys have anything more on this larvae?" she asked.

"We're working on it," Valente said.

"From what I can tell based on your report and the victims' profiles, what we often find with these cases is a psyche split in two: one is a frightened little boy reliving childhood trauma and the other, a sadistic beast bent on revenge for the horrors he suffered, whether real or perceived."

Valente noted how Weist spoke of demented creatures in all their malevolence, yet her tone was gentle and even sympathetic. "Sometimes thorough investigations into their family backgrounds reveal some pretty scary things."

She returned to the table and poured herself a glass of water. "Troubled childhoods, reared fatherless with strong matriarchal figures - mothers, grandmothers, aunts; overbearing mothers, sometimes abusive mothers, mothers who tortured their young boys. In some profiles, there are fathers who never made them feel worthy of ever possessing a woman. If the mind was week to begin with, any one or a combination of those factors could have driven a boy off the edge."

Valente wasn't buying this. "We have something a little different here Dr. Weist. Two men are dead. The victims of most serial killers are women. Someone imitating a killer, or killers from horror books or movies committed both crimes. What is he after? Which profile does this one fit? The delusional serial killer, the domineering one, the thrill-seeking killer?"

Park was surprised. Valente had done his homework.

"I have to admit, the vampire simulation was quite incredible," Weist added.

McCarty laughed. "Simulation? Never heard it put that way."

"And you must be Ed McCarty," Weist offered. "Heard about you from some of the boys downtown. No one walks a grid like you."

McCarty's oafish grin immediately disappeared as he turned several shades of red.

She continued. "I'd say there appears to be a desperate craving for attention with your perp. A failed actor perhaps. Someone who craved the bright lights and the applause but never got it."

"And that alone would drive a man to do what this guy did?" Valente said.

McCarty wasn't going to let her have the advantage. "Hell. I'm a failed and frustrated football player. But I ain't killing any coaches."

"Maybe it's personal," Weist continued. "He's after someone specific but needs to go through others first."

That took Valente by surprise. "Come again?"

"He may have someone he is specifically targeting." Weist sipped more water then turned to Park. "What about your thoughts, Nicole?

"Well, as I stated in my report, thus far, we have a man who has not been able to experience the highs one gets from performing live or on film. We are assuming he has never had the instant gratification and adoration from an audience; he's never had his close-up, so he gets his highs by killing. It is his drug and he gets off on it. And as you suggested, maybe he has a specific target – call it perhaps a revenge motive."

Weist shifted her eyes to the chart, twirling a strand of her hair through her fingers. "I'm going to pose a theory that may at first seem quite unconventional, but that I strongly urge you to consider. We know this man killed two men; one gay, and one straight – one a director, one an actor. Right there you have an unusual profile. As detective Valente said, most serial killers kill women. There are exceptions like Jeffrey Dahlmer who killed gay men, and Williams in Atlanta who killed young boys. But by and large, women are the victims. And most of the killings are rooted in sex. Were either of the body's sexually assaulted or mutilated?"

"No," Valente said.

"Souvenir gathering is a common trait among sexual killers," Weist continued. "These souvenirs can be anything from jewelry and clothing to body parts like vaginas and nipples."

She paused to see if there were any reactions from the group, forgetting for a moment, that they were seasoned vets who had seen just about everything under the homicide sun. Even Park, who had requested out of homicide because of the brutal nature of serial killings, didn't flinch.

Weist took another sip of water. "Videotaping is another method of collecting a souvenir. It is not unusual for some serial killers to videotape the sequence of events in order to relive the encounter over and over again."

"He may or may not have done that," Valente said.

"Could he be hearing voices, like Son of Sam did?" Park said.

"I seriously doubt if he is a delusional killer," Weist said.

"Why?" asked Valente.

"The scenes of the crime are too neat. The crime scenes of most delusional killers are left in total disarray and often the victims are picked at random. Your killer's victims are pre-chosen, he may even have known them, and the crimes suggest careful preparation. It took some doing to find real gorilla hairs."

Valente was momentarily intrigued. He recalled several profiles of delusional killers, like Son of Sam. Another was Ellison Kerry, a Memphis grocery clerk convicted of murdering five women. He claimed that God told him to kill. He decapitated all of them and stabbed them multiple times. Then in interviews he told police that women were evil and that God wanted him to rid the world of this evil.

"We sent a unit to Teague's apartment and it was a mess," Valente said. "The body of a woman was found, presumably Teague's girlfriend. Blood everywhere. Signs of forced entry. There is also evidence to suggest that he fought Teague, overcame him and took him to the graveyard. You have what appears a combination of a careful planner and a disorganized delusional killer. And another thing. He is physically fit."

"Hence my theory," she said. "I think we are dealing with a killer who could match several profiles. And that is very rare. Believe me – very rare. He could be delusional, and playing out a fantasy. But there is something else. Though he left a mess in Teague's apartment, everything that came after suggests a carefully planned event. He probably didn't expect to find the girlfriend. And the physical evidence retrieved from the three sites thus far - St. George's site, the graveyard, and Teague's apartment - they were left there purposely. He's a planner, suggesting a profile common to many serial killers."

"So we have to face a perp who is psychiatrically off the charts," Valente said. "Like I have always said, just what good does all this analysis do us?"

Weist decided not to respond to the comment. She had been warned of Valente's low regard for her profession.

Valente lowered his eyes at her. "Doctor?"

Weist put the glass of water to her lips, but did not drink. She let her top lip caress the rim of the glass. "I am not going to engage you, Detective. I know all about your opinion of us."

"Fair enough. We can move on." Throughout the investigation, Valente had secretly felt that maybe they weren't dealing with a serial killer at all. That perhaps they were dealing with someone wanting to settle a score. "We're also investigating the possibility that he was the lover of these two guys, and that these are crimes of passion or rage."

Weist was not convinced. Love or jealously were rarely, if ever, a factor in serial killings. "I wouldn't make that assumption. I would stick to the assumption that you are dealing with a serial killer. He wants us to know people will be killed in the way they would die in a horror movie. He wants us to know that he is truly a great actor and that the world has made a mistake in overlooking him. And he wants us to know that he will kill again, until he is stopped."

"So you think he's an actor?"

"He could be, or he could fancy himself one."

They were quiet for a moment, digesting Weist's theories. From the moment they were told of the gorilla hairs, Valente had felt there was a connection with the theatre. But that was not the problem for him. A demented actor who watched too much television and dressed up in costume to go out and kill working people in his profession did not pose a problem for Valente.

What nagged at him, and the nagging problem facing all investigations is the *Why*. When you get to the *why* - or the motive-- you will have a better chance of solving the crime. Motive. Motive. Motive. Homicide detectives ate, drank and slept that word. When you have motive, more often than not, you have your perp. So Valente kept asking himself *what's this guy's motive*. He wants the movie-going public to know what they're missing?

Then McCarty surprised everyone with his attempt at psychoanalysis. He had grudgingly read a couple of psych books while in college and was somewhat familiar with cases of people suffering from delusions of grandeur, schizophrenia, paranoia, and as he termed it, just downright sick for no apparent reason.

So with an internal wink at Valente he proudly posed his question. "Does this guy have to be a sicko? I mean, is it possible that he just likes what he's doing? That there ain't no deep-rooted family torture or abuse. He's just a first class prick?"

Weist forced a smile. Secretly, she felt there were some killers fitting that description, though she would hesitate to admit it professionally. "The thrill-seeking serial killer? The pure psychopath? I don't want to believe that. It's not why I've devoted twenty years to this profession."

She took a moment before continuing.

"There are thrill murderers, though rare; people who kill simply for the joy of killing," she said. "But I want to believe that people are born innocent and are later damaged. Many survive in a Darwinian sense, but the weak lose their minds, or are consumed in other ways. I suppose there could be some who are inherently bad, or evil. They came from perfect families, lots of love and attention, but consciously choose to inflict pain on others."

Valente and Park cast a glance at each other. He felt that this was going to be more difficult than either wanted to accept. Catching a serial killer can often take years. Sometimes they are never caught. Did Valente want to spend the rest of his career chasing after one crackpot? How obsessed could he become with the case? At times he cursed the fact that he had developed his investigative skills to the point were he was often assigned cases no one wanted or no one could handle.

"And the mother factor?" he asked.

"Pardon me?" Weist said.

"Do you think he fits that profile? The stuff you were saying about abusive mothers. It's in your book"

This stunned everyone in the room. Naturally, no one had expected him to have read her book. "That would be a blessing wouldn't it? If we could locate the mother before he kills again? Find out what kind of a woman she was, or still is?" Weist said.

Though Valente hated to admit it, he was for the first time in memory becoming intrigued by psychoanalysis. Maybe it was her passion and gentility. Not a trace of anger or attitude in her tone. And he had liked the part in Weist's book about holding abusive parents responsible for the murderous actions of their offspring.

"Again, I believe that the sadistic behavior of most of these criminals is rooted in a nightmarish childhood," she added. "So I would certainly assume that his profile is consistent with that theory. For now anyway. Have you tried to find the mother"

"We're on it. Nothing yet."

"Expand your boundaries," Weist suggested. "I doubt very seriously if she lives here."

So far, their investigation had produced little. Two men killed in horrific, B-movie fashion, a woman who simply got in the way, and Valente kept asking himself *why*. He had just heard from Weist that a jealous lover wouldn't necessarily go to those extremes.

"Permit me to re-emphasize something," she said.

"Of course," Valente said.

"What do all actors want?"

"Money," McCarty said.

Weist actually found the oaf amusing in an early hominid sort of way.

"Attention," she continued. "They want attention. They crave it. Maybe this is his way of telling his mother or father that he is worthy."

"I'm not buying it," McCarty said. "I like my theory. He's a mean son of a bitch who has no conscience."

Weist calmly looked at them. "No. He has a conscience. It's just muddled in a kaleidoscope of illusion, reality and horror."

And then she said something that left a chill in the room. "You must understand that dreams and reality merge so that he has no means of distinguishing what is real from the illusory; what has value and what is worthless."

A brief silence followed. Though intrigued by her, Valente was anxious to get this over. "You have the report doctor. If you think of anything else, please call us. We'll get you updates as they develop."

"I want to help." As she was about to leave she turned to them. "I hope you get him alive. I'd love a couple of hours with him."

Park laughed. "I'm sure you would."

When she walked out of the room, all eyes were on Valente.

"What?" he said.

"You read her book?" Park said.

For a rare moment in his life Valente actually felt awkward. "Let's try and track down mommy."

"You handled yourself admirably," Park added.

"Thanks. I'd rather have a root canal without Novocain than talk to a shrink."

Chapter 41

SHELLY BROOKS STORMED into his apartment cursing the world around him. He had blown nearly a thousand dollars at the track. Barf left him after the fourth race, having blown his own wad. The two had had an argument—Shelly wanted him to stay and Barf wanted to leave. Shelly downed his umpteenth bourbon and soda, and had gotten ugly. Barf knew it was time to go.

Outside Brooks' apartment building, Hollywood nightlife had yet to kick into full, spasmodic gear, but inside, the winds of rage were about to blow. He kicked the side of his upholstered armchair, and threw his racing form at the window. Then he picked up the racing form, rolled it up, and started slamming his couch. He kept pounding the couch until there wasn't much left of the form. His face had turned red and glowed like red lights in a whorehouse. His body was soaked in perspiration.

But once the storm inside him passed, he sat down and wiped his forehead. Shelly looked at his apartment. He was going to miss the place but it was time to move. He was having a modest home renovated in Laurel Canyon that wouldn't be ready for another six months. So he still had time to enjoy his seedy digs on Franklin Street.

Here, he felt he was in his natural habit. Colorful drunks, hookers, and assorted druggies were frequent renters. He didn't care about the druggies, but the hookers appealed to him. Laurel Canyon would definitely be a step up for a guy like Shelly. After years of living in Hollywood, he had decided it was time for a change. If for no other reason, he would have a hot tub that he could fill with two or three hookers and do for real what he had only dreamed of.

He opened a bottle of bourbon, poured himself a drink and went through his address book looking for a late-night call service.

Chapter 42

CONSIDERING THE EVENTS of the past couple of weeks, Valente found the caricature, drawn by one of the police sketch artists, taped to the lower edge of a chalkboard a welcome source of amusement. The caricature was of a gorilla strangling
a vampire. The chart had been removed from the interrogation room where they
had met with Weist and taped to the wall to the right of his desk. He leaned back
on his chair, hands clasped behind his head.

The lab results were added to the profile. Also, an entry had been made that
the FBI in Los Angeles had been notified. A map of Los Angeles highlighting
the areas of the killings was taped to the board.

Valente stared at the information for a long time. Nothing was adding up,
other than the obvious. The perp is killing people in grand theatrical and gruesome fashion. And now there's a bat fly to contend with. Find where that bat fly
came from and maybe we can find the perp's lair, he said to himself.

He picked up Weist's report, and glanced over the pages. The usual theories,
and breakdowns of the various types of serial killers, and examples *ad nauseum* of
past, high-profile murderers. And of course, a note on Ted Bundy. No book, or
report about serial killers would be complete without the mention of his name
or that of David Berkowitz. One entry from her report got his attention, and he
copied it on a piece of paper and tacked it to the board. *Most serial killers are sane.*

Chapter 43

MITCHELL SHANKER'S FAVORITE time of day was the early morning. During that time, the marine layer that often hugs the Southern California coastline gave Mitchell comfort. Then, by early afternoon, the layer burned off, giving way to the dazzling sunshine that annoyed him.

The grayness made him forget the blinding sun. It made him feel whole. He would often sit on the Santa Monica pier early in the morning and watch the fog roll in. But a few rollerbladers and skateboarders zipping past him would always spoil the mood. He had a higher purpose now, but one day he would ambush one or two of them and put an end to their meaningless lives.

Under a cloud cover, he cheerfully arrived at Flashy Veneer, one of Hollywood's more popular costume shops. In addition to its stock of every type of Halloween costume imaginable, the store was also noted for its lavish ball costumes, and endless supplies of masks and capes.

To supplement his income from the lab, Mitchell worked the late shifts from 5 p.m. to its 10 p.m. closing, two nights a week. But on Mondays, his day off from the lab, he opened the store promptly at 10 a.m. He liked the work and clientele but hated the store's slimy owner, Shelly Brooks.

Like the lab, working at Flashy Veneer gave him the ability to escape from the world outside. He could get lost amongst the many masks, as well as the endless array of costumes. To him, this shop offered him a sense of security.

For the first time since he had started working there a few months before, he arrived an hour late, and Mitchell prided himself on being on time. He had learned from years of going to auditions to always be punctual. Casting directors don't like to wait.

When he arrived, greasy Shelly Brooks had already opened the store. The short, round man, with a broad forehead, and a nose that would be a caricature artist's dream, yelled at him as he entered. "I had to open up Mitchell. Why didn't you call?"

Mitchell was instantly on his guard. The tension rose slowly through his spine. "I'm sorry. I misjudged the traffic. I don't usually work the morning shift."

"Plan ahead you moron. This is Los Angeles. Rush hour is all day."

Mitchell rarely saw Brooks. Having piled up a small fortune from his store and from a series of smart investments, Brooks liked to keep his evenings free, partying and screwing call girls. They were the only women who would have anything to do with the arrogant, three-time divorced brute with distinct body odor.

This morning he was miserably hung over having polished off most of the bourbon the night before while having his way with a hooker. "In my office. Now," said the malodorous boss.

Mitchell walked passed the clerks who worked the day shift. They had just spent an hour listening to Shelley bitching about Mitchell.

For a moment, Mitchell thought Brooks had inventoried the hundred or so vampire capes in stock and noticed one missing – the one he had worn for the Teague killing. But then Mitchell remembered that Brooks of late was lapse in taking inventory. Renovating his new condo and going to the track were taking up most of his time. One less cape would probably go unnoticed.

Brooks began barking at him as he entered the office. The room was windowless, musty and in disarray. Brooks' noticeable body stench hung in the air and assaulted Mitchell's senses. Copies of past racing forms were strewn about on his desk. Several copies of *Hustler* were spread out on a corner of the floor.

"Sit down." His breath reeked of booze. Other than the wooden chair behind Brooks' desk, the only place to sit was on and old leather chair, cracked at every seam and covered with old newspapers. "I'm sorry Shelley. I've never been late---"

"I don't care. I want my staff to call me ahead of time when they're going to be late. I don't like surprises, particularly when I've been out all night screwing myself until it hurts. Do you know about that Mitchell?"

"Huh?"

"Screwing."

"Umm. Sure." His uncertain tone was evident.

Shelley cleared his throat. "You got a lot of good looks, but I sometimes wonder about you. You're not a fudge packer are you?"

"A what?"

"Fudge packer."

Mitchell suddenly remembered having heard the phrase once before, a few years back when he had wondered into a bar. A couple of moralists were frothing at the mouth about the evils of homosexuality. They went on about how homosexuals were the bane of society, leading the nation down a path of moral decay. The religious bigots were convinced that homosexuals would bring about the end of America mainly because having homosexuals in the armed forces would undermine national security. Yet, Shanker could never remember an empire collapsing because of gays in the military.

A surge of anger rose in him as he glared at Brooks. Then it passed. But in that fleeting moment, when the anger caused the veins in his neck to bulge, he wanted to destroy the pig in front of him. Brooks spoke to him with a detached callousness.

"I really don't care about your persuasion. We're in Hollywood, right?" Brooks said. "But I got bad news for you. I'm going to have to let you go. I want you to know, it's got nothing to do with you being late, even though I'm still pissed about that."

Mitchell was overcome by a sudden wave of nausea.

"I've got to cut some costs. My nightlife is killing me. Hookers, those worthless pieces of meat, are taking every cent out of my pocket. And I'm renovating a place in Laurel Canyon. Money's tight. You're the newest member, so in fairness to the other staff, you gotta go."

The words fell on Mitchell as though spoken by a man whose soul had left his body, and all that stood there was a fiendish malevolence soaked in whiskey.

Mitchell felt the air seeping out of him. *Kill the bastard.* It was his only thought. As he fought for air, he thought of vanquishing the enemy, ridding the world of vermin like Shelley Brooks. But the rational side prevailed, for the moment. He had expenses. He had big things to accomplish and they required money.

"You O.K?" Brooks said. "You look a little pale."

"Shelley. I need this job."

"Tough break. Sometimes we got to think of number one. And I'm number one around here. You don't pay the bills. I do."

Mitchell thought of all the people he had worked for through the years. There was the job bussing tables because he didn't have the nerve to wait on difficult customers; pumping gas; reading scripts for a two-bit agent who paid him ten dollars a script. He thought of the many low-paying jobs he did while preparing to launch his acting career, and never, in all his years of swallowing his dignity, had he faced a man like Shelley Brooks. The brute would die, and not necessarily because he had just been sacked. Cost-cutting and downsizing happen everywhere. No. Shelley would die simply because he was a shit.

Chapter 44

EVERY FEW WEEKS, Valente needed a dose of Ed McCarty - just the two of them at a bar or at a restaurant.

They had agreed to meet at Don Pasquale's. It was an unusually slow night. There were a couple of tables near the front, and most importantly nobody up on stage making a mess out of *That's Amore*. When Valente walked in, McCarty had already been there an hour and was in deep conversation with Don Pasquale at a table near the back. Valente carried a copy of Ellen Wiest's book under his arm

"I'm sick and tired of this shit," McCarty argued.

"Hello Ed." Valente said, taking a seat next to him. "You look sharp. Nice jacket. What shit are you tired of tonight."

Don Pasquale turned to Valente. "What about me. How do I look?"

"Like an eggplant."

"Huh?"

"What do you want me to say?" Valente said. "Do I look like a poet?"

McCarty finished his third whiskey. "Political correctness crap. The guy's a shrink, and she's a blimp."

"Who?" Don Pasquale said.

"Who are we fooling with all this touchy feely talk?"

"I'm sorry Don Pasquale. I should have warned you," Valente said.

"It's O.K. I love this guy," Don Pasquale said with a broad smile. "He reminds me that we did come from apes." He walks past Valente. "I'll get us some wine."

Valente opened Weist's book.

"You going to read?" McCarty said. But he didn't wait for an answer. "You come to meet me for drinks and you are going to freakin' read?" The whiskey was telling him to finish what he had started. "I heard a newsman the other day talk about setting the time back an hour. Get this. The feel-good shithead said this. 'Tonight we set our time measurement devices back an hour.' Are you fucking kidding me? *Time measurement devices*? What the hell is wrong with saying clocks? Who the hell are we going to offend if we say clocks? When I hear these leftwing assholes talk like that, I want to rip their tongues outta their mouths."

Valente flipped through the pages of his book. "Did he really say time measurement devices?"

"Yeah. And I'll give you a hint. He's the anchor of a major nightly news network. Salt and pepper hair, and has a tendency of doing that sort of thing. Makes me want to puke. Another time, they were doing a human interest piece about young kids who work as bat boys or ball boys at Major League baseball games. In this case it was a young girl. The sissy newscaster referred to her as a ball person. Ball person? Pretty soon we'll take the man out of woman and call them *wo-persons*."

Don Pasquale returned with a bottle of red, and two glasses.

"Ed. Write the book. It'll be a best seller," Valente said, then leaned over to Don Pasquale. "I hate to admit it. But I agree with him and that is when I think *I* need therapy."

Don Pasquale poured wine. 'Well my old friend. In that moment that remains between the crisis and the catastrophe, might as well have a glass of wine."

"*Salute*," Valente said, and they toasted. McCarty was oblivious.

"Aah. Nobody wants to listen to the ramblings of a right wing, middle-aged, beer-bellied, Irish American. We Irish drink too much, right?"

"Don't feel so bad Ed," Valente said. "If I had to eat your food, I'd be trashed every night too."

"I ain't diversified enough," Ed continued, ignoring Valente. "I ain't vulnerable enough. What's happening to this country? America, where women are men and the men are clueless."

Valente decided to shift gears. He wasn't in the mood to listen to him complain all night. "Did you know that in the early Middle Ages, soon after the fall of the Roman Empire, the Church branded actors as outcasts and sought to exterminate them?"

McCarty nearly choked on his whiskey. "How the hell would I know that?" He finally noticed the book in Valente's hand. "You get that out of that book?"

"No. That was a nonsequiter. But it might figure into the profile of our perp. Who knows, maybe he has a beef with the Church."

"Let me guess. You're reading the superstar shrink's book?"

Valente turned the cover of Weist's book towards McCarty. The big guy frowned. His face sunk. "Oh c'mon. You're not reading that crap."

"I've already read it. We established that at Weist's interview when you clowns thought I had lost my marbles. Now I'm reviewing some places I marked. She raises some interesting points." He noticed Ed drifting off. "Ed pay attention. Serial killers, for example. They are becoming a growing problem for us. Per capita we have the highest rate of serial killers in the developed world. Serial killers are very difficult to catch, and they will definitely fool you. They are cunning and clever, and will hide behind a mask. And you, mister I –can-find-a-clue-when-no-one-else can - will appreciate this one. And I quote. *'Severely disturbed individuals who have lost contact with reality generally leave many clues at a crime scene. Serial killers leave few, or none.'*"

McCarty rested his beefy arms on his elbows. "Well that's not news, but bully for her. She's making a lot of money on already established theories. So she's finally going to make a convert out of you."

"Ed my boy. We are all a work in progress. And though I have stated often that I don't have much use for profiling, I never said I wouldn't keep it in our arsenal. Maybe I need to make a half-time adjustment."

"You used to be my hero," Ed said with mock disappointment. He ordered another drink. "But you're right. We have to keep all avenues open."

"Listen to this," Valente said, eyes fixed on another passage in the book. "Serial killers are incapable of showing compassion, remorse or guilt. They enjoy having power and control over people. And they have huge egos."

"Valente, my man. You just read the profile of every producer in Hollywood."

Chapter 45

SHANKER'S BRAIN SCREAMED at him. It was the taste of blood that made his skull ache. He remembered Marilyn, Nicholas Teague's girlfriend. He had not planned to kill her, but watching her die was thrilling. Before killing her, he had gazed upon her naked body and thought he was in the presence of an angel. Never had he seen such physical perfection. And he had learned something else from that night. Killing someone not in the plan was O.K.

He paced back and forth in his living coffin. Cobwebs had gathered in the corners of his ceiling, and the room began to smell of decay. And the basement was not as neat as it had always been. This mattered not to him. His mind was changing. He was changing. Filth was becoming a friend.

A couple of days had slipped by since Shelly Brooks fired him. His boss, the good scientist Clayborne, had accepted a request to serve as a guest lecturer at Louisiana State University. He would lecture, during a one-week visit, on cardiotoxins, found in snake venom, that are specifically toxic to the heart. These toxins may cause the heart to beat irregularly or stop beating, causing death. Black mambas and some cobra species carry the cardiotoxins.

He was glad that Clayborne would not be around. He did not want him in the way. Soon the roar in his head subsided.

Something was becoming very clear to him. Something that had to do with Shelly Brooks and Doctor Clayborne.

⇥◉ ◉⇤

The hour was getting late at Don Pasquale's. McCarty had switched to coffee. Four whiskeys was enough. Valente had already gone home

"I think I'll take a cab." McCarty said.

"Good idea" Don Pasquale said. "Leave your car in my lot."

"Don Pasquale. You're a good man."

"Eh. We try."

"Yeah. Let me tell you something. It ain't easy doing our work."

"Yeah? Try owning a restaurant."

"Restaurants don't kill people…well there is this one in my neighborhood, serves the worse food…"

"Ed. Time to go. I gotta close."

"I always feel like Rodney Dangerfield. You know. Get no respect kind of thing."

"Everybody has those days. It's called life. The trick is to find the joy in things not normally so joyful. Laugh. Laugh at life's stupidities. Like me. I laugh at you." He gives him a playful nudge. "Take your friend…Sam. He comes here one, two times a week, takes off his police jacket, so to speak, and puts on the jacket of a man who wants to spend two-three hours enjoying good food, wine, good cheer. In all the years he come here I think maybe only once or twice I hear him talk about work."

"I think I'm going to wet myself."

Don Pasquale puts his arm around Ed. "You are a good egg. Don't let this work lose your soul. Not worth it."

"I want to hear more about Saint Sam. I wanna be just like him when I grow up."

"Ed."

"I'm kidding. He's a great guy. The best. Now call me a cab because I'm drunk, and if we talk anymore about Valente, I might fall in love with him."

They both laughed. "You stand over there by the door. Get some air. I'll call you a cab."

Shanker returned to the lab late that night.

The lone security guard recognized him and let him pass after Shanker said he had forgotten his gym bag and some papers.

The black mamba rested in its terrarium. Getting the thing out of there was not going to be easy. The last thing he wanted was to anger the hyperactive snake. And he briefly thought about not disappointing his boss. Clayborne had, after all, placed his trust in him.

With great care, he lifted the lid of the terrarium and quickly snared the mamba with a two-pronged metal rod he had brought with him. Shanker then grabbed the snake from the back of its neck and shoved it into a burlap sack. The snake went berserk in there. Shanker tied the sack tightly. It would be days before the doctor would notice the theft. And since the thing had been acquired illegally, it was unlikely the good doctor would report its disappearance. A better plan could not have been hatched.

Chapter 46

WHAT AMAZED SHANKER the most were the hidden talents. And he had many of them. He was incredibly resourceful, and he could turn on the charm when he wanted. He could dupe people easily into thinking they were safe around him, when in truth their impending doom was only moments away. He was after all a great actor.

As he drove up the San Diego Freeway from Santa Monica, while nearing the midnight hour, his emotions were high because of the death he had beautifully staged. A movie could not have been scripted better. Shelly Brook's murder would go down as one of Hollywood's most infamous. Shanker had scripted the entire thing and left a copy next to Brook's disemboweled body in a secluded alcove off Mulholland Drive.

The disembowelment was a nice touch, though not original. There have been many movie disembowelments.

But the snake - that was a stroke of genius.

Chapter 47

VALENTE WALKED INTO the station briefing room at 8:10 a.m., coffee in hand. Eight police officers and detectives had mustered along with Park and McCarty. They all sat at their desks with files in front of them.

Valente took a long sip of his coffee then set it on a desk next to his lectern. "Good morning. I trust you guys had a chance to look at the updated case report. For now, the opinion is that the clues are in the Poe stories which you've already received. You all have your homework assignments. Divide up the stories amongst you. Report back to me in two days."

"All of them? Why not just the detective stories?" asked one officer.

"If we were dealing with an idiot who played the obvious then I'd agree. But we are not dealing with an idiot. We are dealing with a formidable adversary. So divide them up. You can skip *Murders in the Rue Morgue*. I'll study that one."

Another officer called out. "Detective. You mentioned that this guy is imitating the killings in horror films, or books. We could be looking at a number of sources. Why Poe?"

Valente knew that the young officer had a point, and frankly Valente wasn't completely convinced that the answers rested within Poe's stories. But he remembered something a former chief had told him while he was at the academy. Never doubt yourself in front of your men. Never say to your troops *I don't know*.

"The gorilla hairs told me something about him. He is meticulous, careful, calculating, and criminally sophisticated. Poe's mysteries are rich in detail. Poe's villains are intelligent. They are careful, and cautious. And don't forget, Poe invented the detective novel. I think our boy is telling us just that. I think he is telling us to read Edgar Allan Poe."

"But the vampire correlation," another detective called out. "What about that?"

"I never said he was going to make it easy. He's going to plant all kinds of false leads, clues that lead nowhere. That's not an unusual MO. What we have to do is cut through the fat. Any other questions?"

There were none, so Valente dismissed them except for Park and McCarty. "Ed. Did forensics turn up anything else at the graveyard?"

"Nope. Just the bugs, the SAG card and footprints. There were our prints, and a pair of what appears to be boot prints. But not Western. Dress boots with perhaps a half inch heel."

"So at one crime scene he was wearing tennis shoes, and at the graveyard, black boots. What's that tell us?"

"He's in costume all the way down to his footwear?" Park offered.

"Maybe."

Then McCarty remembered something. He hated when that happened - forgetting a detail no matter how important or insignificant. "Wait a minute. We found something else. Alpaca hairs behind the grave stone supporting Teague's body."

"He wears alpaca sweaters. So?" Valente said.

"These sweaters are not sold in any stores. You know, they're the kind sold by street vendors from Peru. And there are only a couple of places where those vendors set up their sidewalk tables."

"That could be a break. You show his mug shot yet to the vendors?"

"I thought I'd maybe save that pleasure for your greatness, your highness."

"Get out of here Ed. Check the vendors."

As they dispersed he stopped Park. "You holding up O.K?"

"I'm fine. Why do you ask?"

"Nicole. It's going to get worst before it gets better. We might get to heaven. But we're going to pass through hell first."

"Are you waxing on me again?" She said with a smirk.

Valente was serious. "A couple of years back you asked for reassignment because of the brutal nature of our work."

"Jesus Christ. I know why I asked for reassignment. Your point?"

Valente chose his words carefully. "I want to know. Is my partner O.K?"

"Sam. It's never easy, but if you are worried about me letting the department down. Don't. I'll be fine."

She stiffened, turned and walked out of the room. He wasn't completely convinced but for now he chose to believe her. He sensed a tough woman still lived underneath her gentile manner.

Chapter 48

AFTER HIS FIRING, he had watched and waited. Nearly a week had passed. Nightly, Shanker watched Brooks leave his late- night hangout, a seedy bar on Melrose Ave., deep in the bowels of Hollywood. It was a dive that served up cheap booze, food and hookers. This was a bar where the lowest form of human life gathered in packs. It was a howling bar of pool shooters, bikers, fat whores with fat breasts hanging over their thick studded belts. It was a place where doomed waitresses stumbled around on their last legs.

Brooks was a living celebration of fat people, another thing Shanker hated about him. Shanker took great pride in the impeccable care he took of his body. He permitted himself the occasional junk food splurge, but normally he ate healthy and exercised regularly. Brooks represented all that was wrong with American eating habits.

One night – *the night* – Brooks staggered out of the bar followed by a drunken hooker. His shirt tail stuck out of his pants, his gut hung over his belt and his oily hair fell over his eyes. He reached for her breast but the hooker slapped his hand away as she staggered away from him. Too drunk to give pursuit, he cursed the whore. He cursed the pavement, himself, then no one in particular as he staggered across the street to a dirt lot. He tried to step over a low hanging chain fence but his foot caught underneath the chain and he fell flat on his face. Blood streamed from a cut on his lip. Now he really cursed.

Suddenly two strong hands grabbed his jacket collar and lifted him to his feet. Brooks' glassy eyes looked into the blackness of those belonging to Mitchell Shanker.

Chapter 49

SHANKER PRESSED A cloth doused with chloroform over Brook's mouth, shoved him into the back seat of his car and fired up the engine.

Shanker drove out of the lot and headed further east on Melrose. Eventually he would drive through the barrio and then to his home, thus completing SCENE ONE of his brilliant screenplay.

SCENE TWO of the script that Shanker had quickly written in his mind began an hour later. Brooks was securely strapped to a gurney, in a room adjacent to Shanker's basement. The same room where he had drawn the blood from Nicholas Teague's body.

Shanker threw a pail of water in Brooks' face. He stirred slightly. First a groan. Then the ceiling appeared as a blur to Brooks. He rolled his head from side to side and slowly sections of the room came into focus until he was able to clearly see his surroundings.

His face contorted to an ugly grimace when he saw Shanker leaning against a counter. "*You*."

Shanker seemed lost in thought. "It is said that the quickest known death took less than five minutes." He stared dreamily up at the one grated window in his basement. There was an odd serenity about him. "If no anti-venom is administered, it is safe to assume that death is almost certainly guaranteed."

Brooks' eyes scanned the room. "Who are you talking to?"

Shanker moved away from the counter, revealing a sealed, rectangular metal container two feet wide and about a foot deep.

"Untie me Goddamnit. Untie me!"

Shanker moved to a wooden table where there was a small entertainment unit. He put in a CD and soon Strauss' *Tales from the Viennese Woods* filled the room.

"Do you like Strauss?" Shanker kept his eyes on Brooks while he pulled thick rubber gloves over his hands.

Brooks was confused, scared and wanting answers. "What are you doing? Untie me."

Shanker picked up a two-pronged iron rod. "I love the Strauss waltzes. Blue Danube is one of my favorites, as is this one. In my next life, I hope to return as a composer of great music."

With his free hand he unlatched the container's lid and carefully removed it. Swiftly he jammed the rod into the container. With one sweeping motion he lifted the serpent out of the metal box. A very angry snake hissed and coiled around the rod. Shanker quickly grabbed the snake at the base of its head, released the rod, and with his other hand grabbed the snake at the tail.

Brooks could only watch, frozen in fear.

"The Black Mamba." Shanker regarded the snake with near reverence. He recalled Clayborne's words. "For centuries it has sent terror through the hearts of Africa. Next to Australia's land taipan, it is the world's most venomous land snake. Two drops of its venom can kill a man in a matter of minutes. Even with anti-venom administered, many still die."

"Get that thing away from me Shanker. Don't do anything stupid."

"Do you know another reason why they are so dangerous? Besides their deadly neurotoxin, the black mamba is very nervous and extremely unpredictable. Most herpetologists don't want anything to do with them because of their jitteriness."

"I'm sorry Mitchell, for calling you a fudge packer."

"It is also the world's fastest snake."

Chapter 50

IN SCENE THREE, Shanker's head pounded. His heart raced. Everything had gone, thus far, as scripted, and Brooks had made a great foil. He played the role of the victim well. The screams, the pleas for mercy – no one could have written his lines better.

The black mamba struck at him several times, as mambas are apt to do. They are rapid strikers, biting at anything around them. When provoked, they are one of the world's most aggressive snakes.

Shanker had released the snake, and watched him strike at Brooks. Then with the rod, Shanker flung the serpent against the bulkhead. The snake was momentarily disoriented. It was in that moment when Shanker felt a wave of fear. Could he finish the scene? Was he capable of one final dramatic moment without crossing over to something farcical? For the line between horror and farce is a very thin one.

Thankfully, the fear passed quickly and Shanker lifted a long knife from the counter and carefully moved closer to the mamba. The snake had turned its attention to finding an opening in which to crawl, and hide. Shanker came up behind it and with a swift blow, sliced the snake in half. Then quickly he cut off its head.

Brooks lay on the gurney, dazed. There were several puncture marks on his face and neck.

Shanker enjoyed the look of terror in his eyes. "From a snake to a snake." Brooks felt the venom attack his nervous system, as his body twitched, then convulsed. "There's a saying Shelly. You can win the rat race. But you're still a rat."

"Give me anti-venom. Please." Shelley shook violently.

"It won't do you any good. You've been bitten far too many times."

Brooks cried out. "God."

"You don't actually believe he's going to help you?"

His cries were ear splitting to the point where Shanker had to leave the room and go upstairs where he waited until the screaming ended. When Shanker was certain that the venom had done its work, he returned to the basement.

Pale and ghastly, Brooks lay on the gurney. Shanker leaned over him and heard a very faint, rasp. He would be dead in seconds. "You played your part well. But I was better."

With the long, sharp knife - the one that sliced off the snake's head - Shanker cut out Brook's bowels

Chapter 51

WITH BROOKS' BODY wrapped and tied in a blanket, he had driven to a clearing off Mulholland Dr. high above the San Fernando Valley where he dumped the body in a tangle of bushes.

He returned to his car and sat there for about ten minutes staring at the blanket, and marveling at how he ended the life of so despicable a human.

His thoughts shifted from Brooks to the sky above him. Strangely, Mitchell looked at the night sky with childlike wonderment. He had felt like this before. These feelings filled and thrilled him. He felt it first after killing Marilyn. And now, again with Brooks' murder. The taste of blood was becoming stronger and stronger, and he liked it. Diversions were going to be fine, he kept telling himself. He thought about that as a convertible, driven by a young brunette drove by. For a moment he wished he could force that car off the road and watch it spiral to a fiery crash below. Diversions were fine as long as they didn't muddle his brain. Thus far, his mind was not becoming muddled. Diversions were fine. Confusion was not. He had to make sure he did not become confused. But the sweet smell of success was all too pleasant.

Mitchell enjoyed these thoughts as he drove home where he would begin to prepare for the big things that awaited. And the loudspeaker in his mind announced to Los Angeles, *Mitchell Shanker has arrived.*

Chapter 52

VALENTE HAD BEEN up for hours going over *Murders in the Rue Morgue*. He was convinced a clue would be found in that story or in another of Poe's works. Though he had given reading assignments to his team, he wasn't going to just stop with *Murders in the Rue Morgue*. Valente read some of the others. *The Cask of Amontillado* intrigued him wherein a man, after being insulted by his friend, buries him alive in a crypt filled with ancient bottles of wine and sherry. There was *The Pit and the Pendulum*, and *The Masque of the Red Death* set against a backdrop of Medieval Europe's plagues and pestilence. But what really grabbed him was *The Black Cat*.

It had been a high school favorite. *The Black Cat* was a gruesome tale of a man who loses himself to the wicked seduction of alcohol. It also may have been the first story that involved cruelty to animals.

Haunted by his brutal mutilation of his once beloved cat, the inebriated protagonist acquires another one. The creature was a large, black cat with a white splotch of hair on its breast. The cat becomes his tormentor, and the man who had once loved animals, determines to destroy the new cat.

One night, while going to the cellar with his wife on a household errand, the cat walked between his legs causing him to stumble and fall down the creaky stairs. In a rage, he lifted an axe to destroy the animal but his hand was staid by his loving wife. Pushed by the interference into an even more maniacal rage, he buried the axe into her brain.

Then he set about to wall her up inside a wall of the cellar, after which he went looking for the cat that caused all this. But the cat was to be found nowhere.

Days passed and still no cat. The wretched fiend had disappeared giving him a measure of solace and comfort.

When the police came to investigate the reported disappearance of his wife, he eagerly cooperated and boastfully showed them the cellar and the sturdiness of its walls. Suddenly, after tapping at the very wall where his wife had been interred, there came a fiendish howl from within. The howl then turned into a wailing shriek – half of horror, half of triumph. At first the police were stunned. In another instant, several stout arms were toiling at the wall. Brick by brick it came down until, to their horror, the decayed corpse of his wife was revealed. And sitting on the head of the corpse was the black cat.

Again, a tale of revenge, only this time a cat was the perpetrator. Considering revenge as a motive was not lost on Valente. Did the killer point them to Poe because he wants the world to know about revenge?

The *Black Cat* also tells the tale of a man so wasted by alcohol that he commits acts of atrocities for sheer pleasure. Poe not only created the detective novel but also foreshadowed writers who told gruesome tales of serial killers. Valente thought about these and other scenarios when his doorbell rang.

Park entered his apartment with her cell phone at her ear. "Yeah. Yeah. He's right here." She snarled at Valente. "Don't you answer your phone?"

"Been up late with Poe. Pretty gruesome stuff. "

"It only gets better." She handed over her phone.

The dispatcher gave him news that sent a shock wave through him. Valente's world was about to take another spin.

Chapter 53

HE CALLED IT the lair of the worm and boldly engraved those words on a rotted beam.

There was a place under the MacLean Theatre, many feet below ground, where few people ventured. It was the area that had once held the foundation of the original theatre. In the old days, this was a large storage basement where flats, backdrops, screens and other large pieces of theatrical equipment were kept. Rows of old costumes hung on rusted aluminum racks. Trunks containing hundreds of yards of cables and ropes were stacked alongside the walls. This was a sub cellar, beneath the actual, functional cellar.

Now, this dark and dreary place served as a breeding ground for rats, termites, slugs and other crawly creatures that also inhabit children's nightmares. In this breeding ground of the awful, Shanker made his final preparations. And from there he could travel in shadows, undetected, through the many nooks and crannies of the old theatre.

⇥⇤ ⇥⇤

Actor Kevin Rodgers had the dark, haunting looks and thinning black hair that bore a resemblance to a young Edgar Allan Poe. He was cast as the lead, in part, because of that resemblance and because of his brooding talent. He combined a youthful innocence with a burning intensity not often found in young actors and it was for this reason that Carly chose him to play the tortured poet who kept longing for his lost Lenore in the *The Raven*.

Kevin had just turned 30 and this would be his first major, theatrical role. After years of one rejection after another, he had found employment with the MacLean Theatre. Worked two shows as an understudy until getting the lead role in what Styles hoped would be a clever and successful adaptation of *The Raven*.

But Kevin was having difficulty with two scenes – the end of Act One and his final ranting where he berates the black bird.

He was on stage late going over the scene for the umpteenth time, or so it seemed. His voice was hoarse, and he was thirsty.

Jennifer, the costume assistant and his girlfriend, found him center stage and carefully walked up behind him holding a bottle of water. "Need a break?"

Kevin was so consumed with his role that he barely heard her. "Huh?"

"Want a drink?"

"Not now." He paced to the far left of the stage. "How much longer can we stay?"

"Honey. We should go. It's getting late."

"Jennifer. I can't get the same effect pacing around in my tiny apartment. I need the stage."

"I guess we can stay a little longer. Carly and Ron have gone home. I have a key."

"Tell you what. Why don't you order some pizza or something and let me finish this one part that is giving me a headache."

Jennifer put her arm around his waste. "Want to get sultry in the Green Room?"

"Maybe," he said with a wink.

The thing was spread-eagled above them on the rafters behind some floodlights. It watched them. It wanted them. It would descend at the appropriate time and eat them. It would deprive them of what it never had. This is how he now wanted to be known. From this day on he was *terror*. He was *horror*. He was *It* – the monster that would destroy them all.

⇢▰◉ ◉▰⇠

Kevin and Jennifer kissed for several moments. He had had enough of rehearsals. Her tender persuasions had finally taken hold of him. But they never made it to the green room.

The thing above them unfolded, and slowly slipped to the landing below.

The monster lifted its tall frame and spread its cape wide, like a bat. He stood for a moment and stared down at them. He was lord and master over their destiny. Their blood would be spilled at his will!

Chapter 54

Valente arrived early at the station. The news from the dispatcher about yet another gruesome, horror-fashion murder had kept him up all night. He had called for an early morning meeting to brief his partners on the latest developments. Park was at the wall chart making the latest entries in Shanker's profile. She had briefed Valente earlier on the circumstances around Shelly Brooks' murder. Their adversary was becoming more and more difficult, and this made Valente anxious. And he did not like himself when he allowed anxiety to take hold. To him, it was a useless feeling that got in the way of good police work.

Park twirled a strand of hair through her fingers when she finished writing on the chart.

"So this man has no connection to the theatre other than he owned a costume shop, party shop… what is it?" Valente said.

"Both," said McCarty who walked up behind them, having just arrived. Coffee in hand, he sat at a chair in front of Valente's desk.

Valente was about to continue when he noticed Campbell leaning against a wall, arms folded, looking like he was monitoring them. This annoyed Valente to no end. He hated when Campbell played hall monitor.

With a scowl at Campbell, Valente continued. "He was a small-time shopkeeper who spent lavishly on hookers, drugs and booze."

"Piece of work. Dropped wads of cash at Santa Anita," McCarty added.

Valente continued. "He sometimes ran with a porno crowd. All in all, a lowlife, but a somewhat successful one. Now, just from that lifestyle alone you've got a huge pool of suspects."

Detectives McCarty and Park listened patiently as Valente again rattled off Shanker's M.O.

"The two earlier victims were both associated with the MacLean Theatre. We're soon going to find out how they were connected, and how our boy Mitchell relates to that theatre, if he does at all. Brooks, on the other hand, had nothing to do with MacLean nor ever been associated with the victims. The only entertainment this guy ever saw was probably peep shows. I don't see a connection."

"Actually, there is." Park said.

The frustration was mounting. Patience was not one of Valente's virtues. "And what might that be."

"Shanker worked for Brooks." McCarty offered.

"When did you find that out?"

McCarty sensed that at any moment Valente would show the infamous Italian temper.

"Kind of weird," he said. "Couple of lovers up on Mulholland found the body. CSI identified him and told me about his shop. So I went down and took statements from the two, day-shift workers. While I was down there, I got a phone call. Guess what else forensics found?"

Valente glared at him.

"Alpaca fibers. I asked if there was anybody else on duty. They said yeah, there was another salesman, Mitchell Shanker, who had just been fired. Apparently our boy stalked Brooks, drugged him, took him for a romantic drive along Mulholland, stopped for a hand job maybe, and then cut the guy open. The thing with the snake? That was a beaut. That was done somewhere else. This guy's got one hell of an imagination."

"*Now* you tell me about him working for Brooks. That should have been the first thing in your report."

"I'm sorry Sam. The alpaca fibers threw me a curve."

"He's changing his victimology," Park added.

Valente had tried not to let Campbell's presence disturb him, but he could not contain himself any longer. "Any reason why you're here?"

"I'm your boss, Valente. That O.K. with you?"

"This is the last one Lieutenant. The last one. When the books are closed on this case I am out of here."

"Fine with me."

Valente let his voice raise a few decibels. "I feel like the killer is right outside our door and we don't see him." He glared at those around him then calmed down. He looked over the preliminary report again. "No finger prints. Size 8 ½ shoe mold like 100 million other men. Tire tracks from tires that could fit any of a dozen models of cars....what about the snake?"

Park looked at her information. "Toxicology report confirms a poisonous snake. A black mamba to be precise. The thing was found dead near the body."

"A black mamba. Aren't they from Africa?" Valente said.

Park nodded.

"Was he murdered up at Mulholland or dumped there?" Campbell interjected.

"Right now, we figure he was dumped there. Trace evidence of chloroform was found in his body," McCarty said.

Park recalled what Valente had said earlier about access. *Our boy has access to places most people don't. He's not just staring at a butcher knife waiting for voices to tell him when to kill next.*

"Access," she said softly.

Valente looked at her, somewhat distracted. "What?"

"Like you told me before. Access."

"Right. Access. How did he get the snake and a drug only someone working in a hospital or a lab would have access to?"

"You think this is in any way connected to that Sheila Barrow case," Campbell said.

"Possible," Valente replied.

"We have to check every hospital?" McCarty protested.

Valente stood up from his desk and regarded the chart again. "Not necessarily. Our boy's an actor or a wannabe. Not a medic. He may have gotten the stuff from an underground source, and you know just the man."

"I do?" McCarty wondered.

"Jüurgen Reiner," Valente said. A wry smile crossed his lips.

"Mr. Octoberfest?"

"Yep. Reiner knows how to play his game to his advantage. He's one of those guys who dances in out of the law without actually breaking the law. If anybody's made an illegal purchase of pharmaceuticals he'll know. If there are black market shipments coming and going, Reiner's our man. He'll just love a visit from us. Put the usual heat on him. Threaten to pull his green card, bust him for any of a number of immigration violations, and make sure that you tell him we know all about the arranged marriage that got him into this country."

Juurgen Reiner had gained entry into the United States as a mail order husband to a lonely divorcee living in Montana. She needed money and had agreed to marry him if he in turn put $15,000 into her savings account. They married. He got his green card, naturalization papers, and five years later they divorced. A classic marital scam. And then Reiner chose an odd line of work. He sort of became an informant so as not to endanger his legal status as a citizen. His cover? He was a manager at a local fish market.

McCarty wrinkled his nose as though he was already surrounded by rotted fish. "I hate going down to that fish market."

"You know Ed," Valente said. "Life is like putting up a Christmas tree. There's always someone around to break your balls."

"You get that out of a fortune cookie?" McCarty got up from his chair and headed out of the squad room. Valente called out to him.

"Any news from those sweater vendors?"

"Market's open on Saturdays. It's Tuesday."

"Our perp is leaving clues everywhere. And we still can't catch him. I want to know about those fibers."

Chapter 55

HE HAD DECIDED that disposing of Jennifer and Kevin could wait. And this was by no means an easy decision for Shanker, because Kevin had the role that he coveted. No one could play doom like Mitchell.

He loved watching them from above, knowing that he could destroy them at will. But there were still other things to do before the grand finale. There was all the subtext.

It has been said by many theatrical scholars that people go to the theatre to hear the subtext. So Shanker had to work on that. Then there was the whole matter of selective murdering. Not everybody dies in a tragedy. So, patiently he had watched Kevin and Jennifer continue to express their affection for each other, until the hour grew late. When they had left the theatre he made his descent.

Shanker stood alone on the dark stage in the dark theatre. Moonlight glowed outside. From the depths of hell came a fury inside him. It was anxiety but unlike any he had known before. For a moment this wave of anxiety frightened him. Nonetheless, Shanker stood tall.

Remember to stand straight, his mother would always tell him. *Casting directors don't like little boys who slouch. Slouching is a sign of weakness. People with confidence don't slouch.* Shanker never slouched. Shanker exuded confidence.

Don't slouch.

"Should I stand over here?" he said to the voice speaking to him from inside his brain. Shanker moved a little to his right. And he stood straight, and tall. His chest jutting outward. A mighty chest he thought. 44 inches.

You look like a prince. His mother often said to him, when she wasn't punishing him. *Like a prince.*

"The Prince of Darkness," he shouted to the empty theater. "THE PRINCE OF DARKNESS." And the monster roared. "I am the God of all Hell Fire. And I will bring hell down on all of you. I have come, and hell will follow."

Like a prince.

"Shut the fuck up you old whore."

Shanker moved to the center of the stage.

"I believe in God who has created me like himself--cruel and vile he made me. Born from a spawn of nature, born into vileness." Shanker paused and glared into the dark, empty seats in front of him.

"So I am evil, because I am human. Primeval slime has left its vileness in me. Yes! This is Iago's creed! *IAGO'S creed!* Truly I do believe that all the evil I do is destined. And that man is the fool of fortune. The cradle holds an infant who is born to feed the worm. Then after life has run its course ... Death. And then? And then there is nothing. And heaven is a foolish tale."

Chapter 56

SOMETHING BESIDES POE kept nagging him. Valente had read most of his short stories during the course of the investigation and he was still convinced that the answers to the puzzle rested within Poe's thrillers. But while he lay in bed staring at the crack that had moved across his ceiling like a stream looking for a river, another author entered his mind.

His eyes followed the crack as it turned down a corner of the wall where it spread web-like in several directions. It was while staring at this tangled web that an idea struck him.

He reached for his phone on his nightstand and punched in Park's numbers.

After a few rings she answered. "We've got to stop these late night conversations. Can't we do this during office hours?"

"Nicole?"

"I'm here."

Valente sat up in bed and stretched. A wave of passion for her momentarily drowned his thoughts. Feelings that he again fought off. "Maybe we should schedule another meeting with Weist."

"You're joking right?"

"No."

"You want us to continue a dialogue with her?"

"Yeah. Yeah. O.K. Nicole, I'm growing. You happy?" He sensed a smile play across her lips. "You know anything about the hero's journey? It's in all good stories or films. I've read it in film revues of great adventure films and critics often mention the heroes journey."

She searched her memory. It had been awhile since she read anything on this subject. "Something about change right?' The hero has to be affected by someone or something, then goes through a process, a journey towards a resolution."

"Yeah. Where was the hero at the beginning of the story, and where does he end up at the end. What is the hero's quest? How do the challenges he faces in the story affect and change him? Usually for the better, one would hope. Look at Luke Skywalker's journey in Star Wars."

"So what are you telling me my dashing knight?"

"Shanker is writing our journey, in his sick mind, that is"

"Come again?'

"He's taking us on a journey, Nicole. This man is no amateur. In his madness he is brilliantly writing a story of revenge, born out of a deep hatred."

Park listened. She was intrigued.

"What happens in all thrillers, or horror movies?"

"Sam. Can you be more specific? A lot happens."

"Yeah but what is the common thread in every single one."

"You have a great villain, or monster."

"Right. And what happens to that monster."

"It's killed."

"That's right Nicole. He's scripting his own death, but like in all horror films, many innocent people will die, one or two of the heroes' buddies might also get it, but eventually the hero will prevail and destroy the monster."

"Well you made my week. One or more of us are going to die. Thanks."

"That won't happen. Not in this movie."

"Yeah?"

"This is Hollywood," Valente said, "and Hollywood is famous for rewrites. So we are going to rewrite his little drama."

"Doesn't all this sound a little like the story line of the movie *Scream*?"

"A little. Only he is not doing a spoof. This is very real to him. The clues are all there. And look at the genre he chose. It is the one where in every case the villain is either killed or apprehended."

"Except in *Silence of the Lambs*."

"I had a feeling you would say that. O.K. There are one or two exceptions, but he's not playing that. He's sticking to the genre in its most traditional form."

"Sam. You've been doing your research."

"No. I've been staring at a crack in my ceiling."

Chapter 57

THE R STREET Fish Market in San Pedro was only open from 6 a.m. to 1 p.m. but during that short time, hundreds of pounds of fish were sold everyday. Fishermen brought their catch daily and displayed the fish on rows and rows of stalls, benches and crates. U-shaped, with parking in the center, the fish market came to life soon after six a.m., with customers already waiting to get their hands on the freshest catch. Many of them hoped for a sale on Pacific Dungeness crabs.

McCarty stood by his car for a few minutes getting up the stomach to walk inside the gut house as the locals called it. This was a small, brick structure where fish were gutted and filleted for customers. The people who worked there had the unenviable job of scaling and filleting hundreds of pounds of fish bought by customers who came through daily. It was a thankless, smelly job, and McCarty dreaded going in there because of the stench. For Jürgen Reiner, it was a good place to hide.

At 6:15 a.m. Solomon Burke, a large black man with a pronounced belly, got out of his car and headed for the gut house where he unlocked the door. He was soon followed by Rosa, a squat Honduran woman, who came on foot from around the other side of the building. No sign of Reiner, yet.

Burke caught a glimpse of the detective, and couldn't help chuckle to himself. McCarty waved his badge as he entered the place and was immediately struck by the stench. "Jesus, does the smell ever go away?"

"In here?" Burke said who always had the faint trace of alcohol on his breath. "You gots to be kidding me. Morning, noon and night - the place is gonna stink. Working in here is like a sentence to stink for life."

"We get used to it, amigo." Rosa said.

"I'm sure you do," McCarty said.

"So. Big Ed," Burke said. "That's your name right?"

"Detective Ed McCarty."

"Oh man don't give me no rank. We're family here? So what's up? I know you ain't come down here this early to buy some halibut."

"You're right. You know why I'm here. Where is he?"

"Reiner in trouble again?"

"Nope. Just want to talk."

"You mean like, 'you have the right to remain silent' kind of talk?"

"Where is he?"

"He'll be here." Burke turned on a hose and ran water over a stainless steel counter that contained some fish scraps from the day before. McCarty went back outside, unable to take the stench any longer. Once outside, he paused and took a deep breath of fresh air. Then he saw Reiner get out of his car across the lot, not more than twenty feet away. Reiner's jovial expression immediately turned sour when he saw McCarty.

"Reiner. Gotta talk to you."

"I have to work."

"You can talk to me for a few minutes. They won't miss you in there."

"But I am manager on duty today. The fish - well they just don't look the same if I am not there to supervise."

Reiner enjoyed the little teasing dance with McCarty. From past visits, Reiner knew McCarty loathed the place, and the last two times that he had come to interrogate him, he left with a nauseous stomach. "Let's talk inside while I get ready?"

"Nice try. You know I can't concentrate with the smell of rotting sea bass in my nose." McCarty spotted a shaded area under a row of palms at the far end of the parking lot. "Over there."

Reiner stood at just over six feet. His brown hair was streaked with silver and fell over a broad forehead. His ruddy face was punctuated by steady, blue eyes that shined with intelligence. A crescent scar lined the lower left side of his mouth, the result of a soccer injury from his youth.

"Are you here to bust me again?"

McCarty shot him a surprised look. "If I wanted to bust you I would have gone to your apartment."

The truth was, Reiner didn't much bother McCarty. It wasn't like he was dealing drugs or killing people. Seeing Reiner occasionally, with his European charm and manners, was a welcome relief from the daily dose of street scum, punks and hardcore killers that assaulted his senses.

Reiner never seemed to be the type to carry the weight of the world on his shoulders. McCarty envied the man's carefree attitude. "We need some information."

"Of course. Why else, huh?" Reiner retrieved a hip flask from his knapsack and cuddled it in his huge hand. "A little cognac?"

"At this hour?"

"Gets the blood moving. It's a medicinal fact."

"Listen Reiner. I don't enjoy this anymore than you. So let's get on with it."

"As you wish." He took a sip of his cognac, while McCarty opened his little notebook.

"Anybody moving illegal animals?"

"Come again?"

"The illegal trade of exotic animals, a snake in this case."

"Snakes are illegal?"

"Poisonous ones are. Particularly this one."

"Which one?"

McCarty had to refer to his notes. "Black mamba."

Reiner wasn't sure he was getting this. He took another swig from his flask. "You know mister Ed. People don't often baffle me. But this is a good one. I am confused. And I don't confuse easily. Someone is selling black mambas?"

"That's what I am asking you," McCarty said emphatically.

"There's an arms transaction in two days at Long Beach - Pier 44 if you're interested. Could be a nice collar for you and the boys. A couple of right-wing crazies are buying enough M-16s to arm a small militia. So I heard. In Cerritos, a source tells me, explosives are being readied for delivery to a group of Mexican rebels. Something to do with indigenous Indians wanting to establish their own state. But, let me think..." Another sip of his angelic cognac. "No. No black mamba deals that I know of."

McCarty wrote this down, particularly the part about the arms transaction. "You been reading the papers?"

"Only the entertainment and the travel sections. The rest in the papers depresses me. And your coverage of world soccer is abysmal."

"Somebody was killed from a mamba bite the other day. Now, from what I know about mambas, they are not indigenous to this area. The L.A. zoo only has one and it's resting comfortably. So I figure the only way a guy could get bitten by a mamba is by someone who wants him dead real bad. Someone who wants to make a statement. Send a message. He could have just shot him. So how did this someone get a black mamba?"

"That is very intriguing, indeed. Very inventive. What will they think of next?"

"Really? Don't screw with me. Not today, and not here where I am about to lose my breakfast from all this fish stink. You got eyes and ears all over L.A. The killer had to have bought the snake from someone."

"I will try to be of service, but I have to say my sources don't usually deal in reptiles. They are more the heavy artillery types."

"You're a real comedian. Get back to me real soon."

"When would you like this information?"

"Yesterday."

McCarty got up from the bench and walked over to his car. As he passed the fish cleaning building he caught another whiff of the foul air from inside. This time his breakfast came up all over his car door.

Reiner's shoulders shook violently from spasms of suppressed laughter.

Chapter 58

VALENTE LEANED BACK on his chair at a table on Don Pasquale's outdoor patio. He looked up at a zillion stars slung across the sky. He did what most people do when taking a moment to contemplate the heavens. He wondered what it must be like to drift through space. Funny how mature, learned people can retreat to a childlike trance when gazing up at a star-filled galaxy.

At first he didn't hear the footsteps. They were a distant patter. It was late, the night was typically crisp, and that magnificent night sky held him in awe.

The footsteps got closer. Valente heard them but paid little heed. Then a figure moved around the front of his table and sat down. Now Valente paid attention.

Valente lowered his eyes and saw a man in a trench coat, a gray fedora hanging low over his head, a cigarette dangling from his mouth. The faint smell of bourbon wafted towards him. "You Mickey Spillane?" Valente said.

The man dropped a file on the table and smiled. "Not hardly, you ugly whop."

Valente narrowed his eyes and then the realization. "Ernie Cochran. What the hell are you doing here?"

"Word downtown was you were looking for a lab. A special lab."

"Haven't seen you in ages. How did you know where to find me?"

"I work for the FBI. Remember? It's my job to find people."

"Yeah. Right. Well, it's been a long week."

"Your request came via Washington. A somebody or-other Thibodeaux? Sounds like the lead singer in a Cajun band."

"He is."

"Huh?"

"Cajun, I mean."

Ernie squashed the cigarette on the ground under his shoe then popped another out of its pack and put it in his mouth. It was a Camel, non-filter. The kind that burns a man's lungs, unless those lungs are cast in iron.

"I'm sure you read or heard all about the Shanker case?"

"Sure have Sam. Just waiting for you to call in the FBI. You know we'll help."

"We're OK for now. I'll call you if I need you."

"Anyway. Dicks in Washington got in touch with us because they traced two labs working with exotic insects here." He pointed to the file. "It's all in there."

"You want some wine?"

"Bourbon."

"Hey Ernie. You got a part in a crime thriller? What's with the hat? The trench coat. The tough-guy talk. You doing Robert Mitchum's life?"

"You see kid. This is what happens when you don't stay in touch with your old buddy. I've been a consultant on a couple of crime movies lately."

"So you go in costume?"

"Naah. Actually, they give me some extra work – for laughs. Just got off the set."

"What film?"

"*Dead Men Don't Run*. It's a Mickey Spillane type of crime story. They wanted some FBI authenticity so I got asked."

"Nice going Ernie. I always thought you had a good mug."

"Check out the report."

Ernie stood up, pushed his fedora back. His blues looked straight into Valente's browns. "You let me know if you need our help. Don't go solo on this one."

"Yeah."

The 55-year old, grizzled vet put his hands inside his trench coat, "See ya, later."

"What about the bourbon?"

"You drink it."

Ernie Cochrane walked back into the shadows from where he appeared. Valente looked at the silhouette disappear around the corner.

Don Pasquale, who had been standing under the doorframe during most of their exchange, came up behind him. "Who was that?"

"That, my friend, was a late-night bourbon wrapped in a trench coat."

Chapter 59

Early evening in Los Angeles saw the sun make its way over the Pacific. And if the smog conditions were just right, a palette of red, brown, purple and yellow would emerge across the sky creating a typically stunning sunset.

Sea gulls flew over the Santa Monica Pier while below a few joggers ran up and down the beach. Park would love a jog right about now. The occasional rollerblader, sporting the latest exercise fashions, zoomed down the cement paths that ran parallel to the beach.

A charming elderly couple sat on a wooden bench, snuggled next to each other and taking in the panorama. They reminded Park of her parents, still together after all those years, and still enjoying each other's company.

Park shifted her eyes from the loving couple to a sailboat gliding out to sea. She leaned on a railing at the far end of the pier and for a moment felt dreamy. As light mists of salt water gently touched her face, she dreamed of retiring on a boat somewhere in the Caribbean. Spending her twilight years in a Margaritaville state-of-mind would be just fine with her.

One thing about working homicide in L.A., no matter how ugly it could get, there was always the beach, or a pier to go to and feed one's imagination. There were tougher places to work a beat.

She had noticed the time on her wristwatch and remembered her meeting with her partners at the precinct. Park had suddenly decided not to fix her face or hair and keep the windblown look for the rest of the day. *Live dangerously* she laughed to herself.

After having settled in at her desk for a few minutes, Park noticed for the first time in memory a look in Valente's eyes that worried her. His eyes always sparkled with confidence, or burned with determination. And even when his cases gave him fits, his eyes told everyone that he had not lost that winning edge. Tonight he looked beaten.

On her way in she had been briefed by McCarty that the FBI report currently on Valente's desk, mentioned RETLAN Laboratories, the local lab doing research on exotic bats. Its chief researcher was a doctor Clayborne. So McCarty and Valente had gone out there. But the visit to RETLAN had been a major disappointment. Clayborne had been congenial, and spoke of Shanker admiringly. "Nice lad. Always curious," he had told Valente and McCarty. "Don't understand why he up and quit."

"He upped and quit because he's a sick psycho," McCarty had said.

"Alleged, you mean." Clayborne retorted.

"Yeah whatever."

When asked if he had ever had a black mamba, Clayborne had calmly said no. When asked about the flies, Clayborne showed them an adjoining lab where exotic animals, including that Mexican bat, were tested for various experiments and chemical analysis, and yes there were flies. Clayborne suggested the possibility that a fly got in Shanker's bag when he went home. It's the only explanation.

"Wouldn't a fly suffocate inside a zipped bag," Valente had asked."

"Insects are amazingly resilient. Once, on a dive trip to Bonaire, a mosquito got into my mask case, which when sealed, is air tight. I took a four-hour flight back to Washington D.C. where I visited my sister, and when I opened the airtight kit to get my dive watch, which I had also packed in there, out flew the mosquito. From the time I packed the kit to when I opened it, I would say eight hours passed. That thing survived nearly eight hours inside an airtight kit."

So Valente sat at his desk staring into a cold cup of coffee.

Park reviewed a copy of the FBI report while casting a curious glance at her partner. She wore a short skirt that always got his attention. But not tonight.

"Hey don't look so glum," she said. "It's out of character."

Over in the next room Randy Nolan, one of the evening dispatchers, was engrossed in a trash novel. Something about a psychopath killing college girls in their dorm rooms.

6:25 p.m. and things were unusually quiet around the station. "I guess killers, drug dealers, and assorted scum are all having dinner," Nolan said to no one in particular. "Getting a hot meal before going off to work the night shift."

McCarty walked by Nolan and glanced over his shoulder. "Stop reading those books. They'll make you weird."

Randy scratched his pronounced belly hanging over his belt. "Are you kidding? This stuff's great."

Park kept staring at Valente, trying to guess what he was thinking. At times, his silence made her feel uncomfortable. "Ed told me that you guys came up empty at that lab – Clayborne's lab?" Valente did not respond. He was barely listening.

He leaned back on his chair, stretched and glanced over at the Shanker profile. "I look at that thing constantly. I want to light a match to it. Gorilla hairs, black mamba, chloroform, a bat fly with an unpronounceable Latin name. Possible connection to a theatre group. Connections to all three vics. Probably a contact working for a zoo somewhere on this planet. We got a name, fingerprints, shoe prints, a workable psyche profile. The bastard is leaving his calling card everywhere. We got all that, and we got nothing."

He looked at his cold cup of coffee with disgust. He wished instead that in that cup was a nice Cabernet or robust Bordeaux. Then he noticed Park's legs from under her tight skirt. Finally, he forced a smile. "Stop looking so sexy."

That brightened her up. She took it as a sign to lighten the mood, and voiced a thought that had been gnawing at her since she had known him. "Did you ever want to be an actor?"

He appreciated her thoughtful diversion. "Not sure. I think I became a cop to fulfill my boyhood dreams of wanting to be a hero. Isn't that what actors do? Play heroes, sometimes?"

Park nodded. She felt good about getting his mind briefly off the case.

He went over to the coffee maker near his desk, and poured himself a fresh cup. "My dad had a rough life," he continued. "he tried his hand at stand-up comedy when I was very young. He was not a happy man. I didn't want to end up like him."

"How do you mean?"

"Unhappy. Miserable."

"So you joined the force because of all the joy and spirituality associated with crime fighting?"

Valente smiled. She could be adorable in the most trying situations. "I became a cop…" They were distracted by the dispatcher's phone ringing. Nolan, who was buried deep in his trash novel, nearly leapt out of his chair when the phone rang.

Valente ignored the phone. He wanted to share a little of his secrets with her. "I became a cop because I wanted to do something good for people. Save lives. I guess most of us join with the best of intentions only to eventually have our spirits crushed.

Park lowered her eyes knowingly. "We've all been there, Sam. It's the unfortunate, ugly side of our business."

"Is there any other side?"

Park had casually glanced towards Nolan, the dispatcher. He was on the phone and she noticed a discernible change in his expression. "Stop being so glum." She kept her eyes on Nolan.

Nolan's face had turned white. "Detective. You need to take this."

The warmth in Valente's eyes suddenly vanished. "Who is it?"

Cupping the receiver, Nolan said, "It's him."

Valente's harsh tone swept over the room. "Get a trace," Then he slowly picked up his receiver, while the dispatcher put the call on speaker-phone.

A mock British accent taunted the squad room. "There is no homicidal ape in Los Angeles. There is no vampire in Los Angeles. There is just me."

Chapter 60

AT ONE OF the last working phone booths on a street corner in Los Angeles, full, reddened lips repeated the words. "No vampires. Just me." Then those lips, thick with red gloss, twisted into a crooked smile.

Back at the squad room. "Who is this?" Valente said. It hadn't taken long for McCarty and other officers to meet around Valente's desk.

"Do I have an audience?" Mitchell Shanker's voice echoed again over the speaker phone. "*Tre magnifique*"

Valente cupped the phone looking at the dispatcher. "Anything?"

"Not yet. We'll get it."

"I've seen all the movies," Mitchell hissed. "I know the drill. You'll try to keep me on long enough to run a trace. And you will. Only I'll be gone, and you'll catch me, *nevermore*. Who was it, *mon capitain*, that said all the world's a stage? Come, come, come."

Biting down hard on his teeth, trying very hard not to explode, Valente responded. "Shakespeare."

"Yabba-dabba-doo! A cultured cop. But I sense anger in your voice. Cannot lose control *mon capitain*. You have a killer to catch." He chuckled, and then changed his tone. "*Now listen to me*," he said with a force that caught the cops off guard. "Three more people must die. The first, on the 15th of March. I just gave you a clue."

Park looked at a wall calendar. It read March 15.

"What is it you want?" Valente said.

"Want? Why nothing from you. I have no quarrel with the police. Police officers have a tough job. And the world needs you."

Park whispered to him. "Attention." Again Valente cupped the phone, and looked at her, momentarily lost. Recalling the words of the criminal psychiatrist Ellen Weist, Park repeated, "He wants attention."

Mitchell's voice changed again, back to a hard rasp. "Three must die. I leave you now...*all my soul within me burning.* Oops. Another clue."

"Why do people have to die?" Valente said.

"Because it's in the script." The line went dead.

"Pay phone. Los Cabos and 3rd," the dispatcher shouted.

Chapter 61

PARK'S FIRST THOUGHT as they sped towards the location was that Shanker was not sticking to any specific region. All of Los Angeles was his territory. A murder in Beverly Hills, a body dumped at a Pasadena cemetery, and another on Mulholland Drive that could be connected to the same perpetrator. And now, a phone call from Los Feliz, east of Hollywood. *I have seen all the movies*, Park remembered him saying, and he certainly had learned something from those movies. Give the cops fits. Don't stay in one place.

He's good," she said softly. "He keeps one step ahead of us."

The pay phone was precisely where the dispatcher had said -- at the corner of Los Cabos and third. Valente drove his car right up over the curb then slammed on the brakes and slid to a stop a few feet in front of the dangling phone. He and Park jumped out of the car. Their eyes instinctively searched the area, but they knew he was long gone.

Trailing squad cars pulled up alongside them. Those officers jumped out of their cars and deployed in the immediate area, checking an alley and an abandoned lot. After a few minutes of scanning the area, they returned with vacant looks.

Valente cursed to himself. "He said the next will die on the 15th of March, tonight."

The two police officers retained that vacant look that Valente did not want to see. They were just as much in the dark as he was.

"He didn't mention anything about the other two deaths, right?" added Valente.

"We're your back-up detective. Remember? We weren't there when the call came in," one of the cops said.

Suddenly, Park blurted. "The *Ides of March*. Beware the Ides of March. It's from Julius Caesar."

Valente turned red from anger. "That one I didn't read."

"In Julius Caesar, the Soothsayer, early in the play, warns old Julius to beware the Ides of March," she said.

The point of the soothsayer's warning was lost on Valente. His mind was racing in too many directions.

"The 15th of March. That's when Caesar was assassinated," Park said with a sense of relief. She marveled at how the perp was testing their knowledge of the classics.

"O.K. O.K. I know damnit. I remember."

It took a second, but then it hit Valente with a stinging force, like a hard slap across his cheek.

He pulled out his cell phone and called the station's dispatcher. "Nolan? Valente here. Check every theatre and movie listing in a sixty-mile radius. You get every acronym you can on this - CSI, SWAT TEAM, ESU, IRD. Campbell gives you any crap you tell him to call me. And another thing..."

"Whoa Sam. Slow down." Nolan said. "What are we looking for?"

"Somewhere in this cesspool of a city, a production of Julius Caesar is opening... tonight."

Chapter 62

Tʏʟᴇʀ Dᴀʟᴛᴏɴ ʜᴀᴅ just turned forty and after years of struggle, his acting career was finally taking a turn for the better. Forty would be a good year, he thought, as he took the Sherman Oaks exit off the 110 freeway.

Three years on a soap opera led to major supporting roles in two films. The latter landed him the role of Hastings in a PBS production of *She Stoops to Conquer*. And now a chance to direct his first play. Something that had never entered his mind, not even in his wildest childhood fantasies. But his agent kept urging him to try it, and through a series of theatrical connections, he was able to convince the play's producers to give Tyler a shot.

Born near the banks of the Gunnison River in Western Colorado, Tyler Dalton had the Western spirit of adventure bred in him. His ancestors were cattlemen, riding herds from Texas to Wyoming. His great grandfather was a Colorado lawman, and his father owned a dude ranch in Montana "to keep that cowboy tradition alive," he would often say.

When Tyler was a boy, he loved hanging out with the true cowboys who worked the ranch for his father. Men with names like "Billy Grange", "Red Tucker", "Conroy Wilkes", and "Studs Ranger."

But as Tyler grew older and taller, the West took on another meaning. Though an expert rider, he had no desire to follow in his father's or ancestors' footsteps. For Tyler, the West meant Westerns as in John Wayne or Clint Eastwood films. And though he never sat on a Hollywood saddle, he carried with him the muscle of the West to every audition.

He drove his shiny, yellow Mercedes convertible into the driveway of his Spanish style, two-story home in Sherman Oaks. He sat in the car for a minute, thinking fondly of his past and listening to his engine purr. A wave of enthusiasm went through him. *What a car.*

Tyler unlocked the front door and was greeted jubilantly by Sundown, his loving German shepherd. "Hey big guy," he said, while giving his dog energetic pats on the head.

Valente was fuming back at the squad room. Little had gone their way. They were not getting any closer to catching their killer, and he felt that for the first time in his career, the perp not only started with the upper hand, the way they all do, but that he would *keep* the upper hand. The frustration was beyond anything he had known in a long time.

McCarty and Park sat quietly while Valente let off steam. Twice he had slammed his fist against the perp's profile chart which had become a permanent fixture behind Valente's desk. And his blood pressure was about to take another jump when Chief Campbell appeared in the squad room and walked to his office. The last thing Valente needed was a confrontation with him.

Quietly, Campbell entered his office as though he were deep in thought. Valente thought that was unusual. He had expected a tirade. In a moment, Campbell stuck his head out of the office. "Sam. Can I see you for a minute?"

Valente figured the tirade would come behind closed doors. He turned to his partners who gave him a look of encouragement. Reluctantly, he walked into Campbell's office.

"Heard about what happened. The guy actually had your number here at the station? Amazing." Strangely, Campbell was not his usual, unpleasant self, which made Valente uneasy. "You don't think he's stalking you. Do you?"

"No. We're the precinct that handles Hollywood calls. I guess he wants Hollywood to handle this." Valente eyed him suspiciously. "What's on your mind lieutenant?"

"Lend my support. This is a tough case, and maybe I've been riding you and your team a little too hard."

Valente had been waiting for the sarcastic punch line but it didn't come. "That's it?"

"Yeah. I know when I push too hard. It's like when I played football. A coach has to drive his team hard. But sometimes he has to let up. Give the players a chance to catch their breath. The other day I rode you hard. It's the nature of the beast. Some people are good at subtlety. I got all the subtlety of a heavy metal band. What's your next move?"

"Don't know yet. I got dispatchers checking all over the area for a production of Julius Ceasar?"

"Julius Cesar?" Campbell said.

"Sorry. You weren't briefed. He gave us another clue. *The Ides of March*. The 15th of March. That's today. It's also when Julius Cesar was assassinated."

"This guy's amazing."

"No. Mother Theresa was amazing. Martin Luther King was amazing. This guy is an arrogant son of a bitch," Valente said.

"He's smart," Campbell added. "Real smart. Knows his theatre."

"That I'll give him," Valente said. "That's what makes this so hard. He's not talking to dogs, or staring at vacant walls waiting for a voice. This guy is clever, calculated, connected, and..."

"Connected? Like with the Mob?"

"No. Haven't you been reading my reports?"

"Yeah, but, well not all of them. Got a lot on my plate. This is a big town with big problems. Fill me in."

Sam gave him the condensed version of the black mamba killings, and the whole thing with Julius Caesar. He also gave Campbell his theory that the man was not working alone. "How else would he have access to gorilla hairs, a black mamba, a bat parasite, chloroform, and whatever the hell else he is cooking up? Sometimes I feel he is right over there in the next room, just looking at us, laughing inside, watching us stumble all over ourselves..." Valente just stopped, exasperated.

"Alright Sam. You got this one all the way. I'm not pulling you off this case. Whatever you need you let me know. O.K?"

"You were thinking of pulling me off the case?"

"My mistake."

"Why the kid glove treatment? You wake up in the middle of the night full of warm fuzzies for me?" Valente said.

"Not a chance. But like I said, I know when I lean too hard. You do your job, Sam. That's all. And keep the lines of communication open with me, and the department. This case is getting bigger than I ever wanted it to. Media is off the charts with this one."

"We're giving it our best."

"I know," Campbell said.

"One other thing," Valente said. "You and McCarty played football. You understand the whole culture of winning. It's in your blood. It's in my blood too. I don't like to lose, Chief. We'll get this guy, if for no other reason -- I can't have a loss on my resume."

Campbell, considered that for a moment, gave him a slight nod of understanding and left his office. Valente lingered for a moment in Campbell's office then returned to the squad room. He noticed Park and McCarty waiting to hear something from him.

Valente looked at them. "You guys put some Zanax in his coffee?"

"Nope," McCarty said.

"Everything O.K?" asked Park

"Just peachy. Our perp has us jumping back and forth between Poe and Shakespeare. I mean color me cynical, but has this ever happened to any of us before? There's a damned connection between those two writers. I just haven't figured it out yet."

Valente rummaged through papers on his desk looking for something. "Damnit. Nicole, what's Styles home phone number?"

"Styles?" and then after a quick memory search,

"Oh him?" She looked through her phone directory.

Meanwhile, Valente found a piece of paper with Styles number scrawled on it. "Here it is. While our dispatchers are busy doing their tracking why not try him," he dialed the number. "I'm sure he's up on the Los Angeles theatre scene."

Styles' voice mail picked up. Frustrated, Valente slammed down the receiver. In angry silence, he tried again. The voice mail kicked in and this time Valente left a message. "Styles. This is detective Valente and its urgent police business. Please call me at the station as soon as you get this."

Valente hung-up. "I hate voice mail. Where's this guy live?"

"Woodland Hills. We don't have time to go out there," Park said.

"I need to talk to him."

"What's on your mind?" McCarty asked.

"My guess is he'll probably know if a production of Julius Caesar is opening somewhere in this area."

"*If* he is right. Sam, we don't know. He could be playing us, as many of these killers often do. For all I know he could be changing his M.O."

"For all you know?" Valente's tone was a blend of sarcasm and cynicism. "You need to do better that that?" She was blindsided by his sudden change in tone but not surprised. Nerves were frayed.

They were interrupted by the phone ringing. Park answered. "Park here... Yes... Just a minute...It's Styles."

Valente picked up his phone. "Styles. Thanks for calling back."

"I am not a happy camper."

"Do you know anyone who is directing or opening in Julius Caesar? Tonight. In particular, anyone connected to your theatre group?"

Valente could hear Styles clear his throat and exhale loudly, obviously annoyed with the disturbance. "I don't know why I called you back. I did this completely against my better judgment. I have dinner guests."

"Styles. We are under the gun. Just answer my question, and you can go back to dinner. Anyone doing Julius Caesar?"

"No. Not in this area."

"You're sure?"

"For crying out loud. No I am not 100 percent sure. The Los Angeles Metropolitan area practically extends to San Diego, and though the cynics in New York would have you believe otherwise, there are numerous theatrical productions going on out here all year long. Everything from main stage to community theatre. It's quite staggering actually. So it's possible that somewhere out here, some theatrical group could be doing Julius Caesar."

A cop from an adjacent office rushed up to Valente's desk.

"Detective. We found one. The Oxford Theatre Company in Newport. Julius Caesar opens tonight, 8 p.m. in Newport."

Chapter 63

WITH THE MONEY Tyler Dalton had earned on the soap, he had decided to spend some of it redecorating his living room. He had begun with a fresh coat of paint, then added a chandelier, walnut book shelves, several paintings by a new Czech painter, a new Italian leather couch with two matching arm chairs, an art deco coffee table, and a wet bar.

Admiring his living room, and with his loving German shepherd panting at his side, he poured himself a glass of scotch. "No Sundown. You can't have any of this."

The phone rang in the kitchen.

⇥ ⇤

Speed was of the essence. Valente careened onto the San Diego Freeway heading south towards Newport Beach. It was a little past seven, and he needed to reach the theatre before the eight p.m. curtain.

Before leaving the station, he had had an unpleasant conference call with Newport Beach's chief of police, and with the Oxford Theatre Company's artistic director.

"We have reason to believe the killer will strike there," Valente had said.

"Right. But how do we know who he's going to kill?" the police chief replied.

The nervous artistic director broke into the conversation. "Detective. There are thirty people in the cast."

The Newport chief added, "Are you suggesting I get an armed guard around each cast and crew member?"

"How do we do this without alarming the public?" said the director.

Soon, the conservation became a blur of muddled voices and ambient noise.

In the car Valente went over his options while recalling the conversation. "Are you sure about this," said Park. "Why the theatre?"

"Damnit! I don't know! Shanker has the advantage. I'm playing hunches, a long shot. You got any better ideas?"

Park remained silent.

"We may not catch him this way. But if he's there and senses a police presence maybe he'll go back into the hole he crawled out of, and we will have spared a life."

They continued towards Newport Beach at dangerously high speeds. Valente's fingers nervously tapped the steering wheel while Park wondered if this night would end with them wrapped around a telephone pole. "Easy Sam."

Valente paid her no attention. His eyes steadied on the road ahead while his mind entertained hope that they might have a break in the case.

The San Diego Freeway never looked so bright to him. The endless ribbon of red tail-lights looked like a lava flow. He loved Los Angeles, but hated its freeways.

The radio in his car crackled with the dispatcher's voice. "Newport police have uniformed units on the way. Undercovers posing as ushers and box office personnel are already deployed."

Chapter 64

TYLER HADN'T HEARD from Carmen Vega in two months and was glad to get the call. They had met several years ago while on a West Coast tour of a revival of the musical *Grease*. He had understudied the lead character, Danny Zucko, and she had played Rizzo.

Carmen was a sensual redhead with a voice Tyler felt could melt granite. They had remained close friends, sharing what they called their theatrical war stories.

"I'm sorry for not calling sooner Tyler. I've been out of town on tour and, well, you know the rigors of being on tour."

"How was the run?"

"Great. I love doing *Damn Yankees*. I make a great Lola. Trouble is Broadway doesn't think so. I don't have enough name recognition. They're going to cast someone else, someone with, NAME RECOGNITION, when the show returns there."

"Sorry Carmen."

"Life in the theatre. By the way, I heard about Arthur St. George. I'm really sorry. It's horrible, just horrible."

"Pretty gruesome if you ask me. Did you know they found gorilla hairs on his body?"

"Yeah I read that. That's weird?"

He opened his freezer and plunked a couple of ice cubes into his drink. His dog, wanting to join him for a drink, or biscuit, jumped up and down excitedly. "Weird. You wouldn't believe the circus this case has become. I mean, the press, the media, psychiatrists on talk shows here - they are theorizing everything – a failed actor out for revenge; a jealous lover scorned by St. George, and also out for revenge; a moralizing religious zealot out to destroy the decadence of Hollywood, and on and on…"

"Do the police have any leads?" Carmen asked.

"I don't know." His dog had placed his front paws on his chest, trying to lick his chin. "Hold on. Gotta take care of Sundown."

He set the receiver on the kitchen counter. "I bet you want a treat?" The dog is just too overjoyed for dog words. Tyler took a biscuit out of a box on top of the fridge and held it up. "Sit."

Sundown sat, panting. Tyler handed him the biscuit and returned to the phone. "Hey Carmen. Sorry. I had to reward my dog for the tough life he lives."

Sundown devoured the biscuit and then drank from his water bowl.

⊷⊨◉ ◉⊨⊶

"ETA six minutes," Valente said.

The squad cars and police van had turned onto a dark side street not far from the theatre. In front of them, a search and surveillance unit from Santa Monica crossed the intersection.

The Newport Beach units had already arrived and hid on a side street near the theatre waiting for Valente's arrival.

Park sat quietly next to Valente. She had hoped his hunch was a good one. She wanted him to have this collar. They all wanted victory.

She unfolded a police printout of Shanker's mug shot. Looking at his eerie photo with the vacant dark eyes sent her to a place she'd rather not go – the victims of all the killers.

What had bothered Park the most was that the names of the victims had all faded away, but the killer's name lived on and on. Everyone remembers the names Jeffrey Dahlmer, the Uni Bomber, the Zodiac Killer. Even Jack the Ripper. No one forgets Son of Sam. Does anyone, outside the victims' circle of family and friends, remember the names of the victims?

With lights turned off, the police vehicles cruised slowly to a stop. The marquee lights of the theatre glowed through the cypress and pine trees ahead of them.

⊷⊨◉ ◉⊨⊶

Tyler had poured a second drink and was feeling relaxed, though melancholy, talking about St. George's death. "I'm going to miss him. He was a good director."

"What a terrible thing to have happened," Carmen said.

"Guys like him don't come around too often. He was a true impresario. Always willing to take a chance. The thing I liked most about him was his total disregard for the conventional. He hated mediocrity. He really enjoyed pushing the envelope."

"I never met him, but I enjoyed reading about him," Carmen said.

"He once told me something that I've never forgotten. It sounded sappy at the time. But now...I don't know. He said 'Life's not worth living if you don't take a chance on being happy.'"

They remained silent for a moment. Tyler knew that happiness for St. George was living life on his own terms and not worrying about what the rest of the world thought. When critics had told him he was nuts for turning a Poe classic into a musical, he loudly reminded them of Victor Hugo's *Les Miserable* and that a classic can be turned into a successful musical, and then told them to all go to hell. Then he wrote one of his famous letters denouncing their profession, "...while you sit in front of your computer screens, angry that you never made it as an actor or director, and thinking up your clever one-liners of punishment, there are those of us who actually have done something with our theatrical careers. And that just annoys the hell out of you."

Tyler had once teased him that inside that stuffy British persona was a true grit cowboy itching to ride a herd somewhere.

Then Tyler broke their silence by asking Carmen where she was calling from and she told him from her apartment in West Hollywood. He hadn't been there in several months but remembered it as exuding warmth and love, a reflection of Carmen's nature.

Sundown's ears perked up. Something got his attention and it wasn't Tyler's voice. Something else got him to get up from his comfortable position on the kitchen floor and saunter into the living room.

"Hey. Let's not get all morose," Tyler said. "Let's toast Arthur, who is undoubtedly in a better place – one where he doesn't have to worry about the anxiety of opening nights."

He heard Carmen's sweat laugh. "Or bad reviews...to Arthur," she said.

A shadow glided stealthily alongside the house, black against white, moving with stark malevolence.

Sundown emitted a low, guttural snarl. He watched the shadow appear and disappear from his sight in front of the Venetian blinds covering the glass doors that led to Tyler's rear patio.

"Thanks for the call," Tyler said. "See you soon."

Tyler leaned against the kitchen counter feeling comforted by his talk with Carmen. He had often thought about pursuing her but for now, women were off the table. Two back-to-back relationships gone south over the past four years, and he felt that for now anyway focus on work. Women can wait. He polished off the last drops of his drink and for a moment was oblivious to his dog's agitation. But then, Sundown's persistent snarling caught his attention.

Tyler glanced over at Sundown and saw that his snout was right up against the porch door sniffing it excitedly. Something was not right.

Chapter 65

THE CAST MEMBERS of the Oxford Theatre Company took their bows during a round of applause from the audience. What no one in the audience suspected was the considerable undercover police presence in the theatre, nor the units posted outside that had arrived earlier.

Some police dressed in civilian clothing had blended in with the audience, while others meandered backstage dressed as stagehands or electricians. One even posed as a stage manager's assistant. Those in the theatre had taken their seats, curiously looking over their programs, pretending to be interested. Others made idle chatter with fellow patrons.

Outside, three snipers, 20 feet apart, lay prone on the rooftop of a building across from the theatre. SWAT team members crouched in bushes across the street, and a close quarter battle entry team hugged the side of the building nearest the entrance.

Valente had gotten out of his car after they arrived, and climbed into the back of an unmarked surveillance van parked near the theatre. He made a final visual check of the perimeter. He felt a measure of comfort by the heavy police presence.

When the lights came up inside the theatre, the cast, who had already been alerted to the situation, were taken to a police van outside and bussed away.

Valente watched carefully as the crowd left the building and walked to their cars. McCarty was among the patrons pretending to have been interested in the performance. He hadn't been inside a theatre in years. His preferred venues for entertainment rarely extended beyond a basketball arena or an ice hockey rink. Casually he walked across the street and joined Valente in the van. He grabbed a cup of coffee that rested in a console under the dashboard.

Valente's eyes scanned the area, watching the doors, turning occasionally to the snipers on the roof, and the SWAT team in the bushes and alongside the building. He put on a headset and punched in some numbers on a phone attached to a console.

"SWAT leader report."

"We're set," said the SWAT leader.

"BLUE ground team?"

The battle entry group leader replied. "Ready."

Valente still felt uneasy. He had never been up against an adversary like Shanker. A phantom killer with an ability to move through shadows unlike anyone he had ever tracked. He had to admire the man's creativity.

Two cops stood in the lobby posing as ushers. Their .38s were holstered under their jackets. They were young bloods, eager and ready to draw at the first sign of trouble. Park was among them.

She looked inside the theatre. The undercover ushers and janitors were cleaning the theatre as though they were old hands at this work.

Three policemen were doing their best imitation of stagehands moving set pieces off to the backstage area. One of them, officer Rodriguez, a tall angular Hispanic, thought he had seen someone duck behind a large screen. He quickly followed him, and after ducking under a riser his suspicions were confirmed. A man was moving in the area as though lost. "You there. Stop."

The lost man was elderly, with thinning gray hair, and when he turned to the undercover he looked clearly startled "Are you with the police?"

"Yeah. You shouldn't be back here."

"I'm sorry. I'm one of the stagehands and was told to meet back here."

Rodriguez moved closer to him, the smell of alcohol was clearly present on the man's breath. He knowingly looked down at the stagehand. "This way."

"O.K. Sorry chief."

Rodriguez called out to another undercover. "Jamie over here. You wanna escort this guy outside? He's lost."

Chapter 66

PARK'S CELL PHONE chirped. It was Valente. "Anything?"

"Everything's quiet here."

"Too quiet as they say in the movies?" Valente added. "I was hoping he'd be more theatrical."

"Yeah. So was I."

"And how are the new stage professionals holding up?"

"Great. If they ever quit the force, they got jobs in the theatre."

"Later," Valente removed his headset, and sat in silence for a moment staring ahead.

McCarty also had fallen silent, both lost in their thoughts.

Too quiet. Valente's words echoed back at Park. Again and again.

Inside the theatre, the undercover cops continued their roles as stagehands and technicians shutting down for the night. A policewoman had been stationed in the lighting booth, keeping an eye on the theatre. Lights were up full. Several undercover cops lingered backstage. No sign of anyone else and this was making Park uneasy.

She checked the narrow passageway that ran parallel with the stage. Above her, the rafters, fly spaces and light booms loomed precariously. A policeman, posing as an electrician, crouched on a catwalk pretending to check the stability of a couple of strobes. He gave Park a thumbs up signaling all-clear. Then she looked into the green room again, not sure what to expect or who to find. The room was empty.

Thirty minutes had passed since the cast had been hurried out of the theatre and into police vans, and no sign of trouble anywhere. She wondered if they had scared Shanker away. Or if he had even been there.

Park returned to the lobby where she was met by two policemen who told her all was secure in the basement. She was about to report to Valente when they heard a phone ringing.

Soon it became apparent to her the ringing came from inside the box office. The ticket windows were shut and the door was locked. The phone kept ringing. Park knew in her heart that this was not a call she wanted to take. "Anyone have a key to that door?"

Valente and McCarty waited for a call from Park or one of the undercover cops for an update. They did not want to take any chances on revealing themselves. Restless, Valente was about to check in again with their SWAT leader when Park emerged from the theater. By the look on her face, Valente knew something had gone wrong.

Chapter 67

TYLER DALTON'S DESERTED street quietly came alive with the stealth approach of Valente's police unit. Four squad cars - two marked, and two unmarked, followed by a crime lab van slowly edged near the house and parked.

Cautiously Valente, Park, and McCarty moved toward the front door with four other policemen in tow. Others moved out alongside the house, staying in shadows.

When they reached the door, Valente noticed that it was slightly ajar. With his revolver in one hand, he slowly pushed the door open with the other. With their firearms drawn, the police followed Valente into the house.

The house was dark except for narrow shafts of streetlight spilling through a couple of the windows. The police had moved into a hallway and fanned out. Two officers went to check the rooms upstairs.

Valente and Park moved into the living room off to their left, while McCarty and a policeman moved further down a hallway.

The living room was deserted. Next. The kitchen. Nothing out of the ordinary. Everything neat and tidy. Dishes loaded neatly in the dishwasher; a used whiskey glass in the sink; empty dog food and water bowls on the floor next to a pantry. Counter tops wiped clean. The place was spotless.

Valente was about to give Park an all-clear sign when he noticed an empty, wooden knife rack. This was strange, he thought. The neatness of the kitchen gave the appearance of someone who kept everything in its proper place. He looked again inside the dishwasher. No knives. He opened a kitchen drawer and saw only butter knives and a serrated bread knife, but not the knives that fit a knife rack.

The sound of McCarty's voice calling them told him all he needed to know.

Valente and Park quickly converged into the dining room. Park was nearly knocked over by one of the younger cops who had entered the living room with McCarty, and bolted for the front door. They all heard him vomit just as he reached the outside steps.

Within moments, the cops who were checking the upstairs had also reached them. All were frozen by the hulking image of McCarty standing between them and a wall.

McCarty stared at the wall. His broad back and shoulders momentarily blocked their view.

In the shadows, Valente inched closer to him. "Ed?" Valente said quietly. "What is it?"

McCarty remained as still as the night outside. Not a muscle moved. Slowly, Valente and Park moved to his side, and the image that had held McCarty frozen sent shock waves through the two detectives.

Tyler Dalton sat in a chair, with his arms strapped behind his back. Eight knives were stuck in his torso in a circular pattern. He looked like a human pin cushion.

Valente fixed his angry eyes on that torso. Then in a slow, harsh whisper, "The kitchen knives."

Blood had streamed down Tyler's stomach, down his pant legs and formed little pools around his feet. His throat had been cut.

Valente turned towards the wall that had held McCarty in a strange freeze. Scrawled in blood was the phrase, *The Evil That Men Do.*

Park cupped her hand to her mouth when she noticed Tyler's dead German shepherd at the foot of the Venetian doors. It's head had nearly been severed from its neck.

McCarty finally turned away from the corpse. "Fucking maniac." He kicked a champagne stand that nearly hit Park. "Son of a bitch."

Valente told one of the police to get the evidence techs inside right away. "This place is loaded with evidence. He wants it that way, so don't touch anything." Then he steadied his eyes at McCarty. "Ed? Don't kick anything else."

"Don't worry. I won't screw up your crime scene."

"This is small consolation, Sam," Park said. "But I believe we're close. He wants us to be close."

"You're right Nicole. Small consolation." Valente was doing all he could to suppress his rage. In moments like this he couldn't help think of all that was wrong with America's judicial system. He would forget his liberal leanings and despise bleeding heart liberals who opposed the death penalty. "You know what my worst fear is? He stops killing, disappears, and we never catch him."

The phone rang. All froze for a moment. Then Valente cocked his head to one side. "Where's that phone?"

Several pairs of eyes darted across the dark living room. A brief search led to a phone on a small end table opposite Tyler's body. Valente answered. The familiar voice taunted him.

"Pretty clever of me huh? You thought I meant the *actual* Julius Caesar by Willie Shakespeare. No, no, no, no, no. That would be too obvious and so out of character. Your boy on the chair was directing an *adaptation* of Julius Caesar titled the *Evil That Men Do* at a modest theater in West Hollywood. I was to play Brutus, but instead he cast someone else." Shanker's infantile chuckle rang in Valente's ear. "I must say. I do impress myself." He took a dramatic pause. "Ah, but enough about me. Don't take it personally *mon capitain.* Like I said, I have no quarrel with the police."

Park and McCarty had moved to the windows to check the streets. Then McCarty hurried outside and told the patrol unit to scour the immediate neighborhood - check parked cars hoping to find him in one. "After you do that, start knocking on doors." And then he saw what he dreaded and loathed. "Who the hell called them?"

Media trucks from several local and cable networks were heading his way. In a few moments the place would be a circus.

Inside, Valente fought back every urge to explode. "You don't need to keep doing this?" he said, careful not to show any anger in his tone.

At first there was no response. Only Shanker's deliberate breathing. Then… "Listen to me very carefully." Shanker paused for a moment to further aggravate Valente.

Valente cupped the phone tighter to his ear. "One more week," Shanker whispered and the line went dead.

Valente felt a wave of anxiety as he turned to the blood-stained wall. The words, *The Evil That Men Do*, seemed to mock him.

Chapter 69

SHANKER RARELY WATCHED television. But tonight he had to see the coverage of his killing of Tyler Dalton so he had brought a television set down to the lair of the worm. Far up above, professionals with whom he had never had a connection, nor ever will, scurried about wooden floors to make final preparations for a play about a black bird.

In the lair of the worm, though, he faced a dilemma. How to top himself. He felt nothing could surpass his killing of Shelly Brooks. He used a black mamba for crying out loud. It was outrageous. And now this bit of genius.

Shanker sat on a wooden bench eating his favorite junk food – cream wafers. Furiously he channel surfed past an endless assault of commercials until he found a channel broadcasting news of the murder.

A blonde reporter, a clone of so many square-jawed media babes, was in the middle of her report. "…another gruesome killing in Los Angeles. Earlier this evening actor/director Tyler Dalton was found murdered in his home. Police investigators are trying to determine if there is any connection between this and the murder of producer Arthur St. George."

He watched the news report with a strange reverence.

"…L.A.P.D. has no leads, and as of yet, no motive. Mr. Dalton was a rising star who had decided to try directing for the first time."

Shanker turned sullen. "To hell with Tyler. You need to talk about me." The news then switched to an interview with Valente leaving the crime scene earlier.

The same reporter held a microphone towards Valente as he pushed past a tangle of microphones and cameras. "Detective. You are the lead investigator in the case, is that correct?" He did not respond. "Can you tell us anything?"

Valente brushed past her. True to form, the reporter was un-phased by Valente's rude behavior. "Is there any truth to the rumour that the killer is an actor killing like the characters he himself would have played?" she said.

Valente stopped in his tracks. He looked at the blond reporter as though she had just leveled him with the news of the century.

Shanker watched in rapt attention. "That's more like it you blond whore. Say Bingo, *mon capitain*. Bingo!"

Valente stared blankly at the cameras. He was thrown off balance by her remark. At first he wasn't certain why he felt so stunned, because he suspected this all along. It was in one of his reports. Even profiler Ellen Weist agreed that could be a possible motive. They both had agreed that this was a unique aspect of the killings.

Then he felt a sudden surge of disdain for the reporter, and for the media at large who often could care less if they threw a town into a panic, and all in the name of getting a story or selling newspapers.

"Officer. Talk to me. Talk to us," the reporter continued. "There's a killer out there. Don't you think the public deserves to know something?"

This time Valente took the microphone out of her hand and looked directly into the camera. "You know what you are Shanker. You're nothing but a little girl looking for her mommy."

A sharp pain hit Shanker right in his gut. Then a hammering through his head. He open wide his mouth like he was going to scream -- so wide that a baseball could have fit inside. But no sound came out. He just held his face in that wide, distorted position for a moment as though he wanted to roar like a lion. When his jaw ached so much where he could no longer keep his mouth open, he relaxed his muscles. The pain in his gut subsided, and the sudden pressure in his head went away. He lowered his eyes at the television set.

Chapter 70

ELLEN WEIST'S DOORBELL rang at 1:15 a.m. Valente knew she wouldn't be happy by the late-night intrusion, but he had nowhere else to go. He felt like his confidence was fast disappearing and that made his stomach turn. So he had hoped that a talk with Weist could shed more light on the murky investigation.

After the ordeal with the reporters, Valente had gone for a drive by himself. He wanted to be far from the crime scene. He had thought about a visit to his favorite haunt – Don Pasquale's, but chose to visit Weist instead. On the way, he stopped under the Hollywood sign. He had always wanted to do that, but until this evening never got around to it. The sign was a great symbol of what he wondered. *C'mon Valente you're smart.* What does this sign represent? *Dreams? Broken dreams? Despair? Futility? The evaporation of hope; the ruination of fragile lives?*

"Again I apologize for the late hour. But I needed to talk to you," he said while she opened the door to her two-level home in Encino. His phone call had awakened her from a sound sleep, but she was gracious nonetheless.

He followed her down a hallway. Modest decor, he thought, as he snuck a peak at her living room. The furniture looked like it was purchased at one of those large chain stores advertising no interest payments for two years.

She did not have the best taste in art either. Several cheesy landscapes and a couple of animal prints lined a wall in the hallway that led to her study.

But this room was more impressive and in stark contrast to the others. An expensive leather couch impressed him as did her mahogany desk, and two stuffed armchairs framing a marble coffee table. A modest, saltwater aquarium stood against the left wall under a framed Monet print. A spotted moray, and two anemone fish, that steered clear of the eel, inhabited the aquarium.

"Saw you on the news. I like your style."

"Style?"

"I love it when someone gets in the media's face. Can I get you anything?" she said

"Scotch if you have any."

"I have a modest Sauvignon Blanc, and some dry sherry."

"I'll have the modest sauvignon."

"Please, make yourself comfortable."

While she went to her kitchen, he sat on the couch and ran his hand through his hair. Soon he was drawn to the spotted moray, and as often is the case with people who come face to face with an aquarium, he quickly became entranced by the soothing movement before him. The moray swam in a slow, undulating motion, in and out of the tank's coral crevices.

She soon returned with a tray of glasses and a bottle of the sauvignon. "You said on the phone that you wanted more of a profile. What do you have for me?"

He told her of the gruesome way in which Tyler was murdered, and the phrase scrawled in blood on his wall.

Weist remained quiet, thinking about the phrase, *the evil that men do.*

She poured his wine. "Suffering is relative," she began, "just like pain, jealousy, and other human feelings. Perhaps no one suffers more than an artist. Even the successful ones suffer because they often feel that they never reach fulfillment."

Though he searched for diplomacy with her, he could not shake his irritability. "I don't have much sympathy for great talents who throw away their lives," he said. "I am supposed to feel sorry for people who were given a gift and throw it all in a gutter? Most people never realize their dreams. Most people struggle and suffer. But some of these stars? I guess having too much money or too much fame was too much to handle. Must be tough never having to worry about where your next buck is coming from."

"Is that a chip on your shoulder I see there?"

"Must be the environment. I'm in a shrink's home, so I guess I feel like I should let out some steam. Look. Maybe coming over was a bad idea?" He downed the wine in one gulp.

"This must be hard for you, coming here," she said softly.

Valente felt that now was probably the time to get something off his chest with her. The hour was late and he was in the kind of mood where he didn't care about much of anything. And he was in the quiet of her home.

"A few years ago I worked a very difficult case. A psycho killing children up in Seattle. I was on loan to their department."

"I read about the case," she said.

"He was smart. Like our perp now. Anyway, we brought in a profiler after we dug up a third body from a shallow grave in a bedroom community north of Seattle. This profiler had convinced us the killer was leaving the type of clues that would soon lead to his arrest. Profiler deduced the killer didn't really hate kids – he hated himself, and in the kids he murdered, he was actually killing himself. This went on for about a year. Eight deaths later, and no closer to catching our man, I suggested we not only fire the profiler but have his license revoked. But the department felt he was doing the best under the circumstances. Know what happened?"

West listened attentively. She had only a vague recollection of the details.

"One morning, the killer came to the station and put a gun to his head, right in front us. Blew out the back of his head. So, you could say, the profiler was right. The psycho wanted to kill himself. Just needed to go through a few kids first. But the profiler missed something. The killer had a note strapped to his chest. 'You will never find the others.' We were dealing with evil incarnate, and the profiler had us believing the opposite. And last I checked, no more bodies have been found."

"Sam we're not all perfect. Like in all professions, there are few who shouldn't be doing what they're doing. After all, there are a few bad cops, aren't there?"

Valente looked at her with understanding eyes. But still, he had his reservations. If profiling is such an inexact science, why have it all? Why put someone on the payroll who is doing very expensive guess work.

"I can practically hear your thoughts," she said good-naturedly. "May I continue?"

"Yes you may. After you fill my glass with more of that modest sauvignon."

Chapter 71

SHE LIFTED THE bottle and poured. Valente's eyes were fixed on his wine glass while she poured. "All the way to the top."

She acknowledged with a slight nod. "As you know, Hemingway was enormously successful."

"Speaking of Hemingway…" he said lightheartedly.

"Talk about a segue," she laughed. "Not only monetarily, but his writing was some of the best in the English language. He celebrated manhood and danger; wrote stories about knockabouts, Indian camps, fathers and sons, and innocent love: tales by a young man about the young yearning to explore the world out there--and live a life of wonderment and adventure. Yet demons danced in his head. Why?"

"I don't know. Maybe they got tired of dancing in Van Gough's head and moved over to his. I really need something useful here doctor. Not your professional opinion about why a famous writer blew out his brains."

"Bare with me Sam. There is a method to my madness," she said with good humor. "I used Hemingway as an example of someone who, on the surface had it all, but who decided to end his life. True, he was also in a lot of physical pain from having survived two plane crashes, but still, he was a giant in his field. So, if giants in their field can suffer, or feel unfulfilled, think of the anguish of the struggling artist, or actor in this case. The ones who never reached that level of success and recognition. They often feel like they never gain any respect until they are successful. A struggling actor feels rejected by society, feels like an outcast, no matter how real or perceived. Daily, he suffers the indignation of watching other actors, many with less talent, get work and succeed, while he goes off to a thankless job. Where is the glory in parking cars?"

Valente interrupted her. "Our man is a frustrated actor, whose mind snapped?"

"I'm not sure."

"That his mind snapped?"

"I'm not sure if he is an actor. He could be suffering from multiple personalities, though I doubt it because true mult pers is a rare diagnosis and they have a lower IQ than your guy. But, in the spirit of not leaving any stone unturned, if he is a mult pers, one of the personalities could be that of an actor."

Valente took another sip. "Ellen. I need something tangible that I can use to catch this guy."

"My dear Sam. I don't catch anyone. I give you consultations based on the best scientific and psychiatric evidence available, but it's still a crap shoot," she said with a smile. "And nothing beats good old fashioned police work. On that we agree. Profilers and psychiatrists have no magic wand."

Valente was amused by her relaxed, informal manner. He figured that at this late hour she threw off her academic suit and became more relaxed.

"Something else to consider," she said. "Many serial killers are not considered to be psychologically impaired. They are in touch with the real world, but have absolutely no feelings for it."

Valente was growing impatient. He had read her book and was not in the mood to hear her quote passages.

"Do you have anything I can use? A similar case-study. A pattern? Something."

Weist felt his impatience - the dedicated detective trying to bring a monster to justice - and genuinely felt bad for him. He had suddenly looked almost childlike in his despair.

"Maybe this can help," she said with a comforting tone. "The profile of the victim is very important in solving serial crimes as you well know. So you have something tangible to work with. All of his victims are related to theater or film. He's not drawing from a diverse pool which would give you bigger headaches. His victims are either actors or directors. Correct?"

"Yeah. Well except for one. We think he killed his part-time supervisor. But the manner in which he was killed was highly theatrical. Almost like something out of the theatre of the absurd."

"Really?"

"He killed him with a poisonous snake."

Valente recounted the details of Shelly Brook's murder, making sure not to leave out the part about the snake. When he finished, he studied Weist's expression. He wondered if the part about the snake might have thoroughly confused even someone as brilliant as her.

"We've got a handful, huh?" Valente said and finished off the wine.

Chapter 72

"BEFORE WE CONTINUE you mentioned earlier you had some sherry. How about we make that my nightcap?"

Weist fought back a yawn, went to the kitchen and returned with the sherry and a fresh glass. She poured.

"Well you made a point. We do have a handful. Rather you boys have one." She poured herself a spot of sherry.

"Going back to what I was saying. Let's assume another thing - that he is a real actor, and not an incarnation of one of his multiple personalities. Or if not an actor, let's suppose someone involved in some capacity with film or theatre - either now, or at some point in his past. Perhaps he was a failed director, make-up artist or costume designer. We can assume this because his knowledge is too extensive for the mere dilettante.

"So maybe he is or was an actor, and because of a long series of disappointments and failures, he lives out his fantasies through these elaborate killings - almost as though he is playing out his own horror film. That Julius Caesar thing was truly amazing."

Valente sipped his sherry. "You sound like you admire this creep."

"I admire the mind and how it works. Wouldn't it be wonderful if we could harness all the good that lies untapped in our minds?"

"Yeah, yeah. Don't go getting metaphysical. Go on...please."

"The *evil that men do*. There is rich subtext there. Do you know the rest of the phrase?"

"No."

"*The evil that men do lives after them.* He wants to make a statement that will live on in infamy. He wants to become a legend." She sat back in her armchair. "Are you investigating his theatre background? If there is one?"

"We're checking all leads." The moray again caught his attention. Fascinating fish he thought. If he ever buys a fish tank he would make sure to get one.

Valente found Weist attractive in a strange way. She was not beautiful, not even close - her overbite was a distinct turn-off, but her intelligence made her sexy. He tried one last time to pursue the angle he had secretly hoped for. "Let me ask you this again. Could this be just a simple case of revenge? That he is not a psychopath?"

"Doubtful."

"Why are you so certain? …" Valente was about to ask her another question when he noticed that Weist had turned away from him and was staring at her mantle. She appeared to be lost in thought. "Doctor?"

Her entire demeanor had changed. She looked as though a brutal reality had suddenly hit her. "Listen to me very carefully, Detective."

He didn't like the detective part; the sudden formality. But she was a therapist, and they too can be weird.

"It is very likely that your suspect is someone who suffered unspeakable damage as a child. Someone who wanted to succeed as an actor more than anything, but who failed miserably. Those failures along with the childhood traumas eventually destroyed him."

"Ellen. I think you've stated the obvious. We can assume Shanker suffered severe trauma."

She silenced him with her index finger, so as not to break her concentration. "In Gogol's *Diary of a Madman*, you have, as your central character, Poprischin, a totally insignificant, downtrodden clerk in St. Petersburg, engaged in a hopeless struggle with the rigid, and highly impersonal State bureaucratic machine of Nicholas' I oppressive regime. Ludicrously for him, he falls in love with the empty-headed daughter of His Excellency, but being an absolute nobody, he cannot possibly compete with the fops and gentleman of the court.

"With his ensuing madness, he sees every door closed to him and gradually becomes convinced that he is the rightful heir to the Spanish throne.

"In the end he cuts up his civil service uniform and makes a royal mantle out of it. He is then carted off to a lunatic asylum, which he takes to be the Spanish Royal Palace."

Ellen Weist felt a small measure of comfort with her analogy. And she also felt very tired.

"Your man could be engaged in a similar struggle. He is the Poprishcin of Hollywood, engaged in a hopeless struggle against the Hollywood machine. He sees every door closed to him, and then ludicrously fancies himself the heir to the throne – in his case--the horror film throne."

She rested her head against the back of the armchair. Her mind had finally reached the point where it could not think any more on matters of psychology. Valente had to admit that though she filled his mind with theory, she had now given him an impressive profile. He quietly finished his drink while they both sat in silence gazing at the aquarium.

Chapter 73

McCARTY HAD BEEN sitting at a bar in West L.A. for nearly an hour waiting for Mr. Octoberfest to show up. He had listened to the ramblings of a vulgar, middle-aged woman bemoaning the fact that she couldn't keep a man. She leaned on the bar spewing her frustrations over her martini.

"I don't get it," she had said in a loud, gravelly voice. "What is wrong with men today? I'm successful, I don't demand a lot of attention; I am independent, intelligent, and charming. What do they want?"

"Maybe they want someone feminine," McCarty said.

"Huh?"

McCarty had grown tired of her complaints. "A woman who does not remind them of a guy."

"Oh? That so?"

"Let me ask you something, lady. Do you want to go out with a guy who acts like a girl?"

"Is that what I do? Remind you of a man?"

"Honey you got stones the size of Texas, and a voice that reminds me of some hard drinking sailors I know. What are you on, your third martini? You think that's attractive?"

"Fuck you, asshole."

"My point exactly," McCarty said.

She grabbed her things, dropped a twenty on the bar, and stormed out with a distinct stagger.

McCarty felt great that he told off the woman. Life afforded him few of those opportunities. Calmer now, he turned to the bartender. "We are a ridiculous species, don't you think?"

Laughing, the bartender said, "Who? Angry women? Drunks? Bartenders, or humanity in general."

"Life is really pretty simple. All good things end. All bad things end. Then you die. In all my Catholic bullshit upbringing, nobody ever told me why exactly are we on this planet? What the hell are we doing here?"

Not knowing that McCarty was a cop, the bartender shied away from engaging him in a conversation, figuring him to be yet another loser with a trunk full of bad memories.

McCarthy leaned on his elbows. "Take an iguana for example. An iguana sticks its tongue out, catches a fly and eats it, and doesn't care what anybody thinks. It doesn't even know it's an iguana."

McCarty finished his drink, and asked the bartender for a glass of water. "People got to put on airs, be who they're not, do things that you only see in movies. Stick eight knives in a guy's chest when one knife would have done the job. You wouldn't believe the shit I've seen people do."

Now the bartender got suspicious. "You're a cop aren't you?"

"What gave me away?"

"Your descriptive style."

"Oh yeah?"

"Naah. You guys walk in here with enough stress to keep shrinks in business until Armageddon. They couldn't pay me enough to do what you do."

No argument from McCarty. He actually gave the bartender a thumbs up.

It was close to last call when McCarty recognized the blond German coming through the doors, brushing past a couple of bloodshot customers who were leaving. A glint appeared in his eye when he saw McCarty. "Ahh. Mr. Ed. Always a pleasure,"

"I got your call. I'm here, and you're late. What do you got?"

"Please. A bit of civility?" He flagged the bartender standing within earshot. "A Cognac, *sil vous plait*. Remy. A little class, detective."

McCarty grabbed his crotch. "I got your class. Right here."

"Have you ever been to France? Germany? Spain? Italy?"

"Gee. You mean like Europe? No. Once to Cabo San Lucas, and I hated it. I don't like the beach too much, but my ex-wife, she liked to roast in the sun. I guess she wanted to speed up the aging process."

The cognac arrived and not a moment to soon. Reiner lifted the snifter, held its stem between his thumb and index finger, swirled the cognac a few times and took a sip. When his little ritual was over he glanced at McCarty to see how many shades of red he may have turned. "My sources gave me something you might be able to use."

Reiner sat down next to McCarty, swirled the cognac again.

"Reiner, I swear…"

"Easy." Reiner took one more sip and continued. "There is a person who deals in the illegal trade of exotic animals. A few weeks ago she sold three piranhas to an exotic fish collector in Bel Air."

"How about a snake?

"Don't know."

"Does this person have a name?"

"Yes. One moment." Reiner pulled out a notebook from his inside jacket pocket, and flipped several pages until he found her name. "Sheila Barrow."

The name rang a distant bell. "Got an address?"

"But of course constable Ed. 4215 Mallory Place - downtown -- not a great neighborhood." He tore the page out of his notebook and handed it to McCarty. "I don't know how old this address is."

"We'll check it out. You done good Reiner. Thanks."

"Does this mean you will leave me alone for awhile?"

"Pay my tab, and I'll think about it."

McCarty lifted his large frame off his stool and left the bar.

Chapter 74

MORE CANDLES ILLUMINATED the graveyard of dreams. Mitchell Shanker stood triumphant. He hissed at the wooden statue of the raven that taunted him from its perch on the windowsill. "Oh you look so mean and angry. Wait until you see what I have in store for your *compadres*. You little shit bird."

Shanker removed his velour jacket and threw it on the floor. "Little does Ron Styles know what I have prepared for him. There is genius at work here my little black bird."

Mitchell Shanker knew that the bird knew him well. The black bird had listened to him night after night recite passages from *The Raven*.

"Ron Styles, with all his credentials, and schooling and theatrical training does not impress me. You forget my nasty little shit bird, that genius has a way of cropping up in unexpected places and that great artists never get their inspiration from a classroom."

The taste of blood was maddening. It made his lips tingle. His eyes went wild with anticipation. "I will kill them boldly, carve them, and serve them as a dish fit for the guardians of Hades. What say you to that, wicked bird?"

The wooden statuette glowed under the candle light. It's long shadow spread across the floor - an inky sinuousness moving slowly towards him. "You loom so ominous," Shanker said. "Do you try to compete with me?"

He removed his clothing and stood naked in front of the creature. "I will make the net that will enmesh them all." He turned away from the bird and spread his arms out to his side. And he swayed back and forth, as though listening to music.

In his realm of madness he found tranquility. But shadows danced in his head, and so Shanker sat in his armchair and lifted a glass to the black bird on its perch. "You grim, ungainly, ghast and ominous bird of yore…tell me, shall I clasp the rare and radiant maiden whom angels named Lenore."

Chapter 75

THE CHEAP WHISKEY felt good. A half-pint, like the bums drink. Valente didn't care. He had wanted a belt since the evening began. He took another belt, then stepped under the police tape in front of Tyler Dalton's stoop.

Valente had no idea what he had hoped to accomplish returning to the scene of the crime. Tyler's house was the last place he wanted to be, he would have rather slept on Weist's couch, but something pulled him there. Maybe it was the remote notion that the killer might return, and Valente would catch him. One on one. Just he and the killer. But that only happens in movies.

Standing in Dalton's living room, his eyes locked on the writing on the wall, *The Evil That Men Do*. Those words were like a magnet, pulling him closer.

While he wondered what it must be like to have your insides gutted, he had the unnerving feeling that the killer's appetite would grow more and more voracious. He could go hunting for others not associated with the theatre. Why stop with actors, or producers, or directors? There was a huge food supply out there. And right now, Shanker was at the top of that food chain.

Valente went back outside and sat on the doorstep. This was the nightmare he had hoped would never become a reality; a serial killer who was unstoppable and very possibly, uncatchable.

Valente had rarely been stumped. He was an ace detective who had cracked several difficult cases. In ten years as a lead investigator, there were two serial killers, a serial rapist, two brutal killers-for-hire, and several garden-variety, drug-related murderers. But Shanker was fast rising to the top of that list. A real Oscar winner, he sourly mumbled to himself.

Chapter 76

PARK CHECKED HER watch. Four a.m. The persistent ringing doorbell had awakened her. She was not a happy camper.

She wiped her eyes, got out of bed and pulled her revolver out of her holster hanging over the bed's footboard.

The bell kept ringing as though Quasimodo was outside. She looked through the peephole, and then relaxed when she recognized the distorted image of her partner. "Just a minute."

She unlocked and opened her door, and Valente staggered in. He moved to the middle of the room where he stopped abruptly. Valente swayed back and forth, praying that the room would stop spinning around him.

"Are you drunk?" Park said in a not so friendly tone.

"Of course. Do you think I smell like this all the time?"

"You drove in this condition? Idiot."

"I'll give myself a ticket." Valente parked himself on her couch, nearly knocking over an expensive looking lamp on and end table. "Easy, Sam. That's expensive."

"Sorry."

"Let me get you some coffee."

Valente mumbled something to her as he fumbled with his shoulder holster.

"English please. I don't understand mumbles."

She put a pot of hot water on the stove in her California-style kitchen.

Valente leaned back on the couch and took a deep breath. The room had stopped spinning. When a person is in a state of inebriation where a part of the brain is still able to send coherent signals to the part that controls speech, the individual has to think quickly. He has to make sure the words are all lined up properly, all in a row, and then with one burst, launch those words into what one hopes will become coherent sentences.

"We couldn't get a normal psycho. No. We have to get a literate one." That took some doing, but undaunted he continued. "He's got me reading Shakespeare. I don't like Shakespeare. Too many damned words."

"We'll get him Sam."

"Macbeth drove me nuts!"

"Sooner or later, he's going to screw up."

"Talk about needing an editor. Did the guy ever stop and think, maybe, just maybe his soliloquies are too long?"

Park fixed him a steaming hot cup of black coffee, and handed it to him. "Shakespeare. Do you really think they talked like that back in his day?"

"Drink your coffee." She sat next to him, and watched him lift the cup to his lips. "Careful. It's hot." As he was just about to take a sip, he put the cup back on the table, spilling some.

"Sam. You are trying my patience," Park said. She rushed into the kitchen and returned with some paper towels.

"I just came from Weist's place, then the crime scene...or was it the crime scene first...?"

"Sam."

"I don't know...he beat us damnit."

"We're going to catch him. Now drink your coffee."

His glazed, brown eyes stared past her. Focusing was getting more difficult. "How long have we been partners?"

She finished wiping up the spilled coffee. "Off and on, three years...I think."

"I've been good, huh?"

"How do you mean?" He leaned close to her, breathing enough alcohol fumes on her to synge her face. "I've never come on to you. Right?"

She recoiled from his breath. "You've been a perfect gentleman."

He leaned closer. She did not recoil.

"I'm going to kiss you. You can kiss me back. I swear I won't tell anyone."

They kissed. She responded affectionately, but then pulled away. "I don't know about this."

"I do." He laid his lips on hers, and they threw each other into a passionate kiss. His hand found its way under her robe, and up to her breasts. And as he touched her nipples, she broke from their embrace. "Sam," She got up and walked to her kitchen. "I always found you very appealing. You are probably the sexiest man in our precinct. But just give me some air."

"Air? Yeah, yeah...O.K. Let's kiss by the window. There's more air over there."

He put his arms around her waist. "I guess I've always had a crush on you."

"Let's take a break." She gently broke the embrace and moved to her kitchen. "More air by the window? That's a first."

Valente collapsed on the couch. He looked at Park, both of her. He was seeing double now. Beads of sweat had started to form on his brow.

"I have some information that you might find interesting," Park said. "I was going to wait until the morning. You know, maybe get a little sleep?"

She handed him a folder from her desk. "Take a look at this."

When she saw that his head was weaving from side to side, and his eyes had that glassy look, she took the folder back. "Never mind. I'll read it to you."

She sat next to him. "The MacLean Theatre burned down about twenty years ago. Investigators determined it was arson but they never found the perp or perps.

"Were they doing Shakespeare?"

"Shut up. Apparently, a certain director, who was a neurotic mess, mounted terrible productions there. Eventually she was fired. Soon after that, the theatre burned to the ground."

"Why didn't you tell me this before?" he said with some effort.

"First. Go to hell. Second. I tried to find you but I guess you were too busy getting drunk. Third. Since I couldn't find you and it was getting late, I decided it could wait until the morning. Fourth...."

"Alright. Point taken. Can I kiss you?"

"No. I think it's time we pay Styles a visit again. What do you think?"

The brain had stopped sending electrical charges to its various components. Valente looked at the report in her hand, then slowly, his eyelids closed and his head fell into the folder.

"I couldn't agree more," she said, rubbing her hand through his hair.

Chapter 77

THERE WAS A low, painful emission from the human heap in Park's passenger seat after her car ran over a pothole. She had never seen Valente so drunk as he was the night before. Getting him off her couch, dressed and into the car the next morning was no small feat. But she had succeeded. He had barely uttered a word during the whole ordeal of getting him dressed, forcing a half a cup of coffee down his throat, and shoving him into the car.

Park jabbed him once in the shoulder. He groaned. "C'mon flash. I need you coherent."

Valente's breathing was slow and labored. "Wake-up." There was no response. "Speak to me, damnit."

An eye opened. The right one. The left one still remained shut.

"Get it together big boy," Park said, her voice splitting his brain in two. A wave of nausea suddenly rolled from his stomach to his throat. "Stop the car," he uttered in a harsh rasp. His tongue felt thick.

"What?"

"I'm sick."

Park swerved off the road onto the emergency lane and slowed to a stop. Valente fumbled with the door handle, shoved his shoulder against the door until it popped open. He fell out and on his back on the gravel. His brain pounded and the sky above seemed to race past him

Somehow he got on all fours and then out came the vomit. When he was through puking, he leaned back on his haunches, sucking in air.

"Nicole. Never put a drunk into a moving car."

She handed him a roll of paper towels. "Wipe your mouth."

A modicum of relief returned to Valente as he reclined in is seat. Occasionally he caught a glimpse of trees racing past him. A touch of nausea crept back, but not enough to make him stop the car. What really bothered him more than the nausea, were the sharp cramps that shot through his torso, his side and his lower back. Probably his liver screaming for help.

In that moment he hated everything about himself. He had succumbed to the very thing he despised the most -- the inexplicable desire for some people to drink themselves into a stupor; to drink until all that is left is the yearning to die.

It wouldn't have been so bad had his drinking been consumed while enjoying a decent meal, in true Italian fashion. But to drink, just for the sake of drinking went against everything he was taught. "I don't know how some people do it."

Park kept her eyes on the road ahead, but gave him her attention with a tilt of her head.

"Drink all day and night. How do they do it and still function?"

"They don't. They're called alcoholics, and their lives are a mess."

"How much further," he said quietly while leaning his head against the passenger window.

"About twenty-five minutes," she said noticing the exit up ahead for Camarillo which would take them to Carpenteria

"Wake me when we're there."

Chapter 78

Carmen Vega had wanted to help the police. She was devastated by the brutal murder of her friend, Tyler Dalton. There had never been much sexual heat between them and she enjoyed that rare plutonic friendship between a man and woman. He was a guy who had no interest in taking her to bed. A relief for the sultry Latino who often felt she spent far too much time blowing off male jackals when she could be using that time for more important things. So when she received a call to come to the station to offer any insight she could into Dalton's personal life she readily agreed.

McCarty brought her coffee and sat down at his small, disorganized desk. He brushed a stack of unopened mail to one side, and moved the phone to another.

"Very sorry about your friend."

Vega turned her head slightly, fighting back tears. "He was a good man. A good friend."

McCarty offered her a box of tissues. "Good friends are hard to come by. Should we begin, oh and thanks for coming down. Believe me on this case, anything can help."

Vega nodded politely.

"Consider this more of a character statement on Mr. Dalton. We want to try and open a window into his personal life and try and determine if Dalton knew the killer. It's a reach, but we need to look into every closet."

Still bruised by the shock of his murder, she was eager to help in any way she could. "You said on the phone that you were at home speaking to him a few hours before he was killed?"

"Yes. Unbelievable. We were reminiscing about Arthur St. George. I was on tour and read about his murder."

"Did you know St. George?"

"No. But Tyler knew him pretty well. It was just awful, and then this…" her voice trailed off.

McCarty felt sorry for her. Theater people were never really his type but he saw gentility in her that he liked. She didn't appear to be like so many of the numerous theatrical prima donnas he had heard about or interviewed.

She collected her thoughts and continued. "Are those killings connected?"

"We don't know yet." He flipped his small notebook to the next page. "How well did you know Tyler?"

"Friends. That's all. We've known each other for about five years, but we have gone long stretches without seeing each other, what with our different schedules."

"Did you know any of his friends, anyone who might seem suspicious?"

"No not really. Just people you meet at the occasional party. We basically ran in separate social circles. Like I said, we were friends, met on a show, and kept in touch, and often just by phone."

From a file on his desk McCarty removed a photo of Shanker and placed it in front of her. "Ever see this guy?"

She studied the photo closely, but he did not look familiar. She shook her head. "Is it him?"

McCarty continued, "Probably. Look, if there is anything you want to let us know please don't hold back. This is not the time to keep secrets. Anything to shed light on Dalton's murder, and on this sick fuck… excuse me."

"It's OK detective."

"Well anyway. Our lead investigator is up at the McLean Theater in Carpenteria continuing the investigation there. Are you familiar with that theater?"

"I've only heard of it but never performed or auditioned there."

"Do you know the director…" he looked at his notes, "Ron Styles?"

"Only heard of him. Never met him. I have been on tour a lot lately. About to go out again next month. I read in the trades that he is going to do "The Raven?"

"Yeah. Something like that."

McCarty kept writing notes. "Valente is not too keen on him. Doesn't trust him."

"Valente?"

"Our lead investigator."

"I also read an article where they found gorilla hairs on St George's body. Are the police seriously thinking…"

McCarty forced a chuckle. "No. No. We are way past that. It was a plant to throw us off, or…" and he took a moment. He did not want to reveal too much detail of the investigation. No need getting her all confused and more emotional. "Probably a plant to throw us off the trail, get the attention off him. Killers do that all the time – plant false leads."

McCarty took a moment to admire her beauty without being obvious. She seemed not the typical neurotic type that paraded through the squad room soon after St. George's death. Vega appeared to be a little more grounded.

His admiring her was not lost on her and she smiled shyly. "Yes? Is there anything else?"

'Oh. No. I was just wondering, though. What drives people into this business – show business?"

Vega's Hispanic roots came out in a burst of laughter, and nerves. Her voice suddenly fell to a husky laugh. *"Madre de Dio.* Who knows. What drives people like you into your business?"

McCarty managed a smile *"Touche."*

McCarty got up. "Excuse me." He went over to the coffee counter and freshened up his cup. He was mulling over what other questions to ask her, or perhaps just let her leave. He felt in his gut she couldn't offer that much. She was out of town when St. George was murdered and had just returned prior to Dalton's killing, and he had already ruled her out as a suspect. He was hoping that maybe through her statements he could determine if Shanker knew Dalton.

McCarty returned to her and set his cup on his desk. He extended a hand, "thanks for coming in. Here are three cards. We are the three principals on this investigation. You think of anything – anything, no matter how small a detail, you call one of us. OK?"

"Yes." She got up.

"Again. Thanks for coming." As she was leaving she stopped and turned back to him. "I suppose I have to ask. I see it on all the crime shows."

"What's that?"

"Am I a suspect?"

"No. Not at all."

Outside the police station Carmen Vega paused and leaned against a lamppost. She exhaled forcefully. Losing a friend like Tyler was going to be something that would take her a long time to get past, if ever. And then the floodgates opened and she sobbed, and sobbed.

Chapter 79

CARLY PACED BACK and forth in Styles' small office nervously smoking a cigarette. They had been arguing script changes for nearly an hour, and temperatures were rising. Styles slammed his copy of the script on his desk when she had refused to listen to his suggestions about some minor changes. "I am about to launch the boldest drama I've ever attempted, so when I suggest to cut a page or two -- Cut damnit."

"Fine. I'm tired of arguing. I think you're wrong, and paranoid, but O.K."

"And another thing. I just don't feel you've got them ready. Schedule a double rehearsal tomorrow."

She had had enough. "That's absurd."

"Absurd? Let me tell you something. Casting Kevin was absurd. I'm regretting you ever did that."

"You're impossible. Nothing satisfies you. The other day you liked him."

"That was the other day. He lacks consistency."

"Ron please —"

"I'm warning you Carly. If this show does not get the reviews I expect, it'll be your last for me."

"Ron. Stop it," she said slamming her fist on his desk. She was nearly nose to nose with him. If her eyes had been daggers he'd have two stab wounds in his face. "You have got to calm down, or you'll give us both a stroke," she said, restraining herself from a full verbal assault. It was difficult because she never cared much for him.

She loved his vision, but not the man behind the vision. The experience of mounting his play had been fraught with daily disagreements to the point where she had twice thought of walking out on the production. The stellar reputation of the company and the work for her that might follow was all that kept her going. "You've been a nervous wreck since this whole thing began. You're doing no one any good, especially yourself."

"I have a lot at stake in this."

"We all do Ron. We all do. Stop acting like you are the only one with something to lose. Every single member of this cast is deeply committed to this effort. You are *not* the only one with professional pride."

"You don't have the debt I have."

"That's right. I didn't take the same financial risks. Nor did Kevin nor anyone else. But stop blaming us for your past bad decisions. Now's a chance to get it right."

Then Styles' expression turned even more sour when he recognized a familiar face in his doorway. He threw up his arms. "Jesus Christ. What now?"

"Got some pictures for you," Park said in an unusually perky fashion.

"Pictures!? I'm in the middle --"

"Yeah I know. And you open soon." She threw a few copies of Mitchell Shanker's mug shots on his desk.

"This is unbelievable." Styles protested again.

Valente slid into the office, still looking and feeling bad. "Can you turn your voice down a few decibels?" He had decided to let Park take the lead for a while since, for the moment, concentration would be difficult.

"Do you recognize him?" Park said.

"Who?" Styles snapped. She pointed to the photos on his desk. Reluctantly, Styles looked at one of them. Carly also picked up a copy of Shanker's mug shot.

"Did he ever audition here?"

Styles gritted his teeth. "Do you know how many people have auditioned for me since I opened this place?"

"I don't care about past productions. Did he audition for this play?"

Park glanced at Carly who had replaced the mug shot on the desk. "Don't know him," she said.

"Pass them around to your people."

"Oh for crying out loud. We don't have time for this," Styles said.

"How about time for a walk down memory lane?"

A rush of anger welled inside Styles. He did not like where this was going. "What are you talking about?"

Park leaned against the wall. "Our people came up with some interesting history on your little kingdom here."

Suddenly Styles expression changed. He looked grim, as though expecting the worst. "What history?"

Valente forced a smile. "You don't look so good Styles. Like maybe you've seen a ghost."

"Tell us about the fire," Park said.

This also grabbed Carly's attention who was about to leave the room.

Styles rubbed the back of his neck as though a huge knot was about to form. He was about to speak but Carly's presence annoyed him further. "Don't you have a play to rehearse?"

"Yeah. Sure. But you've got to fill me in later," she said smartly, and pranced out of the office.

Styles kept rubbing the back of his neck. "There was a fire."

Valente decided to give his partner a break and took over the questioning. The stomach cramps were gone, but there was still pressure between his eyebrows. "We know there was a fire. We also know about a director who caused a lot of trouble for this group."

"I don't know too much about that. I came here later," Styles said.

"But you served as a guest director, occasionally," Valente added.

"Occasionally. Yes. Why? Am I a suspect?"

Park intervened. "You know Styles. You are a very tiresome fellow."

Styles took a moment to collect his thoughts. He had, for the most part, put the theatre's sordid past out of his mind. "I bought the theatre after it burned down, and then restored it. I know that to many people, I appear -- *tiresome*. But I am also a devotee of reparatory theatre. I don't want to see it die. And thanks to a rather large inheritance, I am able to do my part in keeping theatre alive in this sometimes barbaric nation of ours.

Park was oddly touched by Style's revelation, and though he could be a flaming asshole, he was to be commended. "That's very noble."

"Theatre is so important to a culture," he continued. "And in this country, there are those in government who, for whatever misguided reasons, see us as the enemy. When there's a problem with the deficit…kill the actors."

"To the point Styles," Valente said.

"You don't want to talk to me. You need to see Colleen Gilbert. She holds the dark, deadly secret of this cursed theatre."

"Dark secret?" Valente said.

"The fire, the killings." He looked away from them. "The mother."

"You like riddles, huh?" Valente said firmly.

"You haven't had to live with this. For twenty years we thought we were rid of this problem, and now these murders."

"What about Gilbert?" Park said.

"She was the artistic director back then. You need to talk to her because there are things about this mess that I just don't know."

He went to a file cabinet, opened the bottom drawer and pulled out an old cigar box. "If she agrees to see you, I'm sure she will give you the complete story." He found the card he was looking for inside the box. "I haven't spoken to her in some time but I believe she's at this address." He handed Valente a card.

"Now that wasn't so hard was it?"

Styles forced a wry smile as he waited for Valente to read the card.

"You gotta be kidding?" Valente said. "Anacapa island?"

"Like the saying goes detective. Be careful what you ask for…"

Styles walked out of his office with the kind of smirk Valente wanted to knock off his face.

Chapter 80

THE AIR DUCT above Styles' office was an excellent hiding place. No one paid attention to the air duct. Why would they? There had been no reason for suspicion. Not until now at least, and Mitchell Shanker knew that not one of them would have time to give the air duct one minute's consideration. Not after what he had planned for them. *The net that would enmesh them all.*

Shanker had been casing the theatre for several months. There were occasions, during rehearsals, where he would slip unnoticed into the theatre and sneak into the basement. There, he brought in supplies for his grand finale.

Or he would go up to the catwalks and watch Kevin and Jennifer kiss after rehearsals. The urge to kill burned in him

In the basement, he would stealthily move down its long corridor that ran under the orchestra pit. He passed storage rooms along the way. He had found an electrical closet which he studied one day. It held the circuit board for the theatre and other electrical equipment. Could come in handy he had mused though he had little talent for circuitry beyond just pulling switches. Labrythinian places always fascinated him. He loved the eeriness of it. Made his lips tingle.

On one occasion, while memorizing the corridor in the dark, in the event he needed to escape down that way, he found that it snaked towards a door he hadn't noticed before. The door, which was at the bottom of a narrow set of steps, led to the boiler room where by accident he had found an air duct.

One late Saturday afternoon, after everyone had left from an early rehearsal, he slipped into the duct and crawled along its crawlspace. Good fortune had it that this particular shaft led to the box office and eventually the main office.

So, up there Shanker listened. He had heard of Colleen Gilbert. Voices from the past. Not sure from who or from where. But the name struck a chord. So the vermin police were to pay her a visit? On an island off Ventura no less.

Shanker pressed his ear against the grate until the police had left. Then he retreated down the long crawlspace, back to the boiler room and to the rear of the theatre.

How would he get to Colleen Gilbert? The mark of a genius is that no challenge is too great, no riddle unsolvable...and Shanker was a genius!

Mitchell returned to the lair of the worm. After seeing hundreds of horror films, he wanted to transform himself; to become a winged demon, and traverse the night sky in search of prey. He envisioned himself a thing from an ancient curse.

His lair had grown cold and musty. Mildew hugged the baseboards, and large swathes of spider webs hung from the ceiling. He enjoyed passing under the webs at the bottom of the stairs. The faint stench of rotted meat wafted from a closet in the far corner of the room. His nostrils quivered.

Shanker's madness and growing lust for blood had created more confusion for him. He had a specific plan, but the loudspeaker in his head kept announcing that he needed to move on with other deeds...deeds unspeakable. Horrors unimaginable. His breathing was fast. Rivers of sweat drenched his body. And then he remembered stories of monsters he had read – stories of predatorial creatures bound by one desire. To feed.

But a voice from some dark corner of his brain told him to forget Ron Styles, the actors, and The MacLean Theatre. He had done enough and it was time to move on. Then another voice barked at him. *No.* The voice told him he had to finish his tale of vengeance.

He had to complete *the evil that men do.*

END ACT TWO

Act Three

All that we see or seem
Is but a dream within a dream

Edgar Allan Poe

Chapter 81

THE *OCEAN RANGER'S* bow rose a few feet above the waves. It landed with a resounding *whoosh* that sent water 12 feet above on either side of the vessel as it plied through blue seas under pure sunshine. Two dolphins appeared off the starboard bow, and kept pace with the boat matching her 12-knot clip. Then they crisscrossed in front of the bow, and how they avoided being crushed was a thing of amazement to Park who was fascinated by their behavior. This was her first visit offshore California and the first time she had seen dolphins in the wild. The two hurried back along the starboard side and continued pacing the boat. One turned its head lightly toward the boat, as though looking directly at park.

It was a day of seemingly infinite visibility in the Santa Barbara Channel off California's central coast. No typical Southern California marine layer to deal with which had everyone on board in good spirits. The *Ocean Ranger* left Ventura harbor at around 10:00 am and headed due west for Anacapa, one of the Channel Islands.

Neither Valente nor Park had ever been out there. He had often wondered about the island chain, and his questions were answered after he had read through a visitor's brochure given to him before boarding.

Seafaring Chumash Indians of southern California inhabited some of the islands for more than 6,000 years. In 1542, Juan Cabrillo, a Portuguese explorer discovered the islands and wintered in San Miguel. Subsequent explorers came to the channel and, in the1800s, European fur traders searched the islands for the prized sea otter.

In the early 1980s, Congress had named five of the Channel Islands -- Santa Cruz, Santa Rosa, San Miguel, Santa Barbara Island, and Anacapa, -- a national park, and later a national marine sanctuary because of their outstanding natural resources. The islands' waters provide habitat for marine life ranging from tiny plankton to the world's largest creature, the blue whale. The islands are home to several endangered species like the brown pelican. Large seal and sea lion colonies live on the islands, particularly on San Miguel, and elephant seals breed on Santa Barbara Island. The channel is also a favorite destination for whale watchers.

Today, there are no permanent residents on the islands except for one -- Colleen Gilbert.

Park ranger Martin Lopez leaned against the rail of the foredeck scanning the waters through a slick pair of sun glasses. The California sun was permanently emblazoned on his face, and his tall, lean frame could be imposing to some. "She came to the Park service about 15 years ago," he said to Valente who was standing next to him reviewing a map of the islands. "Said she always wanted to work with wildlife."

Valente folded the brochure and put it back in the inside pocket of his windbreaker. He looked over at Park who leaned on the gunwale across from them watching the dolphins do their synchronized leaps and dives. The ship's skipper, Todd Gibbs, a 20-year veteran of the service, was at the helm in the pilothouse above them. Two other park rangers were down in the galley feasting on doughnuts and coffee.

"She lives out there by herself?" Valente asked, looking at Anacapa, barely a small mound on the horizon.

"Yeah," Lopez replied. "She's a recluse. Usually rangers rotate -- a month on, a couple of weeks off. It gets pretty lonely pretty fast out there. But after her first tour, she fell in love with the place. Loved the solitude, and begged us to let her be the island's permanent ranger, so we let her stay. She's sort of our Lone Ranger," he flashed a smile that revealed perfect uncapped teeth. "Been there three years and rarely leaves the island."

Valente pulled out his notebook from inside his windbreaker and flipped to a page. "You said she joined the National Park Service 15 years ago?"

The amiable park ranger nodded. "She once told me over a beer that as a little girl she wanted to be a forest ranger in Yellowstone. She had dreams about living in the wild, and caring for animals. But like most of us, life doesn't always work out the way we saw it as kids. In her case she went from wanting to be a ranger, to a life in the theater. Talk about opposites. Me? I always knew what I wanted to do. Ever since I saw my first National Geographic special, I knew I wanted to dedicate my life to wildlife conservation."

"You ever get a hunch as to why she made an about face years later, and decided to pursue her childhood dream?" Valente said

Lopez wasn't sure how to answer the question. He had known Gilbert for only three years, since she transferred to the Channel Islands National Park. But she mostly kept to herself. She was gracious, and friendly, but very guarded. Lopez let the sun's rays hit him full force in his face. The blast of warmth soothed him. Before answering the question he adjusted his sun glasses. "If you ask me, I'd guess she was running from something, or someone."

"Why do you say that?" Park said.

"I have no idea, m'am. Just a feeling. Maybe it's a look in her eyes. Maybe it's because no one ever gets close to her. It feels like she's hiding a secret."

'And you say she rarely comes off the island?"

"Yeah. She'll come into Ventura for a doctor appointment, an occasional meeting, pick up groceries and personal items, that sort of stuff. But she stocks up pretty well so I'd say once every 2-3 months she'll come ashore."

Valente made a couple of more notes then turned to Park. "Nicole. You enjoying the cruise?"

She hesitated for a moment, wondering why the abrupt change of direction. "Love the dolphins."

Valente looked back at Lopez. "Thanks for the background info."

"Detective," Lopez said while adjusting his glasses again. "Is she in some kind of trouble?"

"Not at all, Martin. But she may have some important information on a case we're investigating."

"O.K." Lopez headed back to the bridge. "We'll be at the landing cove in about 20 minutes."

"Thanks," Valente said. He moved next to Park who seemed to be enjoying the trip. When Lopez was out of earshot he said, "I didn't think we needed to bother Lopez anymore with this case. Hopefully, Ms. Gilbert will give us what we want."

Park nodded.

Chapter 82

SHANKER HAD WATCHED Park and Valente board the Ocean Ranger from a pier in Ventura. He could not get a full frontal view of either of them but he had a general idea of their looks from watching them from the air duct above Style's office. At least he saw his adversaries.

Shanker looked up and down the dock. Was there a boat he could rent? He had twice piloted a small craft near Laguna Beach, and found it fun. The waters today were relatively calm so he felt that he could handle the hour or so journey to the island.

He spotted a near rotted sign about 30 feet from where he was standing. *Boat rental – half day*, the sign read.

Shanker moved closer to the sign but saw no one in sight. Where was the owner or manager? There was an old wooden chair, a jug of water and an umbrella for shade. An aluminum, 14 foot fishing boat with an outboard motor was tied to a pylon on the pier near the sign. Then from behind came a greeting. "Can I help you?"

When he turned, a man with a wide brimmed straw hat, whose face was mostly in shadows, shoved a wad of chewing tobacco in his mouth.

Shanker was briefly startled by the sudden appearance of the man. As he moved closer he saw a face the texture of leather. Several sun spots and what looked like scars indicated a face ravaged by too many years in the sun.

"Umm. Yeah. Like to rent a boat for a bit. Sign says half day rentals."

"Sure," said Sherm Stokely. He spit out some of his tobacco saliva.

"How much?"

Sherm eyed him closely, even a bit suspiciously. "You got any experience handling a boat?"

"Oh sure. Do it every summer. Mostly south, near Los Angeles."

Sherm put a tad more tobacco in his mouth and with his tongue nudged the wad against his inside right cheek.

"I'll need your pilot's license and a $250 deposit. The half day rate is $200 cash. For that you get that boat," he pointed to the aluminum 14-footer, "a full tank of gas, a cooler of water, and couple of energy bars."

"Did you say pilot's license?"

"That's right. Can't have no amateurs driving my boat."

"How much for you to drive?"

"I don't go out at sea no more. Me and the sun don't agree with each other. Two cases of skin cancer. Nearly killed me"

"I need to go back to my car, get my pilot's license, and find an ATM to get the cash."

"There's a bank across the street from the marina with an ATM."

Shanker had to think fast as he crossed the street, dodging traffic. The area was too busy for him to get away with another killing. How could he get that man away from his boat.

Chapter 83

THE LANDING COVE at Anacapa stood at the east end of the island near a land-mark rock formation called Arch Rock. The rock was a favorite amongst tourists looking for a great photo opportunity.

The *Ocean Ranger's* approach was over choppy waters, but once around the arch and inside the cove the boat was gliding over waters as calm as a lake and sparkling clear as a swimming pool.

The skipper cut the engines slowing the boat considerably. Around them were sheer cliffs reaching high above them. Kelp floated on the surface. A few Garibaldi fish swam near the boat, making the visitors marvel at their stunning orange colors.

As they got further into the cove, Valente noticed that the landing was bar-ren except for a shack that, he was told earlier, served as a small field station. A portable restroom stood next to the shack and a washbasin for cleaning scuba gear was situated towards the front end of the pier. Further down to the right, he noticed a long set of stairs, bolted to the cliff, and led to the summit. But no sign of anyone.

The *Ocean Ranger* came up alongside the wooden pier. One of the rangers jumped onto the landing and held a line taught while another carried their visi-tors' travel bags and placed them on the dock.

"Remember. We'll be back for you in three hours," Lopez said stepping out of the pilot house. "Make sure you're at the landing. The last thing you want is to spend the night here."

"Where are you guys going?" Park said.

"Pick up day trippers at Santa Cruz Island, and make a quick supply check of the ranger station there."

Park slung her knapsack over her shoulders and jumped onto the landing.

Valente followed. "Anybody working there?" he said pointing to the shack.

Lopez threw him his bag. "Not today. Like I said. Gilbert's the only permanent one on the island, and once a week we keep someone down here for a half day-shift."

Valente did not like the idea that there was no one guarding the cove.

"You guys got water?" Lopez said.

Park nodded.

"Good. Take those steps up to the summit – all 224 of them," Lopez added with a smirk. "Follow the dirt trail and you'll see the ranger station at the end of the trail. Can't miss it. It's the only structure up there other than the lighthouse."

Valente lifted his bag over his shoulder and started for the stairs. "Detective," Lopez called out. "Do not be late. We are under a tight schedule."

"We'll be here."

Park was already ahead of him, negotiating the near vertical rung of stairs to the top of the sheer cliff.

Waves welled against the landing as the boat moved away from the pier. Valente watched the *Ocean Ranger* disappear around the cove's outer walls.

Alone. He, Park, a mysterious woman who they hoped would help them crack this case, and dozens of squawking sea gulls soaring overhead.

Chapter 84

WHEN SHANKER HAD reached the ATM he noticed Stokely entering a houseboat, presumably his. One of the voices in his head told him what to do.

Sherm Stokely was in his galley looking for a bottle of rum. He held little hope that Shanker would return. Something about him just wasn't right. If you are a boater you would not forget your pilot's license, and Sherm was sure he had seen a look of surprise in Shanker's eyes when asked about his license.

He opened a cabinet above his sink and found his precious liquor, When he closed the cabinet door, Shanker was standing in front of him.

"Found your license?" The last words he would utter as Shanker slammed a crowbar across his head. Stokely fell, and Shanker delivered several more forceful blows to his head until blood streamed out of one of his temples.

⇢▰ ▰⇠

Two hundred and twenty four stairs. The ascent was nauseating, and reminded him of the time in high school he threw up all over himself during football training camp, in the dead heat of August. He was determined not to let that happen again.

When Park reached the summit, she was nearly hit by a swooping sea gull. Two more followed, exhibiting their territoriality. They were not keen visitors.

Valente wondered how early Indians made it to the plateau, 400 feet up from the cove, with no ladders, stairs or roads.

As they walked the trail, he was smitten by the stunning views the island offered. A barren rock formation miles from civilization and surrounded by blue ocean, he could readily understand how someone like Gilbert would want to drop out of life's congestion, and live close to nature.

His thoughts were interrupted by Park "There it is." She was ahead of him at a bend in the trail. The ranger station came into view about 100 feet, up a slight grade. It was a simple white stucco structure with clay shingles, a front porch, and a radio antenna on the roof. On a gravel patio to the right stood a picnic table and chairs.

Two doors marked the front edifice of the ranger station. One was locked which they assumed to be the sleeping quarters. The door to the office was open.

No one was inside. Valente checked the office which also doubled as a visitor center, and Park went to an adjacent room to the office.

Several brochures and folded maps were stacked on the welcome counter. A rack contained several extra brochures and some tourist post cards of the islands.

A large poster of the islands flora and fauna was taped on the wall behind the counter. The poster contained photos and descriptions of the marine species that inhabit the waters around the islands, and the terrestrial wildlife found on the islands. Anacapa, like the rest of the Channel Islands support only four native mammals, the island fox, the island deer mouse, the harvest mouse and the spotted skunk. The western part of the island is home to the largest breeding colony of California brown pelicans.

There was also a wall map of the other Channel Islands next to the wildlife poster. Otherwise, to Valente, there was nothing peculiar about the office. Typical of what he figured a small ranger station and visitor center in a remote area would look like.

Also noticeable was the absence of a bathroom inside. Only an outhouse behind the ranger station.

In the adjacent room, Park found herself surrounded by theatre memorabilia. Theatrical posters and framed photos of Colleen Gilbert lined the walls. She had once been a stunning woman of elegant bearing. Park noticed a haunting and sometimes sad look in Gilbert's blue eyes as though she had been carrying an inner pain.

There was a framed photo on a shelf of herself and Styles in a ribbon cutting ceremony - perhaps the opening of the newly refurbished MacLean Theatre.

Park had recalled several past investigations where she had had the opportunity to glance into the past life of a suspect, a victim, or merely a person germane to a case. This was no exception. Photos can tell a lot about an individual. She wondered what she would learn about Gilbert from this collection.

A cabinet contained several awards and more photos and there was also a small refrigerator and kitchenette in the room.

"She's quite attractive." Valente said moving into the second room.

"Yeah, in a Katherine Hepburn kind of way."

While glancing at the photos on the wall, Valente caught a glimpse, through a narrow window, of the lighthouse at the top of the hill. He wondered if Gilbert doubled as the lighthouse keeper.

They returned to the visitor's room. Park noticed a logbook on the counter. She checked the entries. There were only four names dated five days earlier. Presumably they were the names of the island's most recent visitors.

Valente glanced at the entries over her shoulder. "Not too many visitors up here."

"Just a matter of time, huh?" The voice spun them both around. Framed in the doorway, Colleen Gilbert stood.

Chapter 85

TALL, GAUNT, AND 60ish, Colleen Gilbert was an elegant shadow of a once striking woman. Her sparkling blue eyes and strong facial features were no less striking. She had long brown hair streaked with gray. Wearing khaki pants, a light blue denim shirt and a photographer's vest, she removed a shoulder bag and set it on her desk.

"They told me you were coming. Lopez and the guys back on the mainland," she said. "They told me, but I already knew it would just be a matter of time before you'd come....before Styles would finally spill the beans. The man has no spine."

Park took a step towards her. "I hope we didn't frighten you, and I apologize if we did." The lack of sincerity in her voice was obvious to Gilbert, but she also realized that a cop, who has been through countless interrogations, can become mechanical.

"Frighten? You can't even begin to imagine..." her voice trailed off as though another thought had entered her mind. And while a part of her brain searched for that fleeting idea, she noticed Park staring at her. "Why are you looking at me like that?"

"I'm sorry. I was just wondering-"

"You were wondering why, or how could a respected artistic director go native?"

"I was thinking that."

"You must forgive my manners. I rarely get visitors. Can I offer you some refreshments?"

"Just some water for me," Park said.

"Thanks but, nothing for me," said Valente.

Gilbert retrieved a bottle of spring water from her refrigerator and poured a glass for Park. Gilbert steadied her eyes on her. "Did you always want to be a cop?"

Park had dreamed the dream of most aspiring athletes. An Olympic gold medal that would ultimately lead to fat endorsement contracts, and the subsequent plush homes dotting exotic places around the globe. "A long time ago I wanted to be a gymnast, but I outgrew the height and weight standards to compete successfully."

"I don't follow."

"I got too tall and heavy -- for a gymnast."

"Oh. I see. Well. Our ambitions change with time. As a girl, I wanted to be a pilot. Of course all the school chums thought I was nuts. For a short time I thought I would become a nurse, but that notion died after I witnessed an accident and saw human blood.

"So onward I plowed through secondary school, having thoughts of starring on the screen and stage. Thoughts I never expressed to my parents because of a father who insisted on a so-called real career. Since I always had a love for the marine environment, I got myself a degree in marine biology from the University of Southern California at Santa Barbara."

She drank some water. "Did you know that abalones are a favorite food of lobsters, and that sea otters are important to the survival of kelp?"

Gilbert did not wait for a response. "But the allure of the theatre was intoxicating. My aunt was a dancer with the Rockettes. I think I got my artistic bent from her. I danced in musicals for awhile."

She paused to admire her captive audience. "Now that's something you don't see very often, you're probably saying to yourselves. A marine biologist chucking science for Broadway.

Eventually, the hard work, and long hours took its toll on my body. So I wandered around the administrative side of theatre, landing among others, jobs as artistic director for various theatrical companies. Moved to Chicago to work with a reputable stock company and then the cold winds of Chicago blew me West."

"So after the fire, you applied for the Park service?" Valente said.

"No. I went diving with sperm whales. Always wanted to do that. I found a website years ago. One of those eco groups that push you to the edge of endurance. Sounded cool at the time. Then I went to Tibet. Thought about becoming a Buddhist. That was a laugh."

She eyed them closely, wondering what they made of her. "Let's see. Then I did some volunteer work for Earth Care. For them, I helped monitor sea turtles in the Virgin Islands. Played nursemaid to a female laying her eggs. We erected a pen so the locals couldn't steal her eggs. We stayed up all night, round the clock, until she buried the eggs and went back to sea."

She got up from her chair and returned to the kitchen. She filled a kettle with water, turned on a burner. "Would anyone like tea?" The two officers declined the offer. "Was it Lopez who brought you out here?"

"Yes," Park said.

Gilbert returned to the office and sat in her chair. "He's a good man. By the book. Handsome as all get out. Those perfect teeth. I suppose he told you guys to be at the landing in three hours, or so. Some stuff about high tides and all that?"

"He didn't mention high tides. He said something about picking up day trippers at another island." Park said.

Gilbert rolled her eyes and shook her head. "He's worried about a great white."

"As in shark?" Park said.

"Yeah. Mr. JAWS himself. I spotted one chasing a seal into the cove about two weeks ago. The big guy's been hanging around the area ever since."

"How big?" Valente said.

"18 feet. Maybe 20."

"Jesus?" Valente said, looking obviously concerned.

"Lopez is pretty jittery. The food supply is very plentiful here, what with all the seal rookeries around the islands. He won't be leaving anytime soon."

"You figure Lopez wants us out of here to maximize our safety?" Park said. "I mean we are in a very large, sturdy boat. How dangerous can that be?"

"I think he frets too much. But the last thing he needs is a freak accident, like one of you slipping and falling into the water just when that shark, or sharks happen into the cove."

"There's more than one of them?" Valente said.

"These are protected waters, and typically you find a lot of fish in these waters, including sharks."

The kettle began a slow hiss until it finally went off like an alarm. "Ahh." She returned to the kitchenette "Don't go worrying yourself Detective. You are in no danger. Just don't go for a swim."

Valente shifted in his chair, wanting to quickly get this interrogation over with. He had actually had a desire of touring the island with Park, enjoying the smog-free air; doing some of the nice things he rarely gets to do anymore because of this case. He didn't want to hear any more about great whites, though. Already, he had replayed in his mind the scene from Jaws where the shark tore apart Quint's boat.

"It's his mother you know." Gilbert stood in the doorway of her kitchen. Her mood had suddenly turned somber. "It's all about mother."

Valente and Park regarded her closely, as though they both knew where she was leading them.

"Shanker. Jocelyn Meredith Shanker," she said quietly.

Chapter 86

THE ENORMOUS DORSAL fin scared the daylights out of him. It appeared not more than ten feet from his boat, then disappeared under a swell. Shanker's knees felt week. He knew if he stood up he might collapse from the weight of the fear that had consumed him. Maybe this was not such a good idea coming to the island. There was no way he could do battle with a shark, *no way*, he kept muttering to himself. *No way*.

The fin appeared again, only this time closer and on the other side. The damned shark had passed under his boat. *It's checking me out* –Shanker thought. *How big is this thing?* He was in a boat no more than 14- feet long and the shark could easily have exceeded that length. Images of a blood crazed man-eater shredding his boat turned his stomach.

Shanker remained frozen. He could see Anacapa maybe a half mile ahead. *Think damnit. Think.*

He spotted a fishing vessel about three-quarters of a mile to his right heading back to Santa Barbara. For a moment he thought about signaling them, but then he quickly banished the thought. He could not risk being recognized. Somehow he had to get to shore without arousing the predator in the water. He squinted into the afternoon light glaring off the waves, hoping he could suddenly see beneath the water. Nothing. All had gone still, except for the drone of his outboard.

Then a thought crossed his mind. The flare gun. If the shark attacked he could at least aim the thing at the shark's mouth and hope the flare would neutralize it.

Suddenly he felt a sustained scrape under his feet. The shark's dorsal had passed under the boat, scraping its hull.

At that moment, Shanker vomited over the side. He remained still, trying to gain strength, watching his vomit float past the outboard. And then, a black eye encased in the largest head he had ever seen emerged from the inky darkness below. It was slowly rising towards him.

Chapter 87

GILBERT HAD RECLINED in her chair and sipped her tea slowly. "I made the decision to fire her. She was not a very good director and when her plays continued to get bad reviews, our subscribers became restless, insisting that something be done. I also had a less than sympathetic board of directors to answer to. I had a soft heart and at first, didn't want to fire her. So I tried to find her another position in administration."

She was about to take another sip of tea, when she put the cup down on her desk. "Oh the hell with this."

She dumped the tea in a houseplant, moved quickly to a cabinet and pulled out a bottle of brandy. She poured herself a healthy shot and slammed it back. Then she poured another.

"To make matters worst for herself, she insisted we cast her son in our production of Peter Pan."

"Mitchell?" Valente held up a 4X6 photo so she could get a better look. This guy?"

Gilbert studied the photo. "I haven't seen him since he was a child. Could be him. Anyway she had dreams of Mitchell being a child star. And of course what better show than Peter Pan to get a kid's career going? But he was a dreadful actor. Adorable little boy, but a terrible actor. She would hear none of that. Pitiful woman. Pitiful. Threw tantrum after tantrum over her son. When I told her we no longer required her services, she went ballistic. She flew into a rage, and attacked me. One of my assistants called the police. She quieted for a little while, but still agitated and begging for me to reconsider. When police came, she went batty again, attacked one and was eventually carried out in handcuffs, kicking and screaming. Then I heard she was committed to an institution somewhere in L.A. for counseling, observation…who knows. Don't remember where. I was just glad to be rid of the nut job. And then, the clever woman was able to convince her doctors that her breakdown was due to unbearable emotional strain under financial stress. The hospital released her and two weeks later the theatre burned down. I know it was Jocelyn that burned the theatre."

"Do you have any proof?" Valente asked.

"Of course not. I'm not an arson investigator," she said angrily. "But it was her. Some things you just know in your heart."

'We checked the reports," Park said. "Whoever did it, is still at large."

"Where is she now?" Valente said.

"Disappeared. I am not even sure if she was a suspect in the burning of the theater, so the search for her was not given any high priority, and no next-of-kin in California to follow-up on."

She poured another shot, and stared at the glass for a moment. "I think she took her son far away from here. And now he has come back to draw the blood of his enemies."

Valente wondered if perhaps Gilbert had been on that island a little too long. "You're suggesting the son is avenging his mother's dismissal?"

"Yes. No. I don't know. But I am surprised I'm still alive."

Valente noticed his watch and realized they had to get back down to the landing to meet the Park Service boat. "We're going to post a unit out here, unless you want to come back to the mainland. We can get you protection."

"Let me think about that."

"O.K. Meanwhile, if you think of anything else, let us know."

Park moved towards the door. "Thanks for the hospitality, and for your time."

They were about to walk out of the ranger station when Gilbert's voice stopped them. "I haven't had a good night's sleep in twenty years. I want to sleep again."

Fortunately for Shanker, great whites do not like the taste of aluminum.

When the shark had surfaced, it nudged the boat with its snout as though testing to see if it was a food item. Shanker retreated to the opposite side, fearing the worst. He had visions of the shark coming through the hull and tearing him to pieces. But the shark had merely been curious and went elsewhere in search of food.

Shanker had remained still for at least ten minutes. Was it really worth going out there he thought? Did she really matter? His knees were still weak, and he felt as though he would throw up again so he waited, until his body relaxed. He had shut off his outboard so as not to run out of gas. The boat drifted a little in a northwesterly direction, away from the island.

Finally when he was certain the shark was far from him, he turned on the engine and steered southwest, towards Anacapa. Slowly he regained courage and focus.

Chapter 88

THE NAME HAD stuck in McCarty's head since his meeting with Reiner at the bar. Sheila Barrow. But why? Why was the name familiar? Was she a one-night stand from another life-time? Was she one of the many hookers he had busted?

He polished off the coffee he had been nursing, turned on his computer, and called up the crime reports of the last three months. Punched in her name and there it was as plain as day. She had been a murder victim, the case Valente had been working on until the Arthur St. George case. McCarty was about to cross-reference when Valente walked into the squad room followed by Park.

"Sam. I'm going down to change. Be back in a few," she said. "Hey Ed."

McCarty spun around on his chair. He immediately noticed Valente had that wind-blown, sun burnt look from a typical day at sea under a piercing sun. Little specks of salt still dotted his eyebrows. "Ahoy there Captain, Sheila Barrow ring a bell?"

"The one with all the animals?"

"That's her. I helped myself to your files because I couldn't get her name out of my head. You neglected to file a report my fearless leader."

"Ed. I got pulled off the case to work this one. Remember?"

"Right. Anyway, ran a computer check and it looks like she could have been Shanker's supplier."

"You're sure about that?"

"Not completely, but Reiner's sources say she is, or was, the premier supplier of illegal animals in this area, if not the whole country. She ran quite a network. U.S. Fish and Wildlife Service been watching her. FBI's had a man on her. She kept records too. Lots of them."

"Yeah. If I remember she had quite a set of log books."

"That's correct and there's an entry from one of her books about a black mamba purchase from a Nigerian source."

"Pull up the forensics report. Whose prints were at her crime scene?"

McCarty printed out a report. "Not Shanker's prints if that's what you're hoping for. And no other prints. Her place was clean. The killer or killers are still at large. Reiner thinks the perps might have been someone she had pissed off. And the murder was committed in a way to make it look like the work of a psycho. Pretty slick huh?"

"Is that what Reiner thinks? He should work for us." Valente scanned the computer printout one last time. "Says here toxicology tests found evidence of three drugs in her system: clobenzorax, paxil, and methamphetamine tegretol."

"Tegretol? That's an anti-seizure medication. Man she was a mess," McCarty said.

"I wouldn't be surprised if the killer knew that she was taking these drugs," Valente continued, "and somehow got the drugs in her to calm her down, so he could overcome her without a problem. In a sense, make it look like the killer was invited to seduce her."

Both checked over the report again. "Well one important question is answered," Valente said. "Shanker did not have an accomplice at the zoo." Valente went to the water cooler and filled a paper cup with water. "You know Ed, I'm relieved. I really didn't want to bust anyone there."

"Yeah. I'm with you on that. I like zookeepers. They're a special breed. Not everyone can shovel rhino shit all day and then turn around and put on a happy face to the public."

Again Valente wandered how, if ever, this man gets a date.

"How did it go with the lone ranger?" McCarty said.

"How did you know about Gilbert's nick name?" Valente said.

"I'm a good canvasser, remember?"

"She's scared." Valente recounted Colleen Gilbert's connection to Shanker, and her doubts and fears. McCarty seemed mildly interested, but in truth, little surprised the veteran, jaded cop. After awhile, the particulars of police investigations seem to blur together. Rapes here, murders there, kids killing kids, punks mugging seniors for their social security checks, desperate mothers killing their babies -- it all blurs together to the point where you just put on an imaginary shell and forge through another day at the job.

Valente seemed to hear his thoughts. *It all becomes a blur.*

"Just living the dream, huh Sam?"

"Yeah."

Chapter 89

A FULL MOON shone over Anacapa and Colleen Gilbert barely noticed. As a young girl, she had always been awestruck by a full moon. Whenever one appeared, she would crawl out of bed in the still of night, and sit by her window and wonder what the big face in the sky was thinking. She would even talk to him, and promise to be a good girl if he would give her a lollipop. As she grew older, a full moon still held her in awe.

But tonight her mind was restless. She hadn't spoken to anyone for years about Jocelyn Shanker and the trouble at the MacLean Theatre, and she had felt relieved that she was able to unload some of that burden. Colleen had fixed herself a cup of tea and laced it with a little brandy. She took a sip and felt better. As she reclined she heard footsteps on gravel.

She lifted her eyes slowly towards the front window. The steps crunched on gravel at a slow, steady clip.

A spasm of fear shook her. No one gets on this island but the park service, guided campers, or special guests under park service supervision. And no one, absolutely no one at night.

She was about to pick up her phone when the sound of steps on gravel turned to those of boots on wooden planks. And then silence. Seconds seemed like an eternity and Colleen had no idea what to do. Alone on an island, and someone outside her door who shouldn't be there.

And then her worst fears realized – the door handle turned. A cold sensation shot through her as she backed away from the door.

The door opened and a man in wet pants and a windbreaker walked in. He stood in the spill of moonlight, observing her, almost with admiration. Then he removed his hat.

Colleen stared into his eyes, and instead of feeling afraid there was an odd look of resignation "You must be Mitchell."

⇥◉ ◎⇤

He did not accost her, and was instead respectful. He remained in the doorway, while they regarded each other.

"How did you find me?" she finally said.

"May I sit down?"

"Yes."

"I've known about you, Miss Gilbert. I know all about what you did to my mother. Can't say I blame you. She could be….difficult."

Colleen stared at him for a moment, then sat back down in her chair. She sipped her brandy, and watched him closely. Outwardly, she was a picture of calm. Somehow, she did not appear at all afraid of Shanker. Inwardly, she knew this could be her last day on earth.

Shanker appeared at first nervous, uncertain. "Gilbert. That is a wonderful stage name. A name that does justice to your commanding Anglo features. I might someday change my name to Mitchell Gilbert. After my first hit."

They sat, looking at each other for a couple of minutes. His unease soon turned to aloofness. He seemed distant, lost in thought, and she never took her eyes off him.

"I'm tired, Miss Gilbert. My crossing was challenging to say the least. May I have a glass of water?"

Chapter 90

INSIDE THE MACLEAN Theatre, Valente moved through the orchestra, looking at the bare stage. His eyes played across the empty theater and then the damndest thing. He thought of his father. He had only briefly talked about him with Park, about his days as a stand-up comic.

He wondered how his father endured playing night after night to drunks in south Jersey dives that smelled of foot odor and vomit. An unsatisfying life that often made him miserable. But he never let on to his family. In front of them, he was a jovial prankster full of good cheer and love. What Valente didn't know as a child, but found out as he got older, was that underneath the bravado was a very sad, and lonely man who had suffered greatly for his art. A frustrated man who never got the big breaks. A man who earned his keep chiefly as a bartender.

There were a few stints in the Catskills, and a rare gig opening for mid-level headliners in Atlantic City casinos, but mostly, work was hard to find. Valente's father spent years hoping for the breaks that would eventually put him on top.

Then, late one night, his father drove his car to the back of a grocery store in Newark, N.J. Rolled up the windows, shut the doors, and kept the engine running until finally the carbon monoxide sent him to a place free of pain and suffering.

Valente could never forgive Shanker for his crimes, but he could understand the underlying torment that in one case drove a man to suicide, and in another to commit murder.

The sound of footsteps brought Valente back to the present. Styles stood at the rear of the theatre.

"In some parts of Europe during the Middle Ages, actors were considered possessed by demons. More than 700 years later, certain esteemed members of our modern Congress, wanted to kill funding for the arts, as though we were responsible for our nation's deficit. We in the theatre have never had it easy. Don't let those few who earn millions give you the wrong impression. Most of us spend our lives in drink, depression and poverty."

"I know," Valente said. For a moment he thought Styles had heard him thinking about his father.

"Detective Valente. Shanker is a man who has never had a close-up."

Valente took a beat before answering. "When did you become a shrink?"

"I work with actors." He walked down the aisle, closer to Valente. "You'll catch him, detective. He wants his close-up."

"Tell me something Mr. Styles. Is there a murder in The Raven?"

This took him by surprise. "No."

"How about in your version?"

"No," he said, almost defensive.

"Anything out of the ordinary that I should know about?"

"You know, when you speak to me, I always feel like I am a suspect. Don't you trust me?"

"You want to know the truth? I'm not sure what to make of you."

Styles decided to move on, and not dwell on himself. "Have you read The Raven?"

"Yes."

"It's about obsession. A man's obsession with his lost love, Lenore. Your killer has a very strange, and deadly obsession."

"I can't argue that."

"I have to admit that I am intrigued by the notion of an actor who can only perform when he is a killer. We live in Los Angeles, detective. Sickos here are as common as bimbos."

Valente had grown tired of Styles. He didn't know what he had hoped to accomplish by returning to the theatre, but he felt he needed to walk a potential crime scene. "We will catch him, Styles. Let's just hope it's not here on your precious opening night."

Chapter 91

A FED-EX ENVELOPE sat in an in-box addressed to Homicide. It had been there for several hours, before Neil Crispin noticed it. Young and fresh out of the police academy, he wondered why no one had bothered to deliver the package, but when things get hectic around there, mail delivery was sometimes put on hold. Typical he thought. He took the envelope, and quickly walked down the hallway to the homicide division. Crispin passed a warren of cubicles that led to the squad room, or the asylum as some of the veterans called it.

At the far end of the room, Valente sat at his desk making an entry in the perp's profile on the chalkboard.

McCarty was at his desk, on the phone, basketball tickets in hand, looking for someone to go to the game with. Park was in Campbell's office, discussing the Shanker case.

Eager to make an impression, Crispin hurried his pace until he reached Valente's desk. "I think this is for you, sir," Crispin said, catching his breath.

Valente took the envelope and looked at the address. "It's just addressed to homicide."

"Since there wasn't a name I figured you should look at it."

"Thanks."

"Glad to be of help sir." Valente waved him off and opened the envelope.

"Oh sir."

"You don't have to call me sir," Valente said. "We're very informal around here."

"Um. O.K. I thought you should know that the Fed-Ex had been sitting in the box downstairs for about six hours."

Internally, Valente was smiling. A little brown-nosing hoping to score points with the seasoned vets. "I'll make a note of that."

Crispin remained in front of Valente's desk for an awkward moment, then turned and walked out of the squad room.

McCarty, who had watched the exchange from his desk, had to offer an opinion. "I hope I wasn't that young."

"I think you were born with a cigar in your mouth and whiskey on your breath," Valente said.

"Amigo. You just wrote my epitaph."

Valente opened the package. There was a video tape inside. "Does this creep not know what a DVD is?"

A note scrawled on the cover – "from Hell…" McCarty's typical devil-may-care attitude quickly turned sour. "Are you fucking kidding me! That was Jack the Ripper's signature."

They went into Campbell's office where he kept an old VCR player.

"Do you believe in knocking?" Campbell said.

"Not today," Valente replied. He put the tape into the wall unit.

"Good thing I kept my old VCR player, huh?" Campbell said.

The images were snowy at first, the usual leader stuff, then Mitchell's face came into view.

He looked into the camera, at them. His face serene, his eyes calm, as though there could never be murderous intent behind them.

"I'm really not that bad of an actor. Oh, I can't do everything, but honestly, who can? Some actors do Shakespeare very well; others are quite adept at comedy, some make great action heroes, then there's Julia Roberts and all those teeth." He smiled broadly, mocking her.

"But I think my niche is horror. I don't think I consciously chose the genre. Who truly knows how one gets their artistic passion? Look at a football player turned actor. Where is the art in football? A friend of mine was born into a family of lawyers and accountants and became a concert pianist, until he died of a heroin overdose. He was twenty." He took a beat, staring at the floor. Then slowly he lifted his eyes to the camera.

And The Raven never flitting,
still is sitting. Still is sitting;

His eyes have all the seeming of
a demon's that is dreaming;
And the lamplight o'er him streaming
throws his shadow on the floor;
And my soul from out that shadow
that lies floating on the floor
Shall be lifted -- nevermore.

"I hope you will be there to catch my best and most explosive performance."

The tape ended, and the snow returned.

For a moment they all remained silent, but Valente had heard something unusual on the tape, rewound it, stopped and then started somewhere in the middle. As they watched him, Valente heard it again. A distant groan. Or so he thought. "Did you hear that?"

Without waiting for a reply, he rewound the tape and stopped near the same spot. He hit the play button and again that strange sound.

"What's that?" McCarty said.

"Listen," Valente urged.

When they took their attention off Shanker, who was reciting the verse from *The Raven*, the sound became clearer.

"Is that a roar? Like a lion?" McCarty said.

Valente rewound the tape again to the spot where they first noticed the sound. They all listened, and then it became more obvious. "It is a roar," McCarty said.

"He's at the zoo?" Campbell said.

"No. But that's what he wants us to think," Valente said. "He's an actor in his world of make-believe," Valente said in a near whisper.

"'There's an abandoned petting zoo in Cerritos," Park said. "You don't think..."

"I remember when it closed. Broke the hearts of a lot of kids," Campbell said.

Valente came to a quick decision. He was tired of waiting. Tired of the case. Tired of all of it. He wanted this guy, now. "Nicole. Get a unit to the theatre.

You go with them. "The Raven" opens tonight and he just might make a grand entrance."

"And you?" she said.

"McCarty and I will take a unit to Cerritos and hopefully find this guy's lair."

Chapter 92

Opening Night. The McClean Theatre.

Styles' dream of bringing Edgar Allen Poe's "The Raven" to the stage would soon become a reality. The artistic differences with Carly coupled with repeated threats of replacing Kevin with a more seasoned actor mattered little. All that mattered was getting through opening night.

The orchestra was abuzz with technicians, actors, ushers and stagehands. Styles stood in the center of the theatre observing the controlled frenzy. Two stagehands moved an ornate desk stage left. A writing quill and inkwell were set on the desk, as was a kerosene lamp. Then they pushed a high-backed, brown leather chair in place behind the desk. A bust of Palas stood stage right. Two others placed a palm plant near upstage center, and then the same hung a row of lights.

Carly was in the front row checking the light levels for the opening scene with her lighting director who was in the booth setting the levels. They communicated through headsets.

When the light was turned down to just the right level she turned to the lighting booth at the rear of the theatre and gave her lighting director a thumbs up.

She casually regarded Styles, who pleasantly acknowledged her. A surprise, she thought, that he didn't find something wrong since he could find nothing right for the past six weeks. Styles retreated to the back of the theater when a commotion stopped him.

Preston had burst onto the stage. He started going through his paces, going over his lines to himself.

Carly barked at him. "What are you doing here?"

"I have a critical scene. I just want to make sure I have it right."

"Preston. You appear to Kevin in a dream sequence lowered by a cable. You have two lines. The cable technician handles the rest. What's there to get right?"

Carly had had numerous occasions to calm an actor getting stage fright, but typically they were actors who had major roles, or carried the show. This was a first for her.

"There are no small roles. Only small actors. Right?"

"Who said anything about you being a small actor?" Carly snapped, her patience running thin.

"Well, you implied it."

"Get back into the dressing room. Now."

"I can't sit still."

"Preston," she said firmly.

"I just want to do the best job, Carly," he sad in a pained voice.

"And you will. I have all the faith in the world in you."

"What if the cable snaps?"

"It won't snap Preston."

"You're sure?"

"Styles has spared no expense to mount this show. We are state-of-the-art here as he reminds us daily. You're going to be fine. Do your relaxation exercises."

"Relaxation exercises?" Preston slowly came back to earth. "Right. That'll work." And just like that, Preston made a swift exit.

Carly rubbed her index finger and thumb over the bridge of her nose, as though that would get rid of the tension. Would this play finally give her the recognition she had sought for so long? Ten years in backwater theatres across the West until finally landing a directorial stint with the MacLean Theatre.

She turned with a start as a hand softly touched her shoulder. "No one ever said directors have it easy. Nice job with Preston." It was Styles.

"Thanks Ron. I've got to get moving. Just a few more nips and tucks and we'll be ready."

"You're going to be fine."

"Did you just go Buddhist on me? Why are you being so nice?"

"Oh maybe because I realized that I was being too hard on you. The play looks great. You did a great job. I have all the confidence in the world that this will be a smash." Was he convincing? Who knows?

"Hope you're right."

"Now don't you go neurotic on me. I need at least one sane person in my troupe."

Carly caught her breath, and for a brief moment enjoyed the friendly repartee. But then she checked her watch and realized there wasn't much time left before crowds would arrive.

"Got to go. Thanks for the support."

"Break a leg."

"I hate that expression."

Chapter 93

THE SIGN READ Marc IV Construction. Valente turned his unmarked police vehicle into the gravel driveway. McCarty sat next to him in the passenger seat eating an Almond Joy. A squad car followed.

Abandoned animal pens stood on either side as they drove into a parking area. The welcome lodge of the former Cerritos petting zoo was straight ahead. Valente noticed a crane with a wrecking ball off to the right. It wouldn't be long before this whole place would be raised, making way for yet another mind-numbing sub-division.

They parked their cars in front of the old lodge. The small structure looked as though it were sinking back into its foundation.

Valente stepped out of his vehicle and did a quick visual across the area. The emptiness spooked him, and reminded him of a scene from one of those apocalyptic movies like *The Day the Earth Stood Still*. A few leaves and scraps of paper blew along the graveled parking lot accentuating the stark setting.

McCarty, and one of the two officers from the other car, stepped inside the Welcome Lodge.

"I don't think he's in there," said Valente.

"Wise guy. Just checking."

And as they went inside, something caught Valente's attention. He suddenly felt his heart skip a beat. Far off in the distance, at the end of the zoo, stood a house on a low grade.

Chapter 94

CARLY GAVE HER stage manager final instructions and asked if he was ready. "Got it all Carly. Don't worry about a thing. You sit out there and enjoy the show."

"Yeah. Right."

The stage manager barked. "Carly. Go."

Earlier, Park had quietly maneuvered her vehicle to the back of the theatre with a unit of three police cruisers, a SWAT team, a crime lab van, a surveillance van, an ambulance and two fire trucks. There they set up their command post.

She had gone into the theatre with a team of five plainclothes, similar to the Newport theatre operation, only less obvious. This time they chose economy over numbers.

Park called Valente on her cell. In a moment he answered.

"Yeah Nicole."

"I'm in the theatre Sam."

"Good. Units in place?"

"Yeah."

"Keep them as out of sight as possible."

Willie Jackson, a young detective assigned to this detail, remained in the surveillance van at their command post. There, he would communicate with Park, the SWAT team and the officers in the theatre.

Snipers took various positions around the theatre. Some climbed up trees facing the building, while two others lodged themselves in bushes.

"Command to SWAT. Command to SWAT. You in place?" Jackson said.

The SWAT leader, lodged in a tree where he could see the front of the theatre and the parking lot, quickly responded. "We're set here. Rear group. Report."

Three snipers had made their way to the back of the theatre and took position. One on the roof of a carport, two others in bushes. The one on the roof checked that the others were in place.

"Shooter one, two and three in position."

Styles had returned to his office where he was met by Park, and her team. He could not resist the sarcasm. "I feel so much better."

Ignoring his tone, she assured him that the show will go on. "We'll have several plainclothes in the audience, and we have a SWAT team around the perimeter.

"I wish I could say I feel reassured."

"Just keep everyone together after the show. If he's here, and that's a big *if*, I don't want anyone wandering around. We're not sure what he wants to do, but he is connected to this theatre and everyone he has killed thus far was in some way connected to him."

Styles frowned. "Well I never met nor ever remember auditioning him."

Shanker's shadowy figure moved along the narrow hallway, holding something heavy in his hand. A long basement corridor ran under the length of the theatre, from the front entrance above, to the back exit.

A policeman stood guard at the far end of the corridor. "Command. Officer Beeker reporting. All quiet down here."

"Roger that," Jackson said.

Shanker stopped in the shadows when he heard Beeker's voice. He listened for a moment and when all was quiet, he continued towards the officer. The shadowy glows played to Shanker's advantage. "Hello there,"Shanker called out, which caught Beeker by surprise.

"What are you doing down here?" Beeker said.

"Came down for an extra strobe. This one burned out." He lifted the old strobe he was carrying.

The Brooklyn accent was thick but didn't sound quite right to Beeker. Almost like he was forcing it. He had been around enough transplanted New Yorkers to know the difference.

The approaching Shanker continued. "Wouldn't you know it. On opening night. Ain't it always that way? Something's always got to go wrong right when you don't want it to."

He stepped into the glow of a fluorescent light hanging from the ceiling. Beeker eyed him closely but not overly suspicious. "And another thing. Theatres? They're no different than other businesses. They want to save money so they buy cheap stuff. This thing's a piece of crap. No wonder it burned out. How you doin'?"

The 'how ya doin' was so off Beeker knew instantly the guy was a fake. He was no more New York than a blond surfer dude from Southern Cal. "Good. I don't remember seeing you."

"Last minute replacement. Freddie came down with a cold."

"Freddie?" Beeker didn't remember anybody named Freddie on the theatre staff. "Just a minute." He reached for his cell phone.

With a sudden movement Shanker swung the strobe casing across Beeker's head, knocking him backwards against the wall. He stood there dazed, and felt blood stream down his neck from the ugly gash across his forehead.

He reached for his gun, but Mitchell swung the strobe again, crushing his skull. Beeker fell against the wall and slid to the floor.

Shanker grabbed his arm and dragged him to the front end of the hallway, leaving streaks of blood on the floor behind him. He shoved the officer into a storage closet.

Chapter 95

THE OLD COLONIAL stood in ruin, and the leaves were over grown. The house recalled a bygone era of stately opulence. It was an imposing structure that was sinking into the ground. Paint was chipped or peeling in almost every corner of the house's exterior, and cracks spread across the molding like varicose veins.

After a cursory inspection, Valente assumed that the house was empty. Of course, there was no way of knowing for sure until they went inside.

Plumes of dust rose around them as they entered the large foyer. Several floor boards buckled under the weight of their boots. The place was musty and smelled of dust. A faint and unpleasant odor of decay wafted from somewhere inside.

In front of them was a winding stairway that led to the floor above. A narrow passage underneath a low archway ran alongside the staircase.

To their left was an expansive, rectangular living room. Two of the cops with them, Morales and Brown, took the creaky passage under the archway. Valente and McCarty entered the living room. Not much light filtered into the room. McCarty tried a light switch. Nothing. They turned on their flashlights and swung them from side to side. McCarty noticed Venetian blinds on the windows. He opened one of them to let in the little remaining sunlight.

Morales suddenly recoiled as she walked into a maze of spider webs.

"Damnit," she said wiping the webs away from her face in quick, jerky motions. "I got bit by a damned spider once. Got an infection that nearly killed me."

"No shit?"

"Yeah. Shit. Had a fever of 105. Two days in intensive care. It was friggin' gross."

The narrow passageway emptied into a den. This room was also draped in cobwebs. More dust rose in front of them with every step they took. A large Rubenesque portrait in a gilded frame hung over a mantle. The fireplace had long been abandoned but there were still a few old logs resting on a metal stand. Two Japanese vases stood on the mantle

A cracked leather armchair and a mahogany coffee table were the only furniture pieces in the room. A walnut bookcase completed the décor.

Valente and McCarty moved down the hall and entered the living room while Brown and Morales went ahead of him to continue their inspections. The room was empty except for a broken chandelier in the middle of the room. Valente noticed a gaping hole in the ceiling and figured the chandelier came loose and fell. The entire house reminded Valente of a faded diva. He ran his hand over a mantle where, encased in glass, stood a small ancient vase of some sort. Could have been Roman, Greek or even Etruscan, or maybe a knock-off.

Above the mantle, hung an old painting of a seascape chipped in several places. McCarty judiciously wrote down notes of everything he saw in the room.

Valente was about to leave the room when he heard the faint voices of Morales and Brown further down the hall. Moving out of the room he saw them standing by a doorway. It was opened slightly. Only darkness came from within.

Chapter 96

Soon the Santa Barbara area would be treated to perhaps the world's first-ever, theatrical adaptation of Edgar Allan Poe's "The Raven." There had been staged readings, and a very silly, Hollywood sub B-movie made in the 1960s, but to Styles' knowledge, never a full-blown stage production.

He stood nervously in the lobby greeting some friends, as patrons and members of the media began to arrive. Theater critics from Channels Five, Four, Six, and Nine made their way into the lobby. This was quite unexpected. Styles wondered who had called them. Grantland Marks of the Los Angeles Times was there wearing a modest suit. He nodded to Styles as he entered the lobby

Park stood off to one side, nonchalantly holding a program, but keeping a vigilant eye for any sign of trouble. Carly made her way into the lobby from the theatre, where she quickly put on a relaxed face as she greeted some arrivals.

Styles brushed against her with a suspicious eye. "Carly. Did you call the news stations?"

She smiled proudly. "Yes. I went to college with Amy Shaler over at Fox, and while talking to her I figured, heck why not call all of them."

Contrary to his usual biting behavior around her, he was genuinely grateful. "Thanks. We can use all the exposure we can get."

"I figured you'd like it. After all is said and done, we are in this together Ron."

Styles was about to say something but they were suddenly surrounded by a group who had just entered the lobby.

In the dressing room, the cast was buzzing with usual opening-night jitters. They were at various stages of costumes and make-up, all focusing their energies on the evening ahead.

"Full house?" Preston asked while applying final touches to his make-up.

"Looks like it," Bart replied from the other end of the make-up table. Meanwhile, Jennifer helped Kevin with his ruffled scarf. "I'm dedicating tonight's performance to you," he said softly, and kissed her.

An actress nuzzled up to Bart, unable to fasten the snaps to her dress. "Help me with this." Bart fastened her dress.

Then Jennifer noticed Preston's face.

"What," he said in a near panic.

"Too much rouge."

"You think?"

"Yep."

"I don't know what it is with me and rouge."

The stage manager stuck his head in the room. "Ten minutes."

Kevin bounced up and down in place to loosen up.

"Relax. Honey you'll be great," Preston said.

"Just want to get on stage."

⋅→▭◌ ◌▭←⋅

Valente stood at the landing for a few seconds shining a light down the stairs. He flicked a wall switch next to him but it was dead. Then, step by step he descended. His team followed behind him, one by one.

Chapter 97

His stomach felt like it needed a bottle of Tums. He was a bundle of nerves watching how fast his theatre was filling up. It looked like another sell-out, one he had awaited with some anxiety, and uncertainty.

Then Styles felt a sudden wave of fear, born out of years of theatrical highs and lows, when a hand on his shoulder spun him around. It was Park.

"Jesus. Detective. Can it wait until the lights go down."

"I just wanted to wish you luck. Hope all goes well."

"Sorry. I thought…nevermind. I'm all nerves."

"I hope it goes well," she said smiling at him.

"So do I." Then a beat. "Thank you. I like you detective. Wanted to say that before. You're not like the others. There is gentility about you."

"That's very kind of you. Thanks."

"Are your people in place?"

"We're nowhere, and we are everywhere," Park said. "How's that for being cryptic."

"Great line. I'll have to write that one down."

⇥◎ ◎⇤

They were now in the graveyard of dreams. The place smelled of decay. Curtains of spider webs hung from corners in the ceiling. McCarty stood under one particularly intricate web at the bottom of the stairs. "A tangled web, huh?"

"Jesus what is that stink?" Morales said, following the others down the stairs.

"We'll find out soon enough," McCarty said.

Beams from all their flashlights danced across the room.

Valente moved along a wall full of horror film posters; *Invasion of the Body Snatchers, The Thing, Phantom of the Opera,* several vampire movie posters, and finally a poster of *Theatre of Blood* starring Vincent Price. Something about that poster struck a familiar chord.

Then he stopped in front of the *Psycho* poster. Brown and Morales also marveled at the vintage posters. "Some of these must be collector's items," Morales said.

Valente kept his light shining on the *Psycho* poster. "You know what made *Psycho* so amazing? First movie to deal with a human monster. Before it, horror films dealt with vampires, or creatures like *The Wolfman, Frankenstein, The Mummy.*"

"*Creature From the Black Lagoon,*" McCarty added.

"Right. But it wasn't until *Psycho* that monsters took on a human face."

Shelves of CDs and video tapes lined another wall. McCarty pulled several out, checking the titles. Nothing out of the ordinary. Mostly tapes or DVDs of well-known horror films.

Chapter 98

THE PHANTOM HAD lived deep in the bowels of the Paris Opera. Deep in torment and tortured by a love he could never have. Inexplicably evil yet equally sentimental, he was often referred to as the Opera Ghost. Horribly deformed, yet cunning and musically gifted he moved at will through the opera's labyrinthine corridors. At night, through the walls, he would taunt opera performers he felt unworthy, making them feel apprehensive and even fearful. He could do this undetected because he knew every hidden passageway.

Shanker held no such advantage. He was not as familiar with this theatre as the phantom was with his opera house, so he had to be careful.

One fluorescent light cast its stark illumination at the end of the hallway. The cloaked figure stood under the fluorescence. He looked upward. A piece of the ceiling had been removed exposing an area crawling with steam pipes and ductwork.

His eyes stared into the blackness above him. "And each dying ember wrote its ghost upon the floor," he whispered.

A few minutes remained before curtain and Styles needed one last cigarette. He rushed outside and stood on the front steps of the theatre. Here he would enjoy a smoke, while the last late-comers rushed past him to get to their seats. He also snuck a sip of brandy from a small flask he kept in his inside jacket pocket. He wasn't aware that black eyes were watching him from a basement window.

Chapter 99

THE DESK IN a corner of the room was not as interesting as the plain, brown coffin next to it. It stood there like a tombstone. Dozens of letters had been spiked to its cover.

The officers weren't sure what to do next. All registered differing looks of bewilderment. This was, needless to say, an unusual thing to find, and with dozens of letters attached. Finally, Valente removed one of the letters. He unfolded it and read. *"Stop ignoring me. I'll do better next time. Write to me mother."* He opened another letter. *"The audition went very well. I think I made a lasting impression."* Then another. *"If you would only write, I'll tell you when and where I will be appearing next. Write to me mother."*

"Fruitcake," McCarty muttered.

"So what profile do we have now? Someone imitating Norman Bates in "Psycho?" Valente said thinking out loud. "Is he hearing voices from heaven, or from hell?"

"Don't go getting spooky on me," McCarty said. "I tell you what I know. We got ourselves a pathetic piece of shit, is what we got."

Valente slid his fingers along the edge of the sealed coffin. He wasn't quite ready to open it. He wasn't ready for what might be inside.

⌗

Stage manager stuck his head in again. "Five minutes."

Preston jumped. "That voice is so irritating. God, he announces as though we are off to the executioner. Could you use a gentler tone," Preston called out to him.

⌗

They had stood there for several minutes reading the letters and wondering what was inside that coffin, but none had moved to open it. Then McCarty noticed the lock was off its hinges. He removed the padlock. He cast a hesitant look at the others, then pushed open the lid.

None of the officers in the basement knew what to make of what was inside. Just when they thought they had seen it all. A mannequin, neatly made up to look like an elderly woman, lay prone in the coffin. It was dressed in a nightgown with her wooden arms folded across her chest.

"Mother?" McCarty said.

Valente noticed something under her left arm. It looked like the corner of a magazine, or a thin paperback. He removed it and saw that it was a script. He shone his flashlight on its cover. The title on the cover read "Peter Pan."

"You writing this down?" he said to McCarty.

"Absolutely. Can we get more light in here?"

"Morales, call CSI. Tell them to bring some strobes," Valente said.

Another officer found an old trash bag under the stairwell. "Found the source of the stink. Some rotted chicken."

"Get it out of here." Valente said.

When McCarty finished writing, he replaced his notebook in the inside pocket of his jacket, and then noticed something in shadows on the windowsill. He shone a light in that direction.

"Sam."

They moved closer to the window and saw that the item was an odd-shaped figurine of a black bird perched on the ledge.

"What kind of bird is that?" officer Brown asked.

"No surprises here. It's a raven." And then Valente noticed something peculiar about the statuette. He shined his light closer. The wooden bird was standing on one leg. The other leg was raised over an explosives plunger, claws spread as though ready to depress the plunger.

Suddenly, Valente's face turned ashen. Then a chill swept through him unlike any he had felt in years. McCarty must have felt the same sensation because he too froze.

Chapter 100

STAGE MANAGER STUCK his head in the dressing room. "Places everyone. Places."...
and quickly disappeared.

The actors quickly took their positions back stage.

The house lights slowly dimmed until the entire theatre was cast in darkness.
Then music - the moody and eerie "Gnomus" from Mussorgsky's "Pictures at an
Exhibition." It was a theme that evoked a sense of doom, a creepy piece suggest-
ing the presence of a rodent-like hunchback.

While the music played, Kevin took his position on stage and sat at the desk.
Once seated, the music got him into the tortured mood necessary for the role.
Listening to the music made him forget all of the opening night anxieties.

In the lobby, a few late-comers hurried in and were quickly ushered to their seats,
but not before Park took a close look at their faces. None matched Shanker's
description.

The late arrivals were followed by two undercovers dressed as ushers. Park
immediately recognized them. "Where's Styles?"

"Don't know."

"I saw him about 20 minutes ago," said the other cop. "He said he was going
out for a smoke."

Then, the sounds of thunder and lightning drew their attention to the stage.

Park peeked inside where a single spotlight illuminated Kevin. More sounds
of rain and thunder, and the effects of lightning flashing outside the stage window behind Kevin. Park was impressed by the sound and lighting effects, that
mixed with the music created an intensely dramatic moment.

Slumped over the desk, Kevin slowly raised his head. There was a half empty bottle of cognac next to him. A brandy snifter lay on its side next to the bottle. He wondered whether or not he should pour another drink. For the moment he decided against it. The music faded, and then he began.

"Once upon a midnight dreary
While I pondered weak and
weary. Over many a quaint and
curious volume of forgotten lore...

Up on the catwalk, Shanker's black, shark-like eyes looked down at Kevin. A body lay next to Shanker with a rope tied around his neck. Dreamily, Shanker picked up while Kevin continued...

"While I nodded nearly napping,
Suddenly there came a tapping,
As of someone gently rapping...
Rapping at my chamber door..."

Chapter 101

THEY HAD HOPED to get to Carpenteria within the hour. Plenty of time before the final curtain.

"Come on Nicole. Answer the damned phone," Valente said in a tense voice. One hand on the steering wheel, the other on his car phone. McCarty sat in the passenger seat barking orders in his phone to other units. "Yeah the MacLean Theatre…Carpenteria"

"Bomb Squad on the way?"

McCarty snapped at him. "You getting senile on me. They were the first people I called."

"Ed. I don't want a cavalry charge to that theatre. I want stealth. That bastard is there and I don't want to scare him away."

The police cruiser tore up the San Diego Freeway at nearly 90 mph. Two others followed.

"Will you answer your goddamned phone? Damnit." A car moving too slow in front of him. Valente slammed the accelerator all the way to the floor and passed the car on his left.

The phone chirped making her jump. She flipped it open, "Park here," she listened for a moment. "Jesus. I'm in the theatre Sam, and there's a show going on."

"Clear the theatre."

"What?"

"Clear the…" they were cut off by cellular static.

Valente lost his composure and slammed the phone against the dashboard. "Fucking, fucking, fucking cell phones. Goddamn them and the assholes who invented this shit."

McCarty offered his phone.

"Let me have that!" He punched in her numbers and waited for the rings. She answered. "Nicole. I'm getting interference. Listen quickly. You've got to clear the theatre."

"Why?"

"Just clear it...before this cell shit cuts us off again."

Suddenly, a scream from the audience.

"What the hell was that?" Valente said.

On stage, Kevin had jumped from his chair, horrified. Park stopped in her tracks unsettled by the sight before her.

Style's body dangled over center stage, hanging from a long chord that was tied to a railing on the catwalk above. The body twitched for a couple of seconds and then stopped and swayed from side to side.

The audience at first assumed this was part of the show. A stunned silence filled the theatre, until all the lights went out. Startled voices from the cast and crew backstage told the audience this was not part of the script.

Then pandemonium.

Limbs frozen, Park braced for the worse. A wave of people spilled out of their seats, and scrambled for the exits.

Park tried to be heard above the screaming and shouting. "Please. Careful. Do not panic. There is nothing to be afraid of..." She heard a hiss from her phone, found it was still in her left hand, and raised it to her face. "Park here."

Valente tried to keep an even tone, but the edge in his voice was there. "Park do you read? What the hell is going on there?"

Park was about to respond when the force of a corpulent woman's shoulder slamming into her chest knocked her off her feet. Park fell flat on her back while her cellphone flew out of her hand and slid under a row of seats.

Chapter 102

IN THE LIGHTING booth, the lighting director found the emergency switch and sent a spill of bluish light into the theater. The light did little to ease the panicked crowd.

They had become a shoving, grunting, clawing mass of hysterical people trying to make their way to the street.

Backstage, Carly bumped into Kevin, who stood blank expression staring at the stage. Preston approached from the wings. "My God Carly. Don't go out there. It's horrible," Preston said taking her arm.

She had been in the dressing room reviewing a minor technical problem with the stage manager when she first heard the screams. She even smiled, thinking that an easily excitable person was frightened by something in Kevin's early dialogue. But then when one scream was followed by several, she became unnerved and was about to investigate when she bumped into Preston and Kevin.

Carly pushed her way past the two actors towards the stage, and froze when she saw Styles' limp body swaying back and forth. Hands to her face, she fought to catch her breath.

⋅→▨ ▨←⋅

Valente sped through one intersection after another causing other cars to swerve out of their way. They had long put Los Angeles behind them, had turned off the interstate and were zooming through Camarillo. Ten more miles.

McCarty kept a nervous eye on the road ahead. "How many years in this shit-ass business? You think you seen it all, and then something out of nowhere has to bite you in the ass,"

A slow moving van inched through one intersection forcing Valente to slam on the breaks. His cruiser skidded around the van, sending Valente's vehicle into a spin. His rear bumper whacked a newspaper vending machine sending it flying through the window of a Taco Bell. Valente left a trail of burnt rubber until he was finally able to right the vehicle.

"We're never gonna get there you drive like that," McCarty said grabbing onto his seat.

"Relax. I ain't ready to die just yet." With one hand on the steering column, Valente used his free hand to try and get through to Park from the car phone. "C'mon Park. Pick up. What is going on there?"

Then a frantic stop on screeching tires. Cars slowing down at a busy intersection up ahead. "This is not good." The whaler on his roof continued to flash, and he let it scream until finally drivers ahead gave him a lane. He sped through the intersection.

Chapter 103

WITH THE STAMPEDE unfolding in the theatre, Carly had decided to leave the back way, which was through the basement. Kevin and Preston were in agreement and they descended the narrow stairs that led to the hallway that ran under the theatre. They were halfway down the corridor when all three froze.

The dark figure approached them with a purpose. Until it finally loomed over them under the bluish fluorescent. Carly gasped. "My God. It's him."

Kevin somehow suppressed his panic, but Preston was in the grip of a sickly fear. His knees weakened forcing him to lean against Kevin. They were all consumed by a fear that paralyzes vocal chords and freezes muscles.

Shanker was terribly confused. A volcano erupted inside his head until he finally couldn't take it anymore. "Whyyyyy!!!" The voice began as a roar and then rose to a shrill shriek that made their ears hurt.

Preston screamed but could not move. "We're going to die Carly." Preston then looked up at Shanker. "Please don't kill us."

Shanker's face was soaked in sweat and a mask of confusion. He gasped, then he jammed his teeth together. He lowered his head and stared long and hard at them, like a hungry predator waiting for the right moment to pounce. A thin stream of saliva drooled off the left side of his mouth and down his chin.

He looked particularly long at Preston. Shanker got closer to him. Close enough to smell him. He sniffed and sniffed like an animal checking out a new food item. Preston felt his breath on his cheek. It was a foul breath.

Shanker would have loved to carve them up. He would have loved to spill their blood all over the corridor. But there was too much to do in too little time.

He did not need any more confusion. No more distractions. *No more distractions.* So he lifted his arm and pointed behind them.

"Go," he hissed at them. "Go. *Now.*"

Without a moment's hesitation, the three bolted down the hallway. When they reached the back door, Carly turned back. The dark silhouette watched them for a moment, then disappeared in shadows. Carly breathed a loud sigh of relief, and in that second Preston wet his pants.

"Can we go, now?" was all he could say.

Kevin remained behind for a moment, looking down the hallway until Carly's firm hand grabbed his arm. "Kevin. Don't even think it. Move. Now!"

Chapter 104

SHANKER HAD FOUND one closet similar to the one he had spent so much time in as a child. This was a closet in a subterranean section of the basement. Sort of a basement under a basement at the bottom of a set of stairs descending from a rear door in one of the backstage corridors.

He had kept her there for two days, gagged and bound. No one would have ever thought to look for her here because *here* was rarely ever visited. At one time it had been an electrical closet. Now it stood gutted and empty.

He opened the door and wheeled her out. Colleen Gilbert tried to make herself heard, but her gag was painfully tight around her mouth. While on Anacapa, he had forced her to his boat to return to the mainland where he kept her prisoner in this basement of the theater.

Shanker peeked over a narrow window and barely made out the dark forms of the shooters positioned over the carport and in the bushes. Shanker spotted all three, and thought how pointless. Like he was going to go out there for a smoke or something.

The loud thumping sound above him took his eyes off the shooters to the scene above. The sounds of the human stampede brought him some measure of relief. His scheme, so far, was going off as planned until he heard something from the other end of the corridor.

⊶═◑ ◐═⊷

The woman's three-inch heel nearly broke the skin on Park's hand. She had been on her back for a few seconds, catching her breath, when a panicked woman in spiked heels stepped on her hand. The force of the heel sent a wave of pain and rage through Park.

The screaming was continuous now with people colliding against each other in a surging mass. Park desperately searched for her phone, her eyes roaming the floor under rows of seats.

She rolled to one side as another wave of people rushed past her. A firm hand grabbed her shoulder and lifted her up. It was one of the undercover cops dressed as an usher. "You O.K. detective?"

"My left hand is shot, but otherwise I'm fine." The undercover noticed a nasty welt forming in the middle of her palm where she had been nearly punctured. "Do you have a phone?" Park said.

"Yeah."

The lobby doors burst open as people clawed over each other with panic in their eyes, and fear in their hearts. Some slid or tumbled to the floor while others trampled the fallen. Two undercover cops tried to restrain several panicked people but to no avail. They had never seen anything like this. The stampede ignored the police as though they were cheap props, and ran right through them.

SWAT leader John Harris drove into the theatre's lot just as a screaming mass pushed their way down cement steps. Others jumped over those fallen, racing for their cars in a frenzy. One woman stepped on her gown and tripped down the stairs, hitting her face against the pavement. Blood spurted out of her broken nose.

"Dear Jesus," Harris whispered. Then his phone crackled. It was Valente. "SWAT leader report."

"My men are in place," the SWAT leader's voice crackled over the phone. "What about the people?"

"Let them all go home," Valente said.

"What if he's in that group?" the SWAT leader asked.

"Doubtful. Our star has something real special prepared for us. I'll stake my badge on that."

"Roger," the SWAT leader signed off.

Valente needed further reassurance. "SWAT leader. Let me re-emphasize. Keep your shooters in position. Do not divert."

"Affirmative."

Valente sat impatiently behind the wheel while watching McCarty clear traffic with two traffic cops. McCarty yelled at drivers like they were scum. Working quickly, the traffic cops and McCarty waved the cars off to the shoulder, until a lane for them had cleared.

McCarty hiked back to the squad car and heard Valente on the phone as he got in. "Bomb Squad, report" Valente said.

"We're not far. Turning onto Carmello Drive. Just tell us where to park."

"Find some place dark. I don't want him seeing you."

"By the way. Campbell called my commander. Thought you were going a little overboard on this bomb thing without positive verification," the bomb squad leader reported.

"Who am I speaking to?"

"Sergeant Ben Jeffries. I'm the leader of this crew."

"Jeffries. I hope he's right. And I think you hope he's right."

"Sam. Park here."

"Nicole. We're hearing screaming all over the place. What spooked them?"

"Styles is dead," Park replied with little emotion. "Hung actually. He's hanging from a catwalk, swinging back and forth over stage center. As soon as we clear this theatre, I'm going to cut him down."

"Park. Listen to me. I think he's going to blow-up the theatre."

Park stared into her phone wondering what next. "You're *not* kidding are you."

"No. In a way it's good the people are clearing out. Saves us a lot of trouble and a lot of mess."

⤙▬◉ ◉▬⤚

Park watched the remaining members of the audience rush out of the theatre. And then she caught a whiff of something unmistakable. *Gasoline.* Instinctively her eyes searched the floors for its source. Then Park saw a look of horror in the face of a nearby cop.

Mitchell Shanker, dressed in black with a long flowing cape, wheeled Colleen Gilbert out on stage.

Park drew her weapon. Two undercovers came up behind her, weapons drawn.

Gilbert was strapped securely to the wheelchair with TNT wrapped around her chest. Her face was bruised and bloodied. Her gag had been removed. Shanker stopped at center stage, stood behind her with a sword pointed at her throat.

Something wasn't right about Shanker's appearance, Park thought. She wasn't sure why she had that thought. Maybe she had expected him to be taller and more handsome. Though his face was partially blocked behind Gilbert, the part that was visible appeared to be sickly. Park could have sworn she saw him stumble.

And then she caught another whiff of the gasoline, only stronger this time.

One of the undercovers looked nervously at Park. "You smell that?"

Park nodded. "Find the main fuse box. Get the lights back on."

"Will do," said one the cops, and he snuck out of the auditorium.

Straining to see through the dim glow of the emergency lights, Shanker's eyes found the guns pointing at him. "Put your props away or she takes her final bow."

◄═◉ ◉═►

Valente turned the cruiser onto the final stretch of road to the theatre, only to find another mass of traffic. His siren was screaming loud but many of the drivers ahead of him took their time getting out of the way.

"You there?" she said softly.

"Talk to me."

"He's got Gilbert strapped to a chair with TNT wrapped all around her."

Valente shook his head and looked at McCarty. "It's never easy, is it?" He had to think fast, then he punched in a few numbers on his cell phone. "SWAT leader."

"Yeah."

"Get your best shooter to the lobby."

Chapter 105

SHANKER REMAINED IN shadows behind Gilbert. He could see Park and the two undercover cops, but they could not get a clear shot at him without hitting Gilbert. This made him feel like he was on top of the world. Images of villains relishing their grand moments of glory raced through his mind.

"You try anything and I will kill her," he barked. "I will ram this sword through her neck, in true horror-movie fashion. You have my word on that, coppers."

Park and the officers with her, kept their revolvers aimed at his head, but knew the chances of a direct hit were slim. They needed a bigger target, like the chest. Shanker was not so dumb as to expose himself.

"And now, ladies and gentlemen, I am going to show you how the part should be played." He cleared his throat. "Once upon a midnight dreary. While I pondered weak and weary. Over many a quaint and curious volume of forgotten lore." The voice was deep and affected. "While I nodded nearly napping. Suddenly there came a tapping..." Park now understood why this man never got a part. He flat out stunk.

Shanker looked up at Styles' dangling body. "Had I auditioned, you would have cast me, and I would have been terrific."

Had he auditioned? Now it was clear to Park why Styles insisted he had never seen him. He hadn't been hiding anything. Shanker had never set foot in the MacLean Theatre to audition.

The bomb squad parked their van in front of the theatre. Two members of the team unloaded the remotely operated vehicle they would eventually send into the theatre. Some of them referred to the vehicle as RovoMan. Jeffries, the bomb squad leader called Valente.

When the car radio rang, Valente was speeding between two cars. Barely an inch separated them on either side. He had lost his patience with the traffic and did not care if he sideswiped cars. He grabbed the car radio. "Speak."

"Detective?" said Jeffries.

"Yeah. Yeah. What is it?"

"Jeffries here. Bomb squad."

"Talk to me."

"Rovoman is ready."

Valente was in no mood for inside jokes. "Cut the jargon."

"Yeah. Sorry. The remote unit is ready."

"I don't think we're going to need it. He's got a hostage wired with enough TNT to level a basketball arena."

"We'll send it to the basement just as a precaution."

"Not yet," Valente said. "Wait for my signal."

⊷══◉◉══⊷

The lobby of the theatre had become a minor staging area. Several undercovers stood at the ready by the front door. Two were poised on either side of the entrance to the orchestra with their weapons aimed at Shanker on stage.

Jeffries had entered the lobby with another member of the bomb squad, and took a look at Shanker. "The guy won't surrender, huh?"

"Not yet," said the cop to his left by the door.

Meanwhile the SWAT team's ace shooter, Andy Moyers, made his way past the group. He was lean, muscular and walked with a confident swagger.

Moyers politely asked the two undercovers near the door to move out of his way. He slipped into the back row of the theatre. Moyers raised his rifle and looked through the scope, focusing on the target. Then he got into a crouched position whereby he could rest his elbow on the back of the seat in front of him. He peered through his scope again.

Mitchell and Gilbert were tableauxed in front of Style's body that was still dangling from the rafters. Gilbert was strapped to her wheel chair with the explosives tied around her torso. Park remained crouched behind theatre seats and ready to open fire.

"I don't have a quarrel with the police," Shanker continued. "My quarrel is with these marionettes. You can go. I don't want you to get hurt. Go!"

Then he leaned close to Gilbert. Tears were streaming down the side of her face. "It all began with you. You refused to let me be a member of your company. Several years ago remember?" Then he looked up at the rafters, distracted, as though he heard a voice calling out to him. "Sorry. First it began with my mother." He looked at the orchestra seats. "Did you get my letters, mother?"

Gilbert, choked by fear and pain tried to make an appeal to him. "Mitchell – please."

Mitchell sliced her cheek with his sword. "Don't step on my lines."

Moyers' right index finger gently touched the trigger. Still not a clear shot. The shadows and lights played tricks on his eyes. Shanker was clever staying behind Gilbert thereby not making himself a clear target. Snipers hated that. He heard Jeffries behind him. "Do you have a target?"

"Not yet."

"I was a good boy," Shanker shouted. "But my mother locked me in closets." Suddenly his head was on fire, as though pieces of glass were dancing in his brain. "Stop that," he screamed.

"Put the sword down," Park said. "Deactivate the bomb. No one will hurt you."

Mitchell was momentarily disoriented, but he knew better than to move way from Gilbert. "Bomb? What bomb? You mean these?" he pointed to the dynamite strapped around Gilbert. "These are toys. Props. *Hello?* We're in the theatre. It's all make-believe." With the point of the sword he sliced the rope that held the explosives to Gilbert's torso, and lifted it high above her head. Then, with a fluid motion, he flung the explosives at them. "Take a look."

Now he had a target. At that moment Moyers pulled the trigger. Shanker had exposed just enough of his torso to the shooter when he threw out the fake TNT.

The bullet caught Shanker in the upper chest just under his right clavicle. Screaming, he stumbled backwards, behind Gilbert. Another bullet buzzed over his head and Shanker fell through a piece of scenery, landing backstage.

"Get her out of here," Park yelled to one of the cops, "and cut him down," she added referring to the still dangling body of Styles. Then she sprang up on stage and disappeared around one of the flats.

Chapter 106

THERE WAS THE theatre – a hundred yards away at the end of the tree-line road. Valente couldn't drive fast enough. The whaler on the cruiser's roof was still spinning its bluish light but he shut off the blaring loudspeaker.

McCarty, who felt like he added a few years and gray hairs because of Valente's driving breathed a sigh of relief. "Remind me never to get into a car with you again."

Valente's radio crackled. He grabbed it quickly, instinctively as though it wouldn't ring again. "Yeah."

"SWAT leader here. Shooter made a direct hit."

"Is he dead?"

"Cannot confirm a kill. Not yet anyway. Perp stumbled backstage. One of your people went after him."

→▸▪▰◉ ◉▰▪◂←

Park had moved down the narrow hallway behind the stage. Every muscle in her body tensed. It wasn't until she had reached a juncture that she thought *what in hell am I doing?* Instinct, or perhaps a sense of duty propelled her, but when she found herself alone in the dark, a wave of fear passed through her. If he overcame her, she did not think she had the strength to take him down. She was no Hollywood fabrication of an armed-to-the-teeth heroine with a busty Playmate figure beating off armies of muscle-bound killers. Park was slender, feminine, and hadn't seen the inside of a weight room since she was a high school gymnast.

Something on the floor in front of her got her attention. Back to reality. No more rambling thoughts. There is a killer to catch. At that moment she realized she had broken at least a dozen procedural rules. For one, she had no flashlight and she was in a dark corridor. And she did not wait for back-up.

She inched forward and saw that the shape on the floor was a body. She crouched low, and could make out the face of Eddie, the lively old stage manager. Park felt around his neck for a pulse, then recoiled. Her fingers were sticky with his blood. His throat had been slashed from ear to ear.

To her horror, she remembered what Valente had said about horror films. While trying to stop the monster, good people will die

Chapter 107

VALENTE RUSHED INTO the orchestra after having driven his car right up the front steps of the theatre. McCarty was right behind him. He moved through a flurry of human activity and reached the stage where paramedics attended to Gilbert's wounds. She looked up at him and saw the look of genuine concern in his eyes. Valente wished he had been able to have given her better protection. Somehow she sensed that he was blaming himself. Gilbert warmly took his hands in hers. "It's O.K. detective. It wasn't your fault."

He was about to console her when the smell of gasoline hit his nostrils. "Where's that gasoline coming from?"

"Don't know," a nearby policeman said. "But we've got people looking for the source."

Valente wasn't satisfied with a simple *we got people on it.* "Let me tell you something. If we're smelling gasoline up here, then somewhere, this place must be soaked in the stuff."

And then he had a macabre realization. All Valente could do was snort at the ridiculously obvious. *This theatre burned down once. The bastard's going to burn it again.* "Find the source of that gasoline."

The first streams of smoke appeared through a crack in the floor of the center aisle near the stage.

⋆⇥⊙ ⊙⇤⋆

Park reached the doorway to the dressing room at the end of the hallway. As she expected, the room was empty. She was about to leave when she noticed a door at the far end of the room. Park had been in the room on two previous occasions but had never noticed the door.

It was slightly ajar. Park moved towards it, drew her gun and pushed it open. She saw a stairway led to a door at the bottom. The door was sealed shut with a cross bar.

She got on her phone and called the theatre security guard who had remained with the police in the lobby.

Lonnie Jefferson was 70, with skin the texture of old leather. He was not happy with all of the excitement at the theatre. He just wanted to live out his days as the theatre security guard with his bottle of cheap whiskey nearby. Nothing else mattered to a man who had lived a life of drifting and pain.

The phone ringing annoyed him because he was in the middle of sneaking a drink in the lobby. He picked up the phone inside the box office. "Yeah. Jefferson here."

"There's a stairway in the dressing room. Do you know where it leads?" Park said.

Jefferson frowned. "Not sure. What stairway?" He took a sip from his bottle. "Oh wait. Wait. That one. Umm. Never gone down there."

"Is Valente there?'

"Who?"

Park realized that Jefferson had no idea who any of them were. "Could you please put one of the policemen on?"

"Wait one."

It happened very quickly. A sudden movement from behind.

A force unleashed from hell pulled her neck and hair and spun her around. Several quick blows to her head, face and neck. Park's gun flew out of her hand. She had never seen such speed. Another sharp blow to the jaw and Nicole fell back into the tight stairwell. She collapsed against the wall. Miraculously, she still held onto her cellphone and slipped it into her pocket.

Shanker was on her like a wolf. Her scream was quickly muffled as Shanker lifted her to her feet, hands around her throat. He began to squeeze the air out of her. She wanted to kick him but the blows to her head had taken her strength. He seemed to look through her with the eye's of a demon. His chest was soaked in blood, but the bullet lodged under his clavicle appeared to have had little, if any effect on him. Where did he get his strength she wondered.

Shanker spun her around, and pulled her close to his chest. His hot breath touched the nape of her neck. Then a sick feeling shot through her. She felt cold steel against her throat. *Do not do anything foolish* she reminded herself.

⊷⊷ ⊶⊶

Valente held the phone to his ear. "Nicole? Nicole." Valente looked at Jefferson. "You said it was detective Park right?"

"Yeah. Said she's in the dressing room."

"Park!?"

A cop rushed up the aisle. "Detective. We've got smoke coming though the floors."

Valente was all instinct now as he flew through the doors of the theatre. Passing three cops in a cluster he ordered them to follow him. And then to no one in particular. "Where is the damned fire department?"

Valente and the three cops raced up the side stairs to the stage and down the narrow backstage passageway, until they reached the green room. Valente stopped them. "Check the end of the hallway," he said to two of them." He turned to the younger of the three. "You," Valente read the name off his name tag. "Lehman. Come inside with me."

Bloodied footsteps on the floor. A blood handprint on the wall. To their right, the door. The room felt warm, so did the floors. Valente knew that a fire was raging from somewhere below them. He was about to call in a report to McCarthy when he saw Lehman go for the door to the green room, ignoring everything he had learned in training.

Valente, expecting the worse yelled at him. "Don't open that door."

But Lehman had committed the fatal error. He had forgotten to feel a door before opening it. If the door was too hot and oxygen entered an overheated room, it would ignite, and the backdraft would torch whoever was in there. Just as Valente sounded the warning, Lehman opened the door. A wave of heat, and then fire consumed him. Valente leapt out of the way just as flames rushed past his feet.

->=◉ ◉=<-

"I said, I ain't never been down there," Jefferson looked at McCarty with bulging, exasperated eyes. "How else do you want me to say it. I don't know no other language."

McCarty's impatience was mounting with each passing second. "How long have you been working here?"

"Why. Am I a suspect? I been working here long enough."

"Does anybody have a floor plan of this place?"

Jefferson threw up his arms. "Well why didn't you say that in the first place. There's one in the office somewhere."

The familiar sound of fire engine sirens got all of their attention. A look of relief fell over their faces. "It's about time," McCarty said. He started for the front doors to meet the fire chief arriving outside. Then he turned to Jefferson. "I want that floor plan."

Jefferson shuffled to the office, scowling. "Yessir, bwana."

->=◉ ◉=<-

Valente rolled on his side, hands in front of his face to protect it from the surging heat. The other two cops had returned, one with a fire extinguisher. All froze when they saw Lehman spinning out of control, screaming wildly. He had become a human torch. The shocked officers in the hallway stood back from the fire, helpless.

Then, the one holding the extinguisher turned it on in a vain attempt to put out the flames. But they were raging out of control and too intense for what a little fire extinguisher could accomplish.

"Get back to the theatre," Valente said.

"What about him," said the cop holding the canister.

"There's nothing we can do. That room's a furnace. Move out of here before we're all toast."

They caught a last glimpse of their partner, arms flailing over his head. Lehman fell on his back, his body in flames, burning to a crisp. Then mercifully, his agony was cut short when the ceiling collapsed and crushed him.

Valente got on his phone as they struggled back to the theatre. "McCarty here."

"Ed…"

"I'm already on it. Fire department's on site."

"It's an inferno back here."

"Well get your ass out of there. Any sign of Park?"

"No."

"She's no dummy. She'll turn up."

Chapter 108

SHE CAUGHT A whiff of his hot, rotted breath. His mouth was right at her ear. And then another wave of fear turned her knees to putty. Was this monster going to take a bite out of her?

He held her firm. Park could not believe his strength, as though he had never been shot. "I never had a quarrel with the police," he said. "You had to spoil everything."

Shanker had a suffocating chokehold on her. As they continued down the narrow passageway she smelled smoke filtering through cracks in the walls. "You smell the smoke? Good. Good. While you were looking for me, I decided to turn up the heat. You see my angel. I have been here before. I have been making a plan. The key to a successful production is careful, painstaking preparation. Hitchcock was a master planner. No detail went unchecked."

Further down the monster dragged her. Down. *Beyond the gates of hell.*

"You know what else makes a successful production?"

She shook her head, knowing that he needed the attention, and that being agreeable would buy her some time.

"K.I.S.S. Know what that means?"

Park looked at him blankly.

"Keep It Simple Stupid. Hah!"

Park could not get a bearing on her surroundings as the light from above was fast fading.

"No fancy elaborate plans. No ticking time bombs placed strategically throughout the theater with timers set to go off in some crazy synchronization. Who has time for all that? It was so simple. Took me a day or two, but very often the solutions to the complications we create are staring at us, right in the face."

Park looked at him with wide eyes, trying to stay calm.

"*Gasoline*. It was so obvious."

As they went further down, the smell of smoke was replaced by the scent of decay. The area also felt damp.

"I dug shallow trenches all over this rat trap, and poured in the gasoline."

She struggled with him, but his strength was overpowering. She kept hoping for him to lose strength, or a slip that would enable her to break free.

"This theatre is mostly constructed of wood," he continued, "and it'll go up in flames like setting a match to a haystack."

Park tried to kick him but her feet rarely touched the ground He held her up in front of him.

"The monster always places the beautiful woman in danger."

Again Park struggled but his hand held her throat so tight that any struggle proved futile and expended precious air that she needed. *Where is he getting his strength* she kept asking herself. He pushed through another door, and stood at the edge of a large hole. He forced her head downward so that she was staring into a deep, lightless pit.

"Did you ever read the *Pit and the Pendulum*? Blink once for yes, twice for no."

She blinked once.

"Good. Well I don't have a pendulum, and this is not exactly the same pit. But the best part of the story, you know, is the part about the rats."

Chapter 109

"Park talk to me damnit." Valente held his cell phone firm to his ear, as though that would make her voice come alive. "Nicole."

The monster heard the static and what he thought was a voice. *Where was it coming from?*

He looked into the dark pit where he had shoved Park. There had been no drama in the shove. No histrionics. Just a forceful shove sending her into that pit.

He heard the static again and spun around, and there it was - a small, green light blinking in a corner not far from him. Park's cellphone. He picked it up as though it were a precious stone and held it in his hand gently. Holding the phone down to his side, he walked to the edge of the pit and thought how clever she had been to have brought her cell phone. Too bad it had fallen out during their struggles. Then he touched his lips to the receiver.

Valente stood motionless, a few feet from the stage. The heavy breathing was unmistakable. He could almost smell his breath. And then the taunting rasp. "Is this *mon capitain*?"

Valente dropped his eyes for a moment. He felt a sudden wave of despair. "What have you done with her?"

"Do you know about monsters?"

"Stop with the riddles." Valente took a moment to carefully choose his words. He did not want to add to his foe's anger. "Everyone thinks you're crazy. But I don't."

"Thank you kind sir. I am genuinely touched." Shanker ran his lips over the phone, enjoying the sensation of hard plastic against his mouth. "Just tell me this. Did you like the thing with the black mamba? Was that brilliant?"

Valente wanted to bring down the walls of Jericho with a roar heard around the world. He wanted to destroy this man. But he held his rage in check. "It was genius."

"*Thank you. I love you.* You are playing your role well, my hero. My Captain. It isn't over yet."

"Where is she?"

"She's of no consequence."

"Will you deal?"

"I don't play cards."

"Me for her?"

"Captain. This is not a cop story. Stick to the genre. Don't disappoint me."

"You don't want her. You want me."

"In truth I don't want either of you."

Shanker let the phone drop to the ground. He was about to crush it with his boot, but a thought occurred to him.

"*Mon capitain.* Are you still there?"

Valente still held the phone close to his ear. He felt like he had run out of options. "Yes."

"I can't say what your chances are, but you have my admiration."

Valente heard a crunching sound, a loud mechanical squeal, and then silence.

By now Shanker's entire right side down to his waist was soaked in blood from the gunshot wound to his chest. Nevertheless, after squashing the cellphone, he slowly walked over to the edge of the pit. There was barely any light near him and even less down there. He heard a faint moan, and barely discerned Park's motionless figure. With his left hand he shoved a large wooden cover over the pit, sealing it tight.

Chapter 110

FOR THE FIRST time since the ordeal at the theater began, Valente felt like he was not going to win. His world was coming un-glued.

Fire had engulfed the passageway behind the stage and all of the dressing room. Valente had retreated to the stage. Firemen had arrived and were dispersed around the theatre. He found McCarty near the front of the stage going over floor plans of the theatre with the fire chief.

"Ed. He's sealed us off from back there. Are the SWAT guys still out back."

Ed looked at him with a vacant expression. "I don't know."

Valente was on his phone. "SWAT leader."

In a moment the SWAT leader was on the other end. "Harris here."

"You still in position?"

"Yeah. What's going on in there?"

"He's torching the place," Valente said. "Listen to me. No matter what happens here, you keep your shooters in place. He might be trying to make a break from your end. He's also got Park. So make sure you have a clean shot."

"O.K."

A surge of insecurity welled up inside Valente, like an inner voice telling him this was all for nothing; like Shanker was speaking to him - *You will never catch me.* But he quickly banished that voice and stilled his fears. He had to stay focused. He had Park's life to save. "Ed. Get some people to check the perimeter."

"I'm on it Sam. He's not going to get away this time."

Valente hoped he was right as he watched McCarty leave the theatre with several police.

Park sensed a presence blacker than the pit in which she was imprisoned. Movement through darkness. Faint sounds. But not clearly discernible.

Her head ached from the fall. She felt a sharp pain in her right ankle. Probably broken, or at least badly sprained. She had to think fast, and not think about fear. She would not allow herself to panic. Then she heard it again. And this time there was no mistaking what it was.

<hr />

Shanker was moving purposefully through a narrow passageway when suddenly it happened. A violent trembling in his jaw, followed by a searing headache that spread along the walls of his skull.

He grabbed his head, pushed his palms against his temples and tried to squeeze the pain out of him. He jammed his teeth together, shut his eyes tightly, anything to try and stop the agony. Shanker stumbled against the wall. Fell to his knees still clutching his head. His brain was on fire and there was nothing he could do. The madness was driving him further and further into an unfamiliar world.

Chapter III

AT FIRST THERE were two red eyes staring at her from somewhere in the darkness. Then another pair appeared, followed by others. This couldn't be happening. But a person's life can take a drastic change for the worst in a manner of seconds. The cases keep piling up of innocent people minding their own business whose lives are forever altered by the actions of a rapist, a murderer, a kidnapper.

Yes a life can change, and end in a matter of seconds. But the rats didn't care about any of that. Rats do what nature tells them to do. They feed.

Shanker had thrown her into this pit, and the fall had broken her ankle which she had figured when trying to put pressure on it. Park bled from cuts to her wrists, elbows, and from a particularly large gash on her bottom lip. The scent of blood was like ringing a dinner bell for the rats.

More tiny red eyes appeared but they seemed to hold their ground. Except for one.

The self anointed leader of the group made the first approach. Because of the blackness in the pit, Park could not see the rats, except for their demonic red eyes. She felt the lead rat sniffing her bare ankle, and immediately kicked it away. The leader was flung against a dirt wall. He squealed in anger, and darted back and forth twitching his nose. The others watched, and waited.

Another pair of eyes emerged close to her. The rat darted up her arm and over her shoulder. With lighting speed it took a bite out of her ear. The searing pain made her scream. Then another attacked, so fast...not even the time between heartbeats. More eyes appeared. She heard tiny claws scratching at the ground. She could only imagine the swarming, twitching bodies of disease and filth moving towards her. She released a painful moan. Park could not let her life end this way.

Chapter 112

McCARTY CIRCLED TO the back of the theatre where he spotted SWAT leader Harris' black SUV hidden behind some trees. Other police had taken strategic positions around the perimeter. He radioed Valente and told him all was clear. No sign of him or Park. And just as he turned back, an explosion blew a hole out the back of the theatre, sending wood and debris into the air. A surge of flames followed.

Valente had opted to stay near the stage when he heard the explosion. The fire chief who had briefed Valente on their progress immediately radioed outside and ordered men to the spot of the explosion.

Several police had remained inside and were awaiting further instructions from Valente. A couple of the police called out to him several times but he appeared not to hear them.

His mind was lost in thought, and those thoughts were all a blur. No concrete ideas were forming in his brain. Just images moving around in slow motion. Shanker's lurid video tape; Park nursing his terrible hangover; Ed McCarty holding up Lakers tickets; Josh Arkoff, the bug guy, smiling with glee at his discovery of the Mexican bat fly. There was Thibedeux in his Cajun lab; Ernie Cochrane, the FBI friend smoking a cigarette in his trench coat; gregarious Don Pasquale holding open his arms welcoming him to his restaurant and the words *The Evil that Men Do* scrawled in blood glowing at him.

But then a strange thing. Valente noticed that the police were looking up at something in the fly spaces. For a moment they looked like followers of a cult leader who had beckoned them to look to the sky for a sign of better things to come. And for a moment he felt as though he were somehow connected to this strange apparition. But Valente was too smart for that. *No.* He was not losing his mind. He snapped out of his momentary lapse. Gone were the blurred images. He turned his head and looked up through the rafters.

And there he had appeared from the smoke behind him, as though right out of a special effect.

Shanker had staggered onto the catwalk. Within moments the police had drawn their guns. But Valente lifted a hand. "Don't shoot. Hold your fire."

Shanker held himself up against the left column near the wings. He was badly hurt and bleeding. His shirt looked like a giant inkblot from all the blood. The gunshot wound and fighting with Nicole had finally taken its toll.

Valente climbed the ladder to the catwalk. Shanker leaned heavily to one side. He looked down at the police below and he said mockingly. "I have an audience."

"Where's my partner?" Valente said.

"Your partner?" Shanker said.

"Asian woman. What did you do with her?"

For the first time Valente got a good look at him and he looked nothing like the handsome man in his photos. Here was a man badly deteriorated. A face hollowed by neglect, with deep sockets, lifeless eyes and blistered lips.

"Where is she?"

"Did you ever read the Pit and The Pendulum?"

"No! Enough of your bullshit. Where's my partner!"

"You should have read it. One of Poe's best."

Valente wanted to blow him away but couldn't, not until he told him where she was. "Where is she…tell me." His voice cracked, but he aimed the gun steady at him.

A weak smile appeared across Shanker's lips, then he softly began to sing. *"Think of Christmas, think of snow…think of sleigh bells, off we go…"*

It was around this moment when several of the policemen on the stage felt a surge of heat from below them. The floorboards began to buckle as smoke and flames shot through the cracks. Behind Shanker, a wall of flames climbed up towards him.

"Detective get down from there," one of the cops yelled.

McCarty was right behind. "Shoot him Sam, and get out of there."

"We need him to tell us where Park is."

"Damnit." McCarty kicked the side of a floor light.

Valente was now up on the catwalk. He squarely faced Shanker, and inched closer towards him on. "Where is she?"

Through glazed eyes, Shanker watched his approach, but didn't care. He knew it was over.

Valente felt a mild panic rise in him. His knees weakened. "Tell me where she is." Valente even did something that normally he would never do. He lowered his gun... *"Please."*

Shanker, with failing strength, leveled his eyes at him." *Mon Capitain.* This is your journey. Mine is over." He spread his arms and began to sing... *"We can fly, we can fly..."* Valente moved towards him but a burst of flame shot up between he and Shanker. Valente dropped back, and then watched in horror as Shanker with his arms still spread out, fell into the flames below. *"We can fly, we can fly... we can fly ..."*

Valente had lunged for him, trying to grab him before he fell. "Noooo," Valente howled. His face was a frozen mask of shock.

No one in the theatre moved. McCarty and the few policemen who remained, looked up at the catwalk like they were watching some bizarre celestial event.

For Valente his world had come to a sudden halt. He was still frozen when suddenly he felt the heat from the rising fire brush his face. And he barely heard shouts from the men below to get off that catwalk. Metal snapped, and beams cracked as the catwalk began to fall apart. Pieces of wood with rippling flames fell on either side of him. Cinders rained down on the stage. A large oak beam crashed at the end of the catwalk.

"Get out of there." It was McCarty yelling over the noise of falling wood and metal. One side of a support beam collapsed.

McCarty angled himself on the edge of the stage that hadn't collapsed and inched towards the bottom of the catwalk ladder. But the floor had weakened from the inferno raging below, and about halfway to the ladder, a section broke under his foot. He felt the blaze from below lick his hands. Fortunately the break was a small one and he was able to get his foot out of there before another section of floor collapsed. Sparks and smoke shot outward. McCarty had to jump off the stage and move backwards toward the seats. Looking up he saw flames crawl across the ceiling. He could barely see him through the smoky haze engulfing the stage.

Valente came out of his shock and turned towards the stage. He saw McCarty trying to get nearer to the catwalk. Suddenly the stink of burning cables and rubber overpowered him. Gagging on the stench, Valente looked around for an escape route. And then he saw one. There remained one cable swaying from a riser above. Swinging over the stage on the cable was the only way off the catwalk. Flames were shooting upwards through sections of collapsed floor, and rising from the backstage area.

In moments the catwalk would be a glowing mass of searing hot metal.

He tore off sections of his shirt and wrapped them around his hand. He grabbed the hot cable and pulled. As he had hoped, the cable was still securely attached to the riser.

Holding it securely in his hands and ignoring the heat burning his palms, he swung towards the orchestra as the catwalk collapsed below him. In mid air the cable snapped and Valente fell.

Fortunately, McCarty had seen the figure coming over him out of the smoke and positioned himself to break Valente's fall.

The two fell over a row of seats, Valente with his face buried in McCarty's chest.

"C'mon you maniac," McCarty lifted him by his shirt collar, while Valente held his singed palms together. They rushed out of the burning theatre as a section of ceiling collapsed behind them.

Chapter 113

THE AREA OUTSIDE the theatre had become a busy staging unit. Paramedics attended to several officers who suffered from exposure to the fire and smoke. Fire trucks pumped water over the roof of the theatre, but to no avail. Section after section of the building collapsed. Most heard the furnace explode from somewhere below that sent more flames into the already massive cauldron. The blaze raged out of control and there wasn't much anyone could do until it burned itself out.

Valente held onto McCarty for support as he led him to the nearest ambulance. Halfway down the steps Valente stopped and shouted orders to anyone who could hear him. "I want this entire area searched and that includes the woods back there. You do whatever you have to do, but find Park."

No one, not even McCarty argued with him, and within minutes the search for Nicole was underway.

Forty minutes later, not much was left of the theatre. Valente and McCarty had fallen into a macabre silence as they stared at two walls left standing over a lunar landscape of debris and ash.

Valente leaned against the back of an ambulance, exhausted and in pain. He sucked in oxygen, but his wounds weren't too bad; second degree burns on his hands and a bruise on his cheek. His hands were heavily wrapped in gauze. His eyes moved slowly from the burned ruins of the theatre to the surrounding areas, hoping to see someone come out of the woods with Nicole in tow.

His only hope was that somehow she had crawled out of that burning mess and found refuge in the woods.

Chapter 114

FOR A WEEK the media had a field day with the Shanker case. News coverage of the MacLean Theatre set on fire resembled something out of a scene from a disaster movie, and the networks made sure they had every camera angle covered --- from overhead helicopter shots to minicams following the action on the ground.

The talk shows were in a feeding frenzy. Experts in criminal psychiatry were on every network and cable station, numbing the viewer into submission with their bloated theories.

There was a Larry King interview with Ellen Weist that featured a lengthy explanation about her whole notion of holding parents accountable for the criminal behavior of their offspring. The call-in responses on that topic were quite lively.

Campbell's television was turned on inside his office. McCarty stood in his doorway watching Campbell who reminded him of a scavenger looking for food, as he channel surfed for more news on the Shanker killings. He stopped at one channel just as a photo of Nicole Park was displayed. It was a good photo and did her justice.

McCarty finally turned away. He had had enough of the usual media frenzy. Not an original bone in their bodies, he thought. The same vulture mentality. The same thirst for the morbid cloaked in a veil of truth-telling.

And then something caught his eye. He noticed Ellen Weist's book on Park's desk. And next to it was a copy of the complete works of Edgar Allan Poe. McCarty took the books and put them in a box with the rest of her office effects. This was going to be one desk he never wanted to look at again. He was going to miss her. He was actually going to miss being called Big Ed.

Chapter 115

THE SANTA MONICA pier never felt as solemn to Valente as it did three days after Park's funeral. Rescue workers had found her silver necklace next to her ashen remains in her death pit under the charred rubble. It had taken the workers hours to remove beams, cut through cement, and pick away at collapsed ceilings and plaster.

Valente let the necklace dangle from his fingers while he leaned over the same railing Nicole used whenever she went to the pier for some comfort.

He saw her smile and heard the voice that so sweetly said *paisano*. He recalled what she had said about troubled people. They wanted what everyone else wanted. *Someone to love them — someone to hold their hand in the dark.*

While his thoughts drifted, an unexpected visitor found him. It was Ellen Weist.

"Sam?"

He turned towards her, tears streaming down his face.

"Guys at the station said I might find you here."

His watery eyes glanced at her. He felt no shame in showing his tears. Then he wiped his face and looked away from her. "This was her favorite place. It made her remember her childhood, fishing with her father." He gazed out at sea. "She had always wanted to go to Hawaii. She told me that once." He pointed towards the horizon. "Straight out there."

"Sam. I just wanted to tell you how sorry I am. I've known her over the years, and she was a special person."

Ellen put her hand on his shoulder. They stood there for a few moments looking at the ocean. "I'm not sure why I came down here," she finally said. "But you're a good man, and I wanted you to know that."

"Thanks Ellen." He thought for a moment and then instinctively said. "Got any last minute summations? Any parting analysis?"

Ellen would not let his touch of sarcasm bother her. Not at this time. "Sam. Shanker wanted nothing more than to be noticed, and mostly by his mother. You said in your report he was singing something from "Peter Pan" while he fell into the fire?"

"Yeah. "We can fly" I think it's called, from the cartoon version."

"You also found letters written to his mother and the mannequin in the coffin, presumably of her?"

Valente nodded.

"I could spend my entire career analyzing this one. But for now, let's say his was probably a classic case of a man who deeply hated his mother but still wanted her approval."

In another time Valente would have probably told her to jump off the pier. But he had become better at accepting profilers. Maybe there was something in all that babble. He smiled at her warmly. "I think I want to be alone."

"Of course."

"I appreciate you coming all the way to the pier."

Ellen held his hand firmly then turned and walked away.

Valente watched her for few minutes, and then he turned his gaze back to the sea. For a moment he felt Nicole's lips on his cheek, and he let his imagination keep that moment alive. Nicole will live in him forever. And forever, he will love her.

Epilogue

The rain fell hard on a tree-lined street in Brady, a small town in Illinois.

A white, two-story modest home with paint peeling off in many places, stood a few feet back from the pavement on that tree-lined street.

There was one light on. Upstairs.

She stood at the bedroom window looking at the street below. Her greasy, unwashed white hair fell to one side. She seemed captivated by the raindrops bouncing off the windshield of a car parked in front of her house. Little explosions of water she thought. The old woman lit a cigarette and let it dangle from the side of her mouth. Smoke billowed through cracked, yellow teeth.

There was an open suitcase on her bed, nearly packed. The old, chain-smoking hag picked up a framed photo of her son from her nightstand and gently placed it in the suitcase between some clothing.

"Why haven't you written, Mitchell?"

⤙▪ ▪⤚

Huddled under her umbrella, mother waited in the rain at a bus stop. She wore a yellow slicker with a matching hat. There wasn't a soul in sight. Most people stay in when a hard rain falls. She did not.

The four-block walk in this driving rain did not dampen her spirits. She had a determination in her eyes, and a sense of purpose she hadn't felt in years.

A Greyhound bus approached. It was the one stop it made in Brady. She looked at the white, glowing letters above the windshield, barely discernible through the blinding rain. Squinting, she made out the name of its destination --- *Los Angeles*.

Mother was happy. Soon she would be reunited with her son.

Made in the USA
San Bernardino, CA
25 July 2018